BRACKISH WATER

Neil S. Plakcy

Samwise Books

This book is a work of fiction. Names, characters, places, and incidents either are products of the author's imagination or are used fictitiously. Any resemblance to actual events or locales or persons, living or dead, is entirely coincidental.

Copyright 2022 by Neil S. Plakcy All rights reserved, including the right of reproduction in whole or in part in any form.

Cover design by Kelly Nichols. Editing by Randall Klein.

There are three previous books in the Angus Green FBI Thriller Series:

The Next One Will Kill You

Nobody Rides for Free

Survival is a Dying Art

Chapter 1

Barbershop Boys

I was listening to the radio on my way to work at the FBI headquarters in Miramar, Florida, when I heard the report that would shift the direction of my life for the next month.

"The U.S. Coast Guard has stopped at sea over 3,000 Florida-bound Cuban migrants fleeing deteriorating economic, safety and political conditions in the Caribbean nation since October — more than the last five fiscal years combined," the correspondent announced. "Prominent Republican donor Alvaro Vela Romero has presented the governor with a list of Cuban refugees he wants released from the Krome Detention Center immediately. Included are political activists, former government employees, and three women jailed for selling cafecitos in Havana's Plaza de la Revolución without permits."

Because this is South Florida, the correspondent, a woman of Cuban extraction herself, pronounced *cafecito* and *Revolución* flawlessly. I was studying Spanish myself with an online app, and as I pulled into the parking garage I repeated those words several times until I thought I had the pronunciation correct.

By the time I reached my office, down a warren of narrow hallways, my cell phone was ringing. With a sinking heart I saw the display read "Jesse Venable."

"I just got into the office, Jesse," I said, in lieu of greeting. "I can't talk now."

"Just hear me out, Angus," he said. "It's about this gay kid at Krome. You gotta help me get him out of there."

When the universe sends me two messages within minutes about the same topic, I listen. I dropped my shoulder bag on my desk and sat down. "Talk."

"His name is Yulirus Diaz, and until a couple of weeks ago he worked at the Museum of Decorative Arts in Havana."

A bell rang in my head. "Would he have been a government employee?"

"Christ, I don't know. I got a friend from the time I spent in prison who was close with one of the guards, if you know what I mean."

I knew. Like me, Jesse was gay, though that shared kinship hadn't stopped me from arresting him for receiving stolen goods two and a half years before. And his friend, and the guard, were probably gay, too, even if only situationally.

"What's this have to do with me?" I asked.

"My friend's friend is now a guard at Krome, and he got to know this kid Yulirus. He's a good guy, a sweetheart, and he left Cuba on a raft because somebody was trying to kill him there. He's afraid they're going to send him back, where he's as good as dead. And I'm scared that nobody's going to care about one gay kid when the governor is putting pressure on releasing these people who have political pull."

"I don't have anything to do with immigration, Jesse. Right now I'm up to my ears in spreadsheets for a series of barbershop robberies."

I joined the FBI first as an analyst, based on my master's degree in accounting. Then after taking the training course at Quantico, I'd been made a special agent and shipped to the Miami office to get some experience under my belt.

It had been a tumultuous time. Jesse Venable was small potatoes compared to some of the other crooks I'd faced down. But I felt sorry for him because he was a very persuasive guy, in his sixties, alone, and a survivor of prostate cancer.

"But you're the FBI," Jesse said. "You guys can stick your fingers wherever you please."

"You know that's not true. Especially for me. I work for a senior agent and he's the one who tells me what to do. And he's going to be pissed if I don't finish these spreadsheets."

"Please, Angus. Just keep your eyes open. See if you can do anything to help this kid."

I sighed. "I'll do what I can, but I can't promise anything."

I hung up and knuckled down to work. By lunchtime I'd finished entering all the data we had collected about a series of barber shop robberies that spanned several counties in South Florida and I was staring at the rows of information looking desperately for patterns. I gave up temporarily and navigated the maze of hallways to the cafeteria, hoping some protein would stoke my brain.

My boyfriend Lester is always on me to improve my diet. Just the other day he'd said, "Proteins help neurons within the brain communicate with each other through neurotransmitters that are made from amino acids."

"What does that mean in English?" I had asked. Lester had a degree in physical education and had been a personal trainer for a couple of years before landing his current job.

"It means you need to eat meat and drink milk to be the best G-man you can be."

That was one of his refrains. He pushed me to exercise, practice yoga, and manage my nutrition so I could outrun and outthink the bad guys. Maybe he was right, or maybe going along with him was part of learning to be in a relationship.

I chose a plate of chicken salad that balanced out protein, leafy greens and heirloom tomatoes, and a can of my favorite pineapple-flavored soda, called Jupina.

Little by little I was becoming a Floridian. We never had pineapple soda when I was growing up in Scranton.

I saw Miriam Washington sitting by herself at a table and asked if I could join her. "Of course. Have a seat."

She was a decade older than my twenty-eight, and held a PhD in art history. In addition to her regular responsibilities, she was a member of the Art Theft Task Force, and I had worked with her on a couple of cases, though in all but one I'd compiled data for her rather than being out in the field.

She was a statuesque African-American woman who favored business suits in bright colors—that day's was a deep maroon, the color of blood. She always made me look ordinary, in my dark blue suits. But my hair was red, and I had a tendency to freckles, so to keep people from thinking I was a teenaged Archie pretending to be a special agent, I stuck to boring.

"What are you up to these days?" she asked.

"Robberies at fifteen different barbershops in inner-city neighborhoods from Overtown in Miami up to Riviera Beach in Palm Beach County," I said. "Same MO in each case. Man comes in just before closing with a little boy, insists that the kid needs a haircut for an awards presentation the next day. Gives the last barber left a big sob story, and the barber agrees. By the time the hair cut is finished the shop is empty, and the man pulls a gun and cleans out the register."

"Lots of those inner-city operations are heavy cash businesses," Miriam said. "I can see they'd be worthwhile heists. You have any leads?"

I shook my head. "I'm just compiling the data, looking for any patterns we haven't found yet. The report is due tomorrow afternoon, which means I'll be working all day tomorrow to wrap up the last details."

I took a couple of bites of my chicken salad. "What are you working on?" I asked.

"I met with the SAC this morning," she said, and frowned. "You know that saying about how shit rolls downhill? A pile of it landed on me."

The SAC was the Special Agent in Charge, otherwise known as our boss.

She took a sip of her coffee. "A rich donor has been bugging the governor about releasing more of the Cubans held at Krome. He was born in Havana himself, though he came to the US as a child with his family."

"I heard about that on the radio this morning," I said. "It sounded like there were a lot of them. Are they all your responsibility?"

"No, I've just got one at the moment. He says he knows about a Spanish Old Master painting stolen from a church in the Cuban countryside."

"His intel sounds good?"

"I have to talk to him first. But I doubt it. The refugees at Krome are desperate people. They've already risked their lives to get here, and for most of them there's no going back. Either they've sold everything they own to pay for passage, or they'll be arrested when they get off the plane."

She sat back in her chair. "I feel terrible for them. But you know how our hands are tied unless the governor decides to grant a blanket amnesty. Which is not going to happen while he's running for reelection."

"Or for president," I said.

"So I'll drive down there and interview Mr. Diaz, and then most likely my name goes on a letter back to the governor telling him there's no reason to grant the man amnesty."

I remembered my conversation with Jesse Venable. "Do you mean Yulirus Diaz?"

"I didn't realize they'd released the names of the rafters we're investigating."

"I got a call about him this morning." I told Miriam what I'd heard from Venable.

"The fact that he's gay won't matter in asylum decisions, because Cuba just passed that law allowing same-sex marriage."

"Jesse says he's scared that he'll be killed if he goes back," I said. "Ordinarily, Jesse shouldn't even want to talk to me, since I was part of the team that put him in prison. So for him to contact me means he's very sure of his information."

I leaned forward. "Can I come to Krome with you? Talk to this guy, help you look into the information he has?"

Miriam didn't say anything.

"Please, Miriam? So far every case I've worked on has already been evaluated by someone else. I'd love to see the way a case gets started and how we make judgments about the quality of information."

I was fascinated by art theft and Miriam was a great mentor, and I wanted very much to continue my association with her. "I can help you verify the information from Jesse. Maybe this guy is in danger because he knows something about the stolen painting."

She blew out a breath. "All right, if Vito says he can spare you."

I couldn't stop smiling. "That's awesome. I'll ask him as soon as we've wrapped up these barber shop robberies. When are you going down there?"

"Tomorrow at two o'clock. Which means I need to leave by one."

It felt like my head sunk down to my shoulders. "No way I can finish by then. Can you wait an extra day?"

She shook her head. "Not with the SAC and the governor on my back. Don't worry, there will be other cases. There always are."

She left, and I finished my lunch and walked back to my office. Crap. When I signed up with the Bureau I understood that my work would mainly be behind-the-scenes information gathering and analysis.

I looked at the clock. It was two in the afternoon, and I'd planned to work until at least seven. Lester's current gig was as a sales rep for a line of high-end whiskies, and he was running a product demo that night at a bar in Fort Lauderdale. I had thought about stopping by on my way home, hanging out with him for a couple of hours, but I hadn't said anything to him.

If I stayed at work, maybe I could bang out my analysis in time to go to Krome with Miriam the next day. I knew little about the place, other than that it was where illegal immigrants were housed and processed before being sent back where they came from. Yulirus Diaz was on the governor's list because of the interest of a wealthy Cuban donor. That position might be a negotiating chip toward a green card for a young gay man in trouble. I was intrigued.

Damn, I wanted to join Miriam. But daydreaming about it wasn't going to get my work done. I went back to my statistics, and as is often the case, I got caught up in the zone, where all my attention was focused on my project, and I hardly noticed time passing. I didn't realize it was quitting time until my boss, special agent Vito Mastroianni, stopped by my office. "Don't work too hard, rookie," he said.

I looked up. He was a big guy, his shirt buttons always threatening to burst through their buttonholes. "Say, Vito. If I get this data crunched by one o'clock tomorrow, do you think I could go to Krome Detention Center with Miriam Washington?"

"That's a hellhole of a place," Vito said. "Why do you want to go there?"

"Miriam's investigating the case of a guy on the governor's list. I could learn about how an investigation kicks off."

"I need whatever magic you can work on that data," Vito said. "We have no leads at all. That has to take precedence." He paused. "But if you find something by tomorrow you're okay by me to go with Miriam."

I thanked him and went back to work. Something gnawed at me as I went back and forth from sheet to sheet on my spreadsheet. In every case, the boy who accompanied the man got a haircut. Yeah, that was part of the MO. But it couldn't be the same boy, could it? A kid's hair didn't grow fast enough to need a haircut every two weeks. After a couple of cuts the poor boy would be nearly bald.

Yet the boys were always described as about the same age. I went back to the statements field agents and local police had taken from the barbers. The boys were always between four and six, and they were all Black, as was the man with them. But I began to dig a few details out of the statements.

One boy could have "passed the paper bag test," I read. I had a couple of Black friends at Penn State, and I had heard the term there. If you held a paper grocery bag up to the boy's skin, it would have been lighter than the paper.

Another boy, however, was described by the barber as having very dark skin, like an African. No one else had commented on skin color, but it was clear that there had to be at least two different boys involved.

The barber in Lauderhill remembered the boy whose hair he had cut wore a bright blue T-shirt with a logo of clasped hands. A barber in North Miami recalled the boy wearing a bright purple basketball jersey that was way too big on him. Other than that, the kids had been dressed like kids.

What else could I tease out of that information? I went online and searched for clasped hand logos and found almost nine million results. I narrowed my search to Florida, to kids, to images, and got nothing. And yet an idea kept teasing around the edge of my brain that made me feel like I knew that logo. I closed my eyes and tried to visualize it, and it suddenly came to me.

The Kids' Club of Scranton. My dad died when I was ten, and my mother sent my brother Danny and me to events there so we could hang out with other boys and their dads and role models. I opened my eyes and jumped onto the computer and started typing.

What popped up was a blue and white logo of clasped hands, which I learned had been adopted by the group after a national competition in 1978, years before I was born. The logo was still in use.

On a hunch, I Googled purple basketball jerseys, and found that a Kids' Club in Miami used those for its pre-teen ball club.

What if the robber recruited boys from the Kids' Club? He could be a father to one of the boys, or a volunteer there. Especially with so many single moms looking for role models for their sons, I could see it would be easy for him to take a boy on an outing—including a robbery – and bribe him to keep his mouth shut.

The local police had come up with a composite sketch of the robber, but because he operated in such a wide geographic area they hadn't had many opportunities to show it around.

I went back over my data again, looking for additional clues, but found nothing. It was nearly ten o'clock and I was exhausted. I typed up my report, and a recommendation that the police canvass the Kids' Clubs in the areas where the robberies had occurred. Then I placed my report in an online folder for Vito to review, and called it a night.

The next morning Vito called me in. "Where'd you get this idea about the Kids' Club?" he asked. "My nephew in Jersey City used to go there."

I explained about the haircuts and the T-shirts. "The robber needs to recruit boys for haircuts," I said. "Since two kids are connected with the club, maybe he's a volunteer there or goes there to look for kids he can use."

"Interesting idea. I'll pass it on to the local cops to do a canvass of the two clubs you cited." He leaned back in his chair. "Guess this means you want to go to Krome with Miriam, and then work on whatever case she's got."

"I do, if you can spare me."

"If the cops come up with any data on possible suspects I may need you to do more crunching. But it's Friday afternoon and there's nothing new on the horizon, so for now you can head to the ass end of nowhere with Miriam. But don't blame me if you get caught up in something you don't want to be a part of."

Chapter 2

End of Nowhere

When I got back to my office I looked up the Krome Detention Center on the map. It was, as Vito had so eloquently put it, at the ass end of nowhere. About a forty-minute trip south and west from our office in Miramar, to the edge of the Everglades.

I texted Miriam that I'd be able to go with her, and then did some research on Krome. The technical term was the Miami Field Office, Krome Service Processing Center, though the website breadcrumb trail led from the Immigration and Customs Enforcement site to a section for detention centers.

Friends and family could only visit evenings and weekends, based on the first letter of the detainee's last name, but that was the advantage of being in law enforcement—we could stop by whenever we chose, though I imagined Miriam had already made an appointment with the appropriate authorities.

It was strange that this recent immigrant had come in contact with Jesse Venable. For a previous case, I'd had to befriend Jesse, then betray his trust in order to arrest him and those he worked with. My involvement with his case had ended when he was arrested, though occasionally I had learned through various documents about his trial and sentencing.

Then a few weeks before, he'd called my cell.

"Angus? It's Jesse Venable. I'm in trouble and I need your help."

"I have nothing to do with your case anymore," I said then. "You need to contact your attorney."

"My case is over. Finished, finito, wipe your ass with it and throw it away. I did my time and nearly died in the process."

"I'm sorry to hear that."

"They made me sell my businesses before I went to prison, and while I was sick I couldn't focus on paperwork, and now it's all a big mess. You've got to help me clean it up, Angus. You owe me."

I didn't owe Jesse Venable anything. He was a criminal; he had owned a chain of pawn shops and gold buyers and used them as a front for illegal activities. As part of my investigation, I had done some freelance accounting work for him and convinced him to like me.

But I did feel guilty about taking advantage of him. He was a heavyset man who had lost his prostate to cancer and liked watching cute young guys in tight bathing suits—and naked. I'd leveraged my good looks as part of getting him to trust me.

"What's the problem, Jesse?" I asked.

"The problem is that my knees have gone and I need an aide to hoist me up out of bed or my easy chair. The problem is that the doctor has me on so much medication I can barely concentrate. The problem is that I've lost track of what bills need to be paid and how much money I have in my accounts."

"I can't help with the heavy lifting but I suppose I could take a look at your paperwork," I said. "Just to get you organized again."

"You're an angel, Angus. Bring that hunky boyfriend of yours and you guys can go skinny dipping in my pool if you want."

"Jesse, Jesse," I said. "I'm not coming over to flash my family jewels at you, or my boyfriend's. Just to help with your accounting needs."

"You never get anything you don't ask for."

That was how I got back in touch with Jesse, which had led to his phone call the day before about Yulirus Diaz. Funny how the universe played its cards.

I was staring into space, thinking about the ramifications of getting involved with Jesse Venable again, when I heard Miriam Washington's voice.

"Ready to go?"

I looked up to see her in my office doorway. She wore a black pants suit, no jewelry beyond a watch, and carried a black leather attaché case. If I didn't know her well, I'd think she looked scary. Beside her, I looked cheerful and friendly.

Miriam drove us through the westernmost of the commercial suburbs, where corporate headquarters in gleaming glass buildings were interspersed with gated housing developments, and then turned south on Route 27. Miles of sawgrass marsh stretched to our right, glinting golden in the afternoon sun. It was almost completely flat, broken only occasionally by hummocks, small islands of low trees. The horizon was endless.

"Beautiful, isn't it?" Miriam asked.

"It's amazing that there is this huge natural area so close to Miami," I said. "You'd think they'd have built all the way over to Naples by now."

"They may. They keep trying to push back the urban development boundary—the line in the muck that stands between the Everglades and big business."

Something flustered a group of swallow-tailed kites and they took off in a swarm to our right. For a long time there was nothing but empty space on either side of us, and it felt like we were on a journey to somewhere very foreign. Soon after we crossed the border into Miami-Dade County Miriam turned off onto Krome Avenue.

Then in the distance a towering hotel rose, looking as out of place as a spaceship. "What's that?" I asked.

"Miccosukee hotel and casino," she said. "We're coming up on the Tamiami Trail, Southwest 8th Street, which used to be the main way from the east coast to the west. The Miccosukees live out here, and they were smart enough to get the right to build a hotel and casino on their land before anyone else did."

"All the way out here?"

"Outside of rush hour, it's only about a half hour from downtown Miami," she said. "And you know what gamblers are like. They'll travel for the chance to lose their money in slots and casino games."

We passed the entrance to the hotel and continued a short distance farther on Krome Avenue. The detention center was as unassuming as the casino and hotel were gaudy. A couple of low-rise buildings, painted an institutional tan, surrounded by a barbed wire fence. At least they'd planted a palm tree on either side of the entrance.

We parked by the administration building and saw a cluster of inmates in orange jumpsuits heading out to a basketball court. "See those empty diamond-shaped pads?" Miriam asked.

I looked in the direction she pointed, and nodded.

"This was originally a missile base, ready to protect us from attack by Cuba." She frowned. "Now the only quote unquote attacks come from immigrants looking for a better life."

She pointed in the other direction. "Over there, that's the transitional unit. Detainees who come into the country with behavioral problems are monitored and treated there before they can join the general population. It's the only transitional unit for detainees in the country, so they come in from all over."

"You know a lot about this place," I said.

"I've worked a couple of cases that involved detainees," she said. "I studied French in college and learned Haitian creole when I went on an internship in Port-Au-Prince. So I get tagged sometimes for Haitian cases."

I was envious of her facility with languages. My younger brother Danny was studying Italian in college, and I had met him in Venice the previous summer. I was impressed at how well he could communicate. Though I'd taken the required courses in French in high school, and then at Penn State, my ability to speak was woefully limited to a few awkward phrases and the ability to ask where the bathroom was. My Spanish was only a little better, developing through reading highway billboards and paying attention to the way people I knew mixed Spanish words in with their English.

Miriam navigated us through the campus of low, white-roofed buildings. "People have this idea that Krome is a prison, but it's a short-term center for detainees ICE views as a flight risk or a danger to society. Most of them are here from thirty to ninety days, and they can wait up to three weeks before they have an opportunity to present a defense to deportation before an immigration judge."

"What about the guy we're here to see?"

"Detainees are segregated into three different categories based on their criminal history. Since Yulirus Diaz has none, he's in the most liberal part. But he's still an illegal immigrant, so he has to make a case why he should be allowed to stay here."

She sighed. "He and a dozen other refugees landed on Ramrod Key a couple of weeks ago," she said. "The others had family members who bonded them out, but he has no one in the States to take responsibility for him."

I felt sorry for the guy without even seeing him. How would I feel in a similar situation, fleeing to a foreign country and then getting locked up in a prison?

"There's no legal requirement for immigration judges to appoint a lawyer for foreign nationals who cannot afford one, but he was lucky in that he's Cuban," Miriam continued. "He met with an attorney from a non-profit group that works with Cuban refugees, and he told her that he had information about artwork being stolen from Cuban churches and museums. Somehow word got to the governor's office, and the governor added him to that list you heard about on the news."

We went through the metal detectors, showed our IDs, and

Miriam said we were there to interview Yulirus Diaz, and gave his alien number and booking number.

Diaz was younger than I expected, barely older than I was. He wore his dark hair in a ponytail, though that might have been because it was easiest in the detention center, and he had piercing dark eyes and high cheekbones. He was a couple of inches shorter than my six feet, and had a slim build and muscular arms.

Because we were law enforcement, rather than family or friends, we were able to meet him in a private interview room. Miriam began in Spanish, but quickly ascertained that Diaz spoke good, if heavily accented, English, and switched to that language. "I understand you have some information about art theft," she said. "Why don't you tell us first about your background, and then we'll get to what you know."

He nodded. "I received my Masters of Art History from the faculty of arts and letters at the University of Havana," he said. "For three years now, I work at the *Museo Nacional de Artes Decorativas*, the Museum of Decorative Arts, in the Vedado neighborhood of Havana."

That jibed with what I'd heard from Jesse. At least the kid was keeping his story straight. The word 'straight' reminded me of one of the reasons Miriam had brought me. Did Diaz ping my gaydar?

It was hard to tell at first. When I was coming out of the closet at Penn State, I'd learned a couple of things to look for. First, look at a man's overall features and the way they fit together on his face. There were a number of studies that looked at the matching length of a gay man's index and ring fingers. Gay men tended, according to those studies, to walk with more of a sway than straight men.

And of course if you were at a bar and a man made direct eye contact, that was a clear signal.

Recognizing the signs was harder in Miami than in Pennsylvania, though. Many of the straight Latin men I'd met spoke with a sexual rumble to their voices, and they were more effusive about hugging and kissing than their Anglo counterparts. But despite the fear that was evident in his body language, I saw several indicators that Jesse was right in identifying Yulirus as gay.

Miriam took a couple of notes as Yulirus spoke. She hadn't asked me to do so as well, so I just listened.

"I have a friend, from my program at the university," he said. "His name is Elpidio López, and he did not graduate, because they catch him cheating on exams. But he know much about art." He took a deep breath. "Six weeks ago, he ask me to come out to the countryside with him. He found a painting in a barn, he says, and he wants to know what I think of it."

"Where in the countryside?" Miriam asked.

"Outside Santa Clara, an old colonial city," he said. "Three hours from Havana, in the center of the country."

She nodded and made a note. "What did you find?"

"A Spanish Old Master, centuries old," he said, with awe. "A beautiful painting in an ornate gold frame. Right away I am suspicious. What is such a painting doing in a barn? My friend, he says he travels around the countryside looking for abandoned artwork like this he can sell overseas. But he recognizes this is special and he want my opinion."

"Why you?"

Diaz shrugged. "Because he knows I am expert. He asks me to research the painting, tell him what I think. So I took many photos with my phone, and then back in Havana I looked in many dictionaries of art. Even I was surprised at what I found."

"Which was?"

"Do you know art?"

I expected Miriam to tell him about her PhD, and her experience working in galleries before joining the FBI, but she simply nodded.

"I think artist is Bartolomé Esteban Murillo, one of the greatest of all Spanish Old Master painters," he said.

She asked him why, and they quickly devolved into art speak, talking about the paint, the canvas, the brush strokes. I could see Miriam warming up to Yulirus Diaz and I wondered what that meant about his information, and why the FBI would care about a Spanish painting in a barn in Cuba.

"And the subject?" Miriam asked.

"Jesus and his father, Saint Joseph. Murillo has painted these two in several different scenes, from Saint Joseph holding the baby Jesus, with Mary in the background, to Jesus as a young boy with his father beside him. His earthly father, that is."

"You don't have any of the pictures you took with you, do you?"

"They take my phone," Diaz said. "But if you can get it I can show you."

Miriam looked at me. "Angus? Want to give that a try?"

I stood up. I had to jump through several hoops, including signing a release for the phone and a promise to return it before we left Krome. It took nearly an hour, and by the time I returned to the interview room Miriam and Yulirus Diaz had completed their bonding process, and were talking animatedly about various other paintings.

Diaz tried to turn on the phone, but it had run out of charge since his escape. He looked ready to cry but Miriam opened her attaché case and began to bring out various chargers and cords until one of them fit. Diaz's hands shook as he plugged the charger into the wall and the cord into his phone. His body relaxed dramatically when the phone began its startup sequence.

I was impressed that Miriam carried all those chargers with her, and I remembered that she'd been to Krome before, and had probably run into a similar problem before. She was indeed a smart cookie, as Vito would say.

When the phone finally powered up, Yulirus showed Miriam a photo he had taken of the painting. I looked at it over her shoulder. To the left side stood an older man, who looked somewhat like Diaz himself, with an oval face, wavy dark hair and a beard and mustache. With one hand, he held the hand of a boy about ten years old, wearing a lavender tunic that hung to his ankles. The boy's head was surrounded by a golden aura.

The scene reminded me of the man or men who had taken boys

in for haircuts at those African-American barbershops. This boy's hair was a light brown, and he could use a trim.

A cluster of cherubs amidst the clouds looked down on the man and boy. "May I send this to myself?" Miriam asked Diaz. He agreed, but his phone didn't have a SIM card that was compatible with US carriers. So she opened her briefcase once again and pulled out a slim laptop. She had a variety of different cords in a pocket of the case, and she used one of them to connect Diaz's phone to her laptop. She discovered he had a whole folder of pictures there, and copied them over.

While we waited for the copying process, Miriam asked, "What made you decide to leave Cuba?"

"When Elpidio try to kill me." His voice shook and he appeared on the verge of tears again. If he was an actor, he was a damn good one.

"Excuse me?" Miriam asked. "The friend who showed you the painting?"

"Yes. We spent two hours in that barn, looking at the details of the painting. I am not expert on Murillo, but I studied many Spanish Old Master paintings in graduate school so I knew what to look for. I give him my opinions, and then he drive me back to Havana." He frowned. "I think that is the end. But then one day I am crossing the street near where I live, and a car pull out and try to hit me."

He began to shiver, and Miriam reached out and took his hand.

"I am saved by chicken," he said. "I cry out, and startle this bird pecking at the sidewalk. She flew up and distracted the driver, and I jump out of the way."

"Did you get a look at the driver?"

Diaz shook his head. "But I recognized the car. It was the same one we drove to see the painting."

Chapter 3

False Friends

Diaz went on to explain how he had become very frightened and decided to leave Cuba. "Right away I sell everything. My few pieces of furniture, my record player and all my vinyl records." He had a faraway look on his face for a moment, then recovered. "Sorry, there is no music here, no art. My soul, it is starving."

Miriam and I both waited for him to continue. "I start to ask around, very carefully, you understand. I don't want the wrong people to hear I want to leave. Eventually my cousin's friend tell me about a man with a boat at the port city of Matanzas, east of Havana."

"Direct route to Key West," Miriam said.

Diaz nodded. "It cost me nearly every centavo for the ride. He say he know secret harbor north of Key West. Many tiny islands, hard to patrol."

I tried to imagine how I would feel under those circumstances. To give up everything and flee to another country, leaving behind friends and family? I couldn't do it. My mother, my brother, my boyfriend—they meant more to me than anything. I would stay and fight. But everyone has a different story, and I couldn't judge Yulirus Diaz against my own priorities.

"I only take one small backpack with clothes and personal things," Diaz continued. "I take two buses to Matanzas, and then walk miles to the marina. There were twelve of us, men and women, one couple with two small boys. The boat was tiny but we all climb in. Some sit on benches, others on the floor. I find a corner and sit there with my pack between my legs."

I could visualize Diaz there in the corner, by himself, and my heart continued to hurt on his behalf. Down the hall from us in the interrogation room, someone began yelling in Spanish, and there was the sound of a fight, people banging into walls and falling to the floor, and a man crying in pain.

Diaz's hands shook as he continued. "We leave when darkness fall and go very fast through Straits of Florida. After time we begin to relax. It was so dark outside I could see more stars than I ever see before, even the Milky Way. If I was not so scared I would be filled with wonder."

Miriam's laptop beeped to signal that the process of copying Diaz's photos was finished, and she and I turned to look at the screen. Because Diaz was stationed across from us, we had to figure out what we were seeing. Miriam skipped through a couple of photos of some festival in Cuba, and then stopped on a shot of a large canvas leaning against a wall inside a barn.

The only light came from behind the photographer. Each shot got closer, until we saw the subject matter. Much of the right side was a light-colored sky with puffy clouds. In the front center of the painting, a boy of about ten sat on a stone. He had curly brown hair, and the light was such that it illuminated his face as if he was favored from above. Diaz had described it as a halo, but it was not so simple.

To his right stood a man, perhaps in his forties, in a loose sort of toga, with sandals on his feet. He had a short beard and dark hair.

Diaz must have noticed as we leaned in. "The style is similar to that of *The Good Shepherd*," he said. "Maybe 1660? Same angelic look on boy's face. Same background. The largest difference is the figure of Saint Joseph to his right."

"It's beautiful," Miriam said.

"Even more when you see it in person," Diaz said. "The small details, like the shine on the apple the boy Jesus holds in his hand. The amused look on the face of the sheep in the background."

We looked at several different shots Diaz had taken, closeups of the boy, his father, even the face of one of the sheep, which was charming all by itself. "Interesting," Miriam said, and she closed the screen of her laptop. "But you were telling us the story of how you arrived in Florida."

He nodded. "Just before daylight, boat begin to slow, and we all cluster to one side to look out. Land, with many small inlets of mangroves. Later they say we were on Lower Sugarloaf Key. There was no place to tie the boat, so we had to jump into the water and wade through the muck. As soon as all of us are in the water, the boat goes away, and I am lost and alone. But at least I am free."

He took a deep breath. "The other people cheer and cry. We fight through the mangroves to reach dry land, getting cuts and scratches on our arms and legs."

He looked up at us. "All other people had family in Miami to contact, but I had no one. I guess I think there will be someone to meet the boat and take us into Miami, but I was wrong."

I could only imagine how he must have felt then.

"When we finally reach the road, the husband and wife and the two boys call their cousins. Everyone else split up by families, leaving me on my own. I walk down a street called Sugarloaf Boulevard, as tourists headed to charter boats for deep-sea fishing. I try to keep my head down and look like I belong there."

The fight outside had subsided, leaving behind an eerie quiet.

"Just one block before the A1A highway, a police car pull up beside me and I see two of the men from the boat in the back seat."

After a quick interrogation the officer had determined that he had no papers, and delivered him to the station. Eventually he had been taken to Krome for processing.

"This is all very interesting," Miriam said, when he had finished. "And we certainly appreciate all that you have done to get to the United States. It must have been a terrifying time, worrying that your friend was trying to kill you, and then leaving everything behind."

Diaz nodded.

"But I don't know what you expect we can do for you," Miriam said kindly. "The FBI doesn't handle refugee issues, and the only crime you have mentioned so far is the alleged attempt on your life in Havana, which would be a matter for the Cuban police."

"But I can tell you where the painting is," Diaz interrupted.

Miriam shook her head. "You can tell us where you saw it last. And by your own admission, you are not an expert on Murillo. It could be a competent fake, or something by one of his students." She turned to me. "In art terms, we call that the school of Murillo."

I leaned forward. "To claim asylum, you would need to demonstrate a threat against your life back in Cuba. Did you report the accident to the police?"

He shook his head. "In my country, it is better not to involve the police in anything."

I took a breath. "Would you be in danger if you went back to Cuba?"

"From Elpidio, for sure."

"But not because you're gay?"

He shrugged. "I don't go to clubs, I don't have boyfriend. There is nothing to charge me with."

"What about political activity?" Miriam asked. "Have you joined any protests? Signed any petitions?"

He shook his head. "I am only focus on my job."

Miriam sighed. "You may have heard from people in Cuba that it's easy to get amnesty in the United States," Miriam said. "And for many years, because of the animosity between your government and ours, it was."

A smile began at the edges of Diaz's face.

"If you had some history of activity against the government, we could report back on that. If you had evidence that you'd been persecuted for your sexual orientation, that's another thing we could put in our report. But without either of those, all we can do is indicate that you allege you know the location of a painting—one that hasn't even been reported as stolen."

Diaz's eyes grew wider and that smile disappeared.

"Your name came up on a list that the governor sent to our agency, asking us to investigate each case individually," Miriam continued. "Ordinarily, you'd never have the opportunity to meet with someone from our agency, the Federal Bureau of Investigation. We have a very specific charter to guide us in what we investigate, and immigration and amnesty are not in our portfolio."

Miriam looked at me and frowned, then put her laptop back in her attaché case. "But I'm sorry, without either of those, there is nothing we can do."

Diaz's eyes grew wild. "I cannot go back to Cuba! He will kill me!"

"You will have to convince the immigration judge of that."

Diaz's shoulders sagged as he understood that we would not be able to help him.

My brain was buzzing with everything Diaz had told us. I held up my hand to Miriam. "Hold on a minute."

I turned to Diaz. "You said that your friend looks for artwork he can sell overseas," I said. "Do you know where he gets what he sells?"

Diaz shrugged. "Once we talk about security in museums, and he ask me many questions about alarm systems and security guards. But in my country, there is no money for these things except in Havana."

I leaned in close. "Do you think he steals these pieces?"

"Sometimes he brag about how easy it is to walk off with paintings or pieces of sculpture," he said. "He watch when the guard go to smoke. Or he take big backpack with him."

I was very familiar with the charter Miriam had mentioned, and trafficking stolen art across international borders was definitely in our purview.

"Do you know where he sells the art?" I asked. I looked into Diaz's eyes, hoping he was smart enough to understand where I was going.

He did, because he smiled slightly. "Some go to Spain, but I know he tell me he find art for a man in Miami. Once he deliver the painting himself, but he also fly to Antigua to meet this man when he was on a cruise."

That was what we needed. I turned to Miriam and spoke in a low voice. "Diaz is in the United States now. Suppose he contacts his friend and asks if he can help deliver the Murillo to someone here."

"If it is a real Murillo."

"Even if it's not, that's still smuggling, right? And it's a case for us."

She spoke in a similar quiet voice. "Angus, I understand you feel sorry for Diaz and want to help him. I do, too. But we can't manufacture a case where there is none."

I took a deep breath and was about to plead with her, but she turned back to Diaz.

"If you have direct knowledge of artwork being smuggled from Cuba to the United States, we can look into that, and ask that you be given temporary status to remain while we investigate. Do you have such knowledge?"

Again I looked directly at Diaz. He began to smile again. "I do."

Chapter 4

Island Visit

Miriam and I left Diaz with a promise to get back to him and walked back to the car. It wasn't until we were back on Route 27, surrounded by endless acres of sawgrass marsh, that she said, "I understand what you did with Diaz, and why. But now we're going to have to prove the case."

"What happens if we can't?"

"Then he goes before an immigration judge. If he can't prove a real need for asylum he'll be sent back to Cuba, whether or not he's on the governor's list."

"And if he's lucky his friend will forget about him and he can rebuild his life," I said. "But that won't be easy since he quit his job and sold everything he owned."

"So cynical for one so young," Miriam said.

That might be, but it put more pressure on us to make sure he could stay in the United States.

We were almost back to the office when I got a text from Vito. "Need to see you as soon as you get back."

"Crap," I said. "I was hoping to get an early start on the weekend since I finished those spreadsheets last night."

Miriam went through security but instead of driving into the garage, she dropped me off at the entrance to our solid glass building. The retaining ponds and stands of sawgrass that lined the path were one of the ways the building had been strengthened against any kind of vehicular attack.

Once inside, I made my way to Vito's office. "You made a good call, rookie," he said, as I slid into the chair across from his desk. "The Broward Sheriff's Office sent out a couple of officers to canvass the Kids' Clubs in Broward with a composite sketch of the robber, and they hit pay dirt almost immediately. The guy's a staffer in the Lauderhill center, and he was supplementing his income with some help from the boys. He'd offer their moms a free haircut if the kid would go along with him, and made the boys swear not to tell anybody what was going on."

"Well, that sucks," I said. "I mean, I'm glad they caught the guy. But I wish it had been someone who was more of a villain, not some guy who works with at-risk kids."

That reminded me of a guy I had met on a previous case, who worked at a shelter for at-risk youth called Lazarus Place, and turned out to have less than honorable reasons for being there. Not everybody was as good as they seemed to be. Even your friends could turn on you—as in the case of Yulirus Diaz.

When I got back to my office I called Jesse Venable. "Miriam Washington and I met with Yulirus Diaz at Krome," I said. "I need your help if we're going to get him amnesty. Call around. See if anyone knows about paintings and sculpture brought in from Cuba."

"Miriam Washington. She doesn't like me."

"It's not a popularity contest, Jesse. We're talking about saving a man's life. And don't tell me you don't know any smugglers. You spent decades running a pawn shop. You know more crooks than a hundred public defenders."

I stopped for a breath. "He said that his friend regularly sells to a man in Miami. That once they met when the buyer was on a cruise passing through Antigua."

"Like that's any kind of a clue. You know how many people are on one of those big ships? And how many cruise lines go to Antigua?"

"I don't, but I'm sure I could find the statistics. Right now it's all we have to go with."

I sat back in my chair. "You know art," I said. "And you have your own specialty." Jesse's focus was on the male nude, and his house in Weston was full of photographs, sculptures, watercolors and paintings of naked men. It was like a visual Grindr. "Ask around if anyone in your broad circle of acquaintances focuses on Cuban art."

"Christ, there's whole galleries of that shit in Miami," Jesse grumbled. "But I'll ask. You and the handsome hunk still coming over here tomorrow afternoon to look at my paperwork?"

"I'll be there. I can't speak for the handsome hunk yet. It's not like we're married or anything."

"Take my advice, Angus. You get hold of a man like that, you never let him go. I wish I'd been so lucky when I was your age."

When I hung up with Jesse, I logged into the FBI computer system and caught up on my emails. It's as if the server for our office knows when I've stepped away from my desk and floods me with incoming messages.

One of them caught my eye. There was a growing number of LGBTQ folks in law enforcement in South Florida, and we'd met a couple of times for happy hours to share experiences. The email was about a happy hour the following month, and it reminded me that one of the guys I'd met through the group was a lieutenant commander stationed at the US Coast Guard base in Miami Beach.

Before I could second guess myself, I picked up the phone and called him.

"Brian Quirk."

"Brian, it's Angus Green from the FBI. Do you have a minute?"

"For a rainbow brother in blue? Of course. What's up?"

I sketched out the situation. "When you intercept boats coming from Cuba, do they ever carry art as well as people?"

"As far I know, only incidentally," he said. "Where a refugee is carrying some family heirloom. Most of the craft we intercept are makeshift, often more rafts than boats. In those cases the people are lucky if they carry enough water."

"But it's possible?"

"Anything is possible. But if you're talking about high-value art, you're looking at a high-value boat as well."

"Explain," I asked.

"I've got a meeting in half an hour," he said. "But if you want to come over here in about an hour, I can give you the dollar tour of our facility and tell you everything I know."

"That'd be awesome, Brian."

Miami Beach wasn't exactly on my way home from Miramar, but for the chance to see another agency's base, and learn what Brian knew about smuggling, I'd make the detour.

I sent both Miriam and Vito messages about where I was going, and I left the office a few minutes later.

I took the Turnpike to I-95 and fortunately most of the Friday afternoon traffic was leaving the city rather than heading toward it. Even so I took the express lane down to the MacArthur Causeway, the long, flat road that led to Miami Beach. The sun was at my back and glinted off the water of Government Cut, where the cruise ships docked. To my left were a series of low bridges that connected private islands where celebrities like Gloria Estefan and Jennifer López had houses.

I turned right off the causeway onto Terminal Island road, which led past the ferry to Fisher Island, yet another home for the rich and famous, and then stopped at a guard house where I had to show my ID and be verified for my meeting with Brian.

It wouldn't be an exaggeration to say that roads, buildings and parking lots covered every inch of the small island. Boats of all kinds were docked along the water's edge, while others were in drydock. The buildings were all low-rise, the tallest no more than four stories.

But as I got out of my car, I smelled the ocean, and I could see how working on Terminal Island could be intoxicating. After I gave my name to the receptionist I stood by the window of the waiting room looking out at the water until Brian came to get me.

He was a trim guy in his early forties, wearing dark blue slacks and a light blue short-sleeved shirt with epaulets. "Do you want to see the base while we talk?" he asked.

"I'd love to."

He led me outside, where once again that smell of ocean water hit me. "You must love the water," I said.

"Kind of a requirement for the Guard," he said. "I grew up in Southern California, and my father was an executive with a government contractor and also a recreational fisherman. We used to go out in his boat every weekend when the weather was fair, which was pretty often."

We strolled through the parking lot and he pointed out various buildings. "When it came time for college I knew I didn't want his life—stuck in an office all the time, only going out on weekends." He laughed ruefully. "And yet here I am. At least I'm a lot closer to the water than he was."

"You were in the service during Don't Ask, Don't Tell, weren't you?"

"For a few years. But I was firmly in the closet then so it didn't matter. Then when that act was repealed, a couple of men I worked with came out, and that gave me the courage to follow."

"Clear sailing since then?"

He laughed. "The military is like any organization. You have good people and bad people. But things are getting better all the time."

We came to the end of the island where we saw a massive tanker, the size of a city block, heading out through Government Cut. "But you asked about smuggling art," Brian said. "I did some thinking, when the meeting I was in dragged on. Here's one idea."

We turned left, and began walking in the shadow of high-rises from the tip of Miami beach. "Take your average forty-foot cabin cruiser," he said. "Those boats are optimized for storage space, and yet you can still find hidden compartments if you look. I heard about one boat that was being inspected after a trip to Mexico, and the drug dog alerted. The officers broken open a bulwark and discovered faint traces of cocaine. But they also found Mesoamerican artifacts that were being smuggled."

"Wow."

A boat like the one he was describing was slowly exiting the marina across from us, though when it cleared the bulwarks the driver raced the engine.

"And that's only one case," Brian said, when the noise had passed. "You own a reasonably nice boat, it's expected that you might have some artwork on the walls. Our agents are trained to recognize a Picasso lithograph worth half a million dollars against one worth a couple thousand. And that clay pot on the counter could be an Inca olla or a replica from a junk store."

"So let me posit a situation for you," I said. "Suppose you want to get some stolen paintings out of Cuba. How would you do it?"

He was quiet for a moment, and I looked out at the wake the powerboat had left. I had a visceral memory of jumping on a boat just like that one as it left a dock in Fort Lauderdale, during the case where I'd arrested Jesse Venable.

"If I had access to a decent boat, I'd have someone build in a secret storage compartment," Brian said finally. "Then I'd get a tourist visa to Cancun and travel there. I could offload the artwork in Cancun and sell it through there. Or I'd swap out my travel documents so the boat doesn't appear to be from Cuba, and then continue on to the United States."

We talked for a while longer as we circled back to where I'd parked. "Thanks for all the advice, and the tour," I said.

He waved his arm around to encompass the island. "I consider myself one of the luckiest men I know. I have this view every day, and whenever I can I get out on the water. I'm able to serve my country without hiding who I am. I married a great guy two years ago, and we get to live in paradise."

"I'm grateful to the men who paved the way for me, at the Bureau and in government service in general," I said.

"You have a boyfriend?"

"I do. He's great, and very supportive of my career. He has a background as a physical trainer, and sometimes he goes overboard in pushing me physically."

"I know what you mean. My husband's a marathoner, and I've been down every jogging path on Miami Beach with him, in every kind of weather."

He reached out to shake my hand. "Do good, Angus. I hope you can help this guy at Krome."

"I hope so, too," I said.

Chapter 5

A Lot to Unpack

From Terminal Island I drove up to Fort Lauderdale to meet Lester at another of his restaurant demonstrations. The place was a new one on US 1, with a fancy bar back lined with upscale liquors. There was a big area for mingling in front of the bar, and rows of small booths along both sides for more intimate conversations.

The clientele was primarily a species I like to call *homo hipstericus*. The guys either had their hair pulled up into top knots that reminded me of Pebbles Flintstone or cut in elaborate styles with poufs on top and razor cuts along the back and sides. They wore linen shirts with the tails out over khakis and sneakers that cost more than my rent.

The women were opposite in every way, from their salon-styled hair to their extravagantly high heels. They wore form-fitting dresses with low-cut necklines and thigh-high slits. It was a wonder they could move at all, but the message was clear. The guys where there to hang out with their bros, while the women were on the prowl for men with six-figure incomes, six-packs, and at least six high-limit credit cards in their wallets.

They were the perfect crowd for the small-batch whiskies Lester represented, and he worked them like a pro. He was six-four, bulging with muscles, with a twenty-four-karat smile. He made the guys want to be him, the women want to sleep with him. But sorry, folks, he plays for my team, and with me exclusively.

I watched from the corner while he poured, talked and mixed custom cocktails. After a while I stepped up and became his social media guy; I photographed the drinks and the bottles and the customers, posting to his accounts on Facebook, Instagram, TikTok and more.

In exchange he slipped me a cocktail now and then. My current favorite was the Tallulah—whiskey, coke, peanut syrup, and a couple of salted peanuts. I sipped slowly so I wouldn't get drunk, savoring the tanginess of the peanuts once they'd been marinated in the whiskey and coke.

Did liking that drink make me as much of a hipster as the dudes clustered around the bar? It was a slippery slope, I admit.

By the time Lester shut down at midnight, I had a pleasant buzz but I could still drive. Lester followed me back to my place, a fifties house in the not-yet-gentrified part of Wilton Manors, which I shared with a roommate.

The gentle buzz was making me horny, and as soon as we got into my bedroom I tackled Lester and began kissing him like crazy. "I can taste the peanuts on your lips," he said, when we took a break.

"You make good drinks."

"Is that all I'm good at?"

"Why don't you show me what else you can do?"

I was awake before Lester the next morning, and I walked out to the kitchen where my roommate Jonas was waiting impatiently for the coffee maker to complete its bubbling. "You going to your class today?" I asked.

Jonas had been taking a management class to increase his chances of promotion at the call center where he worked, supervising operators. He hated it and was desperate to get out of there.

"Last class," he said. "Online final exam, and then I'm done."

"Good for you. What's next? Another class?"

"This finishes my certificate." He looked down at the coffee machine, which was still brewing. "But I'm kind of making some plans."

I sat at the kitchen table. "Really? What kind?"

"You know that girl Camilla I told you about?"

"The blonde in your class with the British accent?"

He nodded. "Well, we've gotten to be friends, and..."

"Jonas. You're not turning straight, are you?"

He laughed. "As if. Camilla's a lesbian anyway." The machine finally finished its work and Jonas stuck his travel mug under the spigot. "She has this idea about starting a store to sell textiles and cookware from Provence."

It was as if he was talking to the coffee maker, not me.

"I love that stuff," I said. "Such beautiful patterns. And it fits the esthetic here in Florida, too."

He turned back to me. "That's what Camilla says. She's already found a great space in downtown Delray Beach, lots of foot traffic. And she has sources for all kinds of great stuff."

"And? Why does this matter to you?"

"Because she needs a business partner," Jonas said. "I took courses in accounting, management and marketing, and I worked in a couple of different retail stores while I was in high school and college."

My immediate worry was what would happen if Jonas quit his job and the store didn't make money, and he had trouble making his half of the rent. But I didn't want to rain on his parade. "That's great. So you'd quit your job?"

He nodded. "My dad has agreed to provide us the start-up funding we need."

"Your dad? He has that kind of money?"

Jonas had always seemed like he was teetering on the edge of financial instability.

He looked down at his coffee mug. "He's kind of rich." Jonas had grown up in Plantation, a suburb of Fort Lauderdale, and gone to a private high school and to the University of Florida, but I hadn't realized that his family was more than ordinarily well-off.

"He majored in chemistry in college, and he was going to go to medical school but then his father died, and he wanted to do something in medicine that didn't require a long internship and residency. So he decided to become an optometrist."

I nodded.

"He kept tinkering with chemistry and eventually he invented these eye drops for people with macular degeneration. He licensed the formula to a drug company and he makes royalties from them, besides his practice."

"That's great. And he's willing to subsidize you?"

"He wants me to be settled," Jonas said. "He thinks I'm kind of a loser because I don't have the science brain that he has. He wanted me to go to medical school, you know, but I flunked chemistry in high school." He looked up at me. "I think I did it just, you know, to give him the finger. My smart dad, the chemist, and I couldn't even pass the class in high school."

"Jonas, that's pretty childish, don't you think?"

He shrugged. "What can I say, I was a teenager. And it was all tied up in my figuring out I was gay, too. They sent me to a shrink who said that I was trying to send them a message not to expect anything from me."

My heart went out to him. Jonas had had a tough time in high school; he was near-sighted, pear-shaped, and waved his hands when he talked. He'd been pegged as gay early on, and subjected to teasing and torment when he was in high school.

"Is this thing with Camilla something you really want to do, or is it another way to get back at your father?"

"Jesus, Angus. You don't mince words, do you?"

"I'm your friend, Jonas. If I don't talk to you like this who will?"

He crossed his arms over his chest. "I like working in stores," he said. "But my dad was always so down on it. Like it was just something I was doing to earn some money before my real career started. But I enjoyed talking to customers and knowing about merchandise, and I like doing things like bookkeeping and ordering."

"Then it sounds like a good idea," I said. "When are you going to open the store?"

"We want to hit as much of the winter season as possible, while snowbirds are still here buying and furnishing properties." He took a deep breath. "Next month."

"Next month! You've had all these plans and you never mentioned them to me."

"I wasn't sure how it would all come together. But we're buying a two-story building a block off Atlantic Avenue, the main drag in Delray. It has two little apartments above the store, and Camilla and I are moving in there. The money we save on rent will keep us from having to take too much money out of the store at first."

It was all too much to take in. "You're moving out?" I said, and I could hear the squeak in my voice. "What's going to happen to me?"

"The lease is up in June. You can renew it in your name if you want." He shrugged. "Or you can move out. Rents in this neighborhood are going up fast, so I'm sure he can get a new tenant in at a much higher price."

He grabbed his coffee cup. "I've got to get to class. We can talk more when you think about what you want to do."

I sat in the kitchen for a couple of minutes after he left. I was glad that he had something to move towards, though I worried that he hadn't thought through all the implications of his plans. Thirty percent of new businesses failed in the first year, often through lack of capital, poor planning or lack of demand. The number went up to fifty percent over five years.

And moving in with his business partner, even if they had their own apartments, could spell trouble. He hardly knew Camilla, just from studying with her and spending a couple of nights out on the town. What if they had business trouble, and couldn't get away from it by going home because they lived next door to each other, and right above where the trouble was brewing?

I had obviously hit a nerve when I asked him if this was a way to needle his father. Even before I learned his father was wealthy, I'd seen that Jonas had a sense of entitlement. That's one of the big reasons why he hated his job. Nobody respected him there or contributed to his sense of self-worth.

"You're deep in thought. And you don't even have coffee in front of you."

Lester appeared beside me. "There's coffee in the brewer," I said. "Jonas made it before he left."

Lester kissed my cheek and then turned to the coffee pot. "You want?"

"Sure. So Jonas had some big news."

Lester poured out two cups and pulled down the chocolate syrup from the cabinet. He poured a swirl into each cup and handed one to me. "Spill."

"He's quitting his job to start a store selling tablecloths and dinnerware with a lesbian. He's moving out at the end of our lease, into an apartment on the top floor of the store in Delray Beach."

"Wow. That's a lot to unpack."

"I know. Hence my pensive mood."

We sat across from each other and sipped our coffee. His always tasted better than mine, probably because of that chocolate syrup I always forgot to add. He had other good qualities, too, besides his prowess in bed and his ability to make good drinks of all kinds. I was lucky I had met him.

Neither of us spoke much in the kitchen, and we left for the gym after we finished our coffees. He has a degree in physical education and worked as a high school gym teacher for a year after graduation, and he's an awesome physical trainer.

He was great at coming up with interesting workouts. Usually we spent time on the treadmill, then race-walked around the track. We combined weights with stretching, and added some yoga for good measure. That morning we did little more than a couple of laps around the track, because the Saturday morning crowd of weekend warriors were crowding the weight machines, and both of us were distracted. I was thinking about what Jonas had said, and where I would be living.

I liked Wilton Manors, and I had made friends there. But it was a long haul to the office in Miramar, and the commute was a bear. I usually stayed at work until at least seven, to miss the bulk of the rush hour traffic, but I still ended up in the occasional bumper-to-bumper delay, leaving me exhausted by the time I got home.

"You want a smoothie?" Lester asked, when we finished with the pull-down machine. There was a smoothie bar at the front of the gym, decorated with posters of pretty landscapes with inspirational messages like "Be who you are or someone else will be."

We got our drinks and sat on hard plastic chairs at a table by the front window. "I have some news," Lester said.

I felt a sinking sensation in my stomach. That kind of sentence never goes on well.

Lester must have seen something in my face, because he quickly said, "It's good news. Really."

I sipped my banana-strawberry smoothie. "Tell me."

"Larry has got himself a new gig with Diageo," he said. Larry was his boss; Diageo was a British company that was the world's largest producer of alcohol. "Which leaves his job open." He sipped his smoothie, which I thought was disgusting—it was green, full of kale and spinach and some blueberries and Greek yogurt. "And they've offered it to me."

"That's awesome!" I wasn't comfortable kissing Lester in the smoothie bar, so I held up my hand for a fist bump. "What does it entail?"

"I'm going to work out of the office in Doral," he said. "Larry has a network of reps like me all over Florida, going out and doing demos and spreading the word about the brands. I'll be in charge of training and supervising them, and working on stuff like social media and brand image."

"That's awesome, Lester. Congratulations."

"I haven't said yes yet. It's a big change and I'm not sure I want an office job. Plus there's the commute. It's miserable getting from Lauderdale down to Doral. The traffic is heavy all the time. And no matter what highway you take, something is always under construction."

"Have you thought about moving down there?"

He nodded. "Doral is a cool neighborhood, lots of apartments and condos and bars and restaurants. It's just crowded."

"I've been down there a couple of times, and I have to say I agree with you," I said. "So what other options?"

"Well, the other day I was there and I drove around looking at neighborhoods and developments. There are a couple of rental communities right off the Turnpike." He looked down at his smoothie. "And I checked out the prices, and the commute to your office."

"My office? Tell me more."

"It's about twenty minutes or so to the FBI office. And I was thinking maybe you and I could get a place together. Shorten both our commutes."

My heart zinged. I liked Lester, and over the time we had been together those feelings had been deepening into love. But moving in with someone was a big deal, a grown-up thing. I wasn't sure we were ready, but there was only one way to figure it out.

"We should totally go over there and look around," I said. "See if we can find something that suits both of us."

Lester's face widened into a grin. "That would be awesome, G-Man."

Chapter 6

Setting in Motion

Lester wanted to go right to Doral and start looking at apartments, but I had promised Jesse Venable that we'd come out to his place in Weston so I could help with his paperwork. "Tomorrow?" I asked.

He shook his head. "I'm working a brunch at a fancy restaurant in Fort Lauderdale from eleven to three," he said. "But we have time. I don't start the new job for a month, and you've still got time on your lease with Jonas."

"In the meantime we can think about what we both want," I said. "Apartment? House like Jonas and I have now? We can start with places close to the highway to minimize commuting and work outward from there."

"Sounds like a plan."

We finished our smoothies and drove back to my house, where we showered and changed. It was sunny and bright and I told Lester that Venable had suggested we go swimming after our meeting.

"Skinny dipping?" Lester raised his eyebrows.

I shrugged. "I'm still a Federal agent, so I'm not sure I ought to get naked in front of a felon. I have a weenie bikini I can wear that will at least leave something to his imagination."

"If I wear one of those there won't be anything to imagine," Lester said. My boyfriend was well-endowed, to say the least, and he was what we in the gay world call a show-er rather than a grower. He was big in all the right places, but he didn't get much bigger when he got an erection. "I'll stick to a pair of boxer briefs."

If they were tight-fitting, they would show Jesse Venable enough to get him salivating, though that was about all. He had confessed to me the year before that his prostate surgery had destroyed the nerves which caused him to get hard, so all he could do was look.

We had taken to leaving a few things at each other's place—toothbrush, razor, a couple of pairs of underwear and T-shirts and swim trunks. I wondered how it would be if we lived together and didn't have to bother with that kind of thing.

Shortly after noon, I drove us out to Venable's house in Weston, a fancy suburb almost due north of where my office was.

When I met him, Venable was a hugely overweight guy, fond of oversized track suits and triple XL t-shirts. The man who greeted us at the door was a shadow of his former self.

He was still a big guy, but he had lost nearly a hundred pounds between prison and his illness, and he looked gaunt despite his weight. He leaned on a walker and as he moved I saw the excess skin on his arms sag.

"Angus!" he said, and his face lit up with pleasure. "And the handsome Lester as well. This is a good day."

Neither of us could hug him, because of the walker, so we settled for shaking hands. He led us into the living room, where a Haitian woman in a white dress and white headscarf sat on the sofa watching TV on her phone. "That's Fabienne," he said. "My aide."

She looked up. "No, I am Mirlande. I don't know why he call me that." Her accent was heavy and hard to understand.

"I can't keep track of them," Venable said. "Different ones every day. If I didn't need the help I'd fire all of them." He thumped his walker.

"You want to go outside and get some sun, Lester, you're welcome to," Venable said. "I'm going to take Angus into the office to look at all this paperwork."

Lester went to the bathroom to change into his bathing suit, and I followed Venable to the office. The desk, which I remembered had been neat when I worked with him before, was cluttered with unopened mail. "This is just the tip of the iceberg," he said. "I got emails up the wazoo I haven't even looked at." He shrugged. "I just don't have the energy or the focus."

He looked at me plaintively. "Can you help me out, Angus? I'll pay you double what I was giving you before."

I sighed. I didn't want to get involved with Jesse Venable again, but I felt sorry for him. He was clearly overwhelmed, and maybe if I got a handle on things, he'd be able to take over his own affairs again soon.

"Why don't you go watch Lester swim," I said. "I'll see what I can do here. Leave me the password and sign in for your email account."

"You sure I can trust you?"

I couldn't tell if he was being serious or sarcastic, so I said, "Which one of us is the felon and which one is the federal agent?"

"Point made. The passwords for all my accounts are on that list attached to the monitor."

"Great cyber security, Jesse."

"What? One of those Haitian gals is suddenly going to know enough English to log into my accounts and steal from me while I'm sleeping?"

"Whatever." I sat down at the desk and started sorting through the mail. After a half hour I had a pile of bank and brokerage statements and credit card bills, and the trash can was overflowing with offers for hearing aids, air duct cleaning and CBD gummies in the shape of circus animals.

I logged in to Venable's checking account, which was woefully low considering how many bills he had to pay. Fortunately he had a lot of money parked in his brokerage account, most of it in a low-rate money market account. I made a ten-thousand-dollar transfer to his checking account, and then made sure that all the other passwords and log-ins worked. I snapped a picture of the password sheet with my phone, then piled all the paper statements into a fiber tote bag he'd gotten when he bought a lot of fast food from Boston Market.

I went into the bathroom and changed into my bathing suit. Lester's shirt, shorts and boxer briefs were piled neatly on the counter, and I added my clothes and slipped on my weenie bikini. Then I looked in the mirror.

Because I have fair skin, I have to minimize my time in the sun, but I had a bit of color on my face and my arms and legs, the result of lots of walking and running with Lester. My biceps were bigger than they'd been a year before, my six-pack more evident. Not that I'm vain, but if I was going to put on a show for Jesse I wanted to do a good one.

I padded out through the living room, where the aide was still watching her program, and wondered what she did for him. Did she have to help him to the bathroom? Wash him in the shower? That had to be humiliating for him.

Lester was on a lounge chair drying off in the sun, talking to Venable about art. "You should have an inventory of all your pieces," Lester said. "Especially if you have strangers coming in and out. Some of your small pieces could disappear in someone's handbag and you'd never know."

"You want to help with that?" Venable asked. "I'll pay you."

Lester shook his head. "Don't have the time. I'm starting a new gig soon." He talked about the job while I jumped in the pool. The water was refreshingly cool and sparkled in the sunshine. I did a couple of laps, feeling my muscles stretch, and then stood up in the shallow end and walked out, water streaming down over me.

I sensed Jesse's eyes on me. It wasn't much different, after all, from going out to a club and dancing shirtless, showing off my body to whoever wanted to look. I had to admit my feelings were more toward exhibitionism than generosity—and after all, who knew how long my looks would last? God forbid I might end up like Jesse someday.

I shook that thought off and sat down beside Lester. "You work on the art task force, Angus. Do you know anybody who could help Jesse catalog his art?" Lester asked.

I turned to Jesse. "What about Yulirus Diaz, if we can get him sprung from Krome. He has a master's in art history from the University of Havana."

"You met him. Is he cute?"

"Jesse. If he can help you, does it matter?"

"Hey, you can't blame me for wanting eye candy. God knows I don't get it from the aides."

An idea started forming in my head. "What do they do for you anyway? Medical stuff? Or just help you get around?"

"Mostly they fix my meals and give me my medications," he said. "They're supposed to do light housekeeping but that doesn't mean much to them."

"Maybe you can kill two birds with one stone," I said. "Suppose I can get Diaz released, and he came to live with you. He could help you out with what you need around the house, and catalog your art. And you could talk to him, too."

"Jesus, I would love that," he said. "It gets so damn lonely without anybody around who can make decent conversation. Fabienne out there is as dumb as they come."

I resisted reminding him that her name was Mirlande, because after all, the next aide would have a different name anyway. "Let me see what I can do," I said.

Jesse wanted us to stay for dinner. "I can order in a terrific Italian meal."

But Lester had a demo to run that evening, and I wanted some more private time with him, so we said goodbye.

We left Venable's house around four and drove back to Lester's.

He threw together a big salad for us to share for dinner, and while he did I sat on his couch with my laptop and Googled how Jesse Venable could sponsor Yulirus Diaz.

The news wasn't good. Since Diaz wasn't his relative, it was almost impossible for Venable to sponsor him. There was one small loophole that allowed Venable's business to sponsor Diaz for a green card, but as far as I knew Venable had been forced to sell his operations before he went to prison.

If we could get Diaz released, at least we'd have a place to put him. If he moved in with Venable, they'd both benefit.

Before I could think that through dinner was ready, and then I accompanied Lester to his bar demo, once again acting as his social media guy, soliciting comments from customers about the whiskey, hashtagging the hell out of everything.

We slept over at Lester's that night, and Sunday morning I went home and he prepared for his brunch program. Jonas was asleep in his room, so I settled at the dining room table with my laptop and started looking for information on Bartolomé Esteban Murillo, the artist whose painting Diaz claimed to have seen in that barn in rural Cuba.

He was a seventeenth-century Spanish artist who spent most of his life and career in Seville. I found over a hundred examples of his work online, a mix of religious iconography and slice-of-life paintings of children and nobles. He had painted numerous images of the holy family, including a couple of Jesus and his earthly father, Saint Joseph, which fit with what Diaz had described to us.

The paintings were darker than I generally favored, shadowy backgrounds with the subjects illuminated in front. I was surprised at how many of the paintings had "after" or "style of," "circle of" or "attributed to" or "copy of" after their names. Only a couple dozen of them were clearly marked as his work. I made a note to ask Miriam about that the next day.

It seemed like Murillo was a saleable artist; the places where I could check auction results without setting up an account showed sales from nearly a half-million pounds for an original to ten or fifteen thousand for a painting of his "school."

That evening Jonas and I talked more about his store. "This afternoon Camilla and I got iced coffees and sat out on Atlantic Avenue, watching the foot traffic," he said. "We counted people with shopping bags and cross-referenced them with people we saw who match the demographics of our customers. Most people were going in and out of stores, and at least fifty percent of those we watched bought something."

"That's excellent research," I said. He was so excited about it that I was reluctant to rain on his parade. And to his credit, he'd crunched the right numbers, and all the demographic data supported an audience for his merchandise.

He showed me photos of items that Camilla had already ordered, and I thought about my potential apartment with Lester. I could see setting a table with those dishes, those cushions on the sofa, that rug on the floor.

Maybe Jonas's research was right—especially as it included young gay couples setting up their first apartment together.

Monday morning, after I checked my email inbox and dealt with anything I had to, I walked over to Miriam's office. Our building is a warren of narrow corridors and small offices, with the occasional hallway opening up to a big window. Miriam was at her desk, typing away, and I waited a moment for her to look up.

"Angus. I was just going to contact you. Have a seat."

Miriam had hung all her diplomas on her wall, along with photos of art she had recovered in the course of her work. "I was intrigued by our conversation with Mr. Diaz on Friday," she said. "So I did some research Friday afternoon on thefts of Spanish Old Masters. There was a big case in California last year when a Velazquez that was last seen in Cuba before the revolution turned up at an auction house."

She sat back in her chair. "Velazquez was a rough contemporary of Murillo. This painting was purchased a hundred years ago by a wealthy Spaniard, and it traveled with his family to Cuba. The family couldn't take it with them when they fled, but they say they left it hidden somewhere in Havana. Unfortunately the man who hid it died and didn't leave the location."

"So someone in Havana found it and got it out of Cuba and to the US," I said.

"Indeed. A couple of years ago I went to a conference on international art theft and I met a man who works on these issues for the Cuban government. I spoke with him this morning, and he doesn't know anything about a Murillo, but there have been several other thefts recently, all of them from small museums and churches around the island."

"Other Old Masters?"

She shook her head. "A Tomas Sanchez, a Roberto Fabelo, and a Carlos Estévez. Not names you have probably heard of, but they're in the vanguard of contemporary Cuban artists. Any collector who specializes in the art would want their works."

"Interesting."

"I've been in touch with one of my counterparts at Interpol as well, and she's seen clues that some of this art might be coming through Miami. Which makes this a bigger case than just a single painting that might or might not be an Old Master. And because there are a lot of data points to collect and analyze, I could use your help. You have a knack for drawing interesting conclusions from spreadsheets—as evidenced most recently by what you figured out about those barbershop robberies."

"As long as you can clear it with Vito. I don't want him to feel like I'm ignoring the work he needs me to do."

"I'll square it with him."

"I got a start on my own on Friday afternoon." I told her about my conversation with Brian Quirk at the Coast Guard. "He mentioned Antigua, which Diaz did also."

She nodded. "Cubans can visit a number of Caribbean islands without a visa. And Antigua is a frequent port on Caribbean cruises. There are no customs agents at cruise terminals—that's all handled in the US. So an American could easily accept a handoff of a small piece of art in John's, for example, and then pack it with his luggage for getting off the boat. Add a phony sales ticket from a known gallery in St. John's and no one would be the wiser."

More pieces of the puzzle surrounding Yulirus Diaz were falling into place. "I followed up with Jesse Venable after we spoke with Diaz, and asked him to snoop around anyone who has a particular interest in Cuban art."

"Good. But remember, the Murillo—if it is a genuine Murillo—isn't technically Cuban art—it's Spanish art that happens to be located in Cuba at the moment. Same with the Velazquez. So we need to keep our eyes open for other artists, especially the three I mentioned." She eyed me. "Your boyfriend has an interest in art, doesn't he?"

Though the Miami office of the FBI was an open, welcoming place, not every agent would be comfortable bringing up a gay man's boyfriend in conversation. I was glad that Miriam was.

"He is."

"Maybe he can give you a quick tutorial on the kind of art held in Cuba before the revolution and what we can be looking for."

"He'd love that." I paused, thinking about what I wanted to say next. "What if we ask Diaz to get in touch with his friend Elpidio and let him know that he's in the US now, and might be able to help sell the Murillo here?"

"And there we get into entrapment."

I shook my head. I'd read enough regulations and watched enough training videos to know what that meant. "It's not entrapment if Diaz can phrase it correctly. Suppose he simply lets Elpidio know that he's here. And then we see if Elpidio asks him for help."

"It's murky territory, but it could work. However, it would be awkward with Diaz locked up in Krome."

"I have an idea about that. Venable is out of prison now and in bad shape." I told her about visiting him on Saturday. "What if Venable hires Diaz to be his aide, and to help him catalog his paintings? Jesse is miserable not having anybody to talk to and he's at risk of having art stolen because he has this ever-rotating series of strangers coming into his house."

"You've thought a lot about Venable. Why?"

I shrugged. "I feel sorry for him. He's not a bad guy, even though he committed illegal acts. He did his time for them, and he's suffering."

Miriam was quiet, and I waited her out. I was asking her a favor on behalf of someone she'd put behind bars in the past, and she had no real reason to agree.

"If we can establish that Elpidio López is already smuggling art into the US, then we'd have a case," she said finally. "But we can't let him make arrangements for the Murillo painting until we get approval from an immigration judge. Is that clear?"

"Eminently. But can we speak to the judge and get Diaz out and into Venable's house while we investigate?"

"One of the things I love about you is your passion to help people," Miriam said. I felt my cheeks redden. "But you have to remember that you are a federal agent, first and foremost, and your responsibility is to the Bureau and the American people rather than to any individual, whether a US citizen or not."

The sweetness and then the bite. I swallowed hard. "I understand that."

She picked up the phone. "I'll call Krome and see what I can set in motion."

Chapter 7

Convincing

While I waited for Miriam to get us an appointment in front of an immigration judge at Krome, I did more data evaluation on the barbershop case. The police in various jurisdictions from Miami to Palm Beach were interviewing barbers again, showing them photographs, trying to find the kids the villain had been bringing with him. Though they had a suspect in custody, they wanted to find each kid and take a witness statement. Since this was a multi-jurisdictional case, we remained involved, and I had to add new data to my spreadsheets every day.

Monday evening I read up on Doral. It was a new city, little more than a dozen years old, nestled between the Palmetto Expressway and the Turnpike. To the west you quickly hit the urban development boundary, meaning we were close to the Everglades with little risk of mammoth projects jumping up in that direction.

The town's name came from a couple who built a golf course there—Doris and Al Kaskel. After a building moratorium in the 1980s, the area began to boom, first with more hotels, golf courses and spas, then with commercial and residential units. Its proximity to the airport—only a mile away—was a big selling point. That would be great for Lester, if he began flying around the state to train employees and host demos.

It looked like a comfortable area for a couple of gay guys, with several "top ten" lists of gay bars in the neighborhood. I started searching for apartments for rent in west Doral. Call it residential porn—it was addicting to look at photographs and layouts and imagine living there with Lester. Some had kitchens that opened to the living room, while others had balconies that looked out on artificial lakes.

I assumed we'd share a bedroom, but a second bedroom laid out as an office could benefit both of us. Lester would undoubtedly have work to do from home, and I still had a small base of clients I did freelance accounting work for. Plus the extra space would keep us from spending all our time in each other's back pocket.

I did have some fears, though. He and I had only been dating for a little over two years, and we'd been very casual at first, only seeing each other once a week or so for most of the first year we knew each other. It was only after I'd come back from Italy the previous summer that we'd gotten serious. Now we spoke every day and saw each other a couple of times a week. Even so, it was a big step to move in with someone when there was so much we didn't know about each other.

How did he feel about money, for example? So far, we'd been splitting our dates, though I had noticed that he was always eager to pick up the tab at more expensive restaurants. And he paid a lot more for his apartment in a fancy building than I did for my half of the rundown house in Wilton Manors.

That was a conversation we had to have. Money breaks up a lot of marriages and even more unmarried couples.

There were things I knew, though. Lester was pushy about physical training. Would that carry over to other areas? He was usually the one who picked the restaurants where we ate, always concerned about calories and nutrition, even when I wanted to splurge on a gourmet burger or a piece of cheesecake.

Lester controlled a great deal of what we did together. So far it hadn't mattered to me—I enjoyed working out with him, visiting museums and art festivals, and of course having sex with him.

Was I losing some part of myself in attaching to him? What would happen if I lost interest in art, or I wanted to start country-western line dancing and he didn't?

We met for dinner Tuesday night at an Italian restaurant called Bona in Wilton Manors. When a friend with a Boston accent referred us there, it had sounded like the name was Boner, and Lester and I giggled about that when we decided to eat there.

He had been to the office in Doral that day, and he was wearing his one business suit. "Guess I'm going to have to start dressing more like you, G-Man," he said, when I mentioned it as we sat down. "You want to go to Sawgrass Mills with me this weekend and do some shopping?"

"Sure. But I thought we were going to look at apartments."

"First things first. Starting Monday I have to go to the office three days a week, and I can't wear the same suit every day."

"You're not going to be the easiest guy to shop for," I said, before I picked up my menu. "Your shoulders are so broad and your waist is narrow, and your biceps will explode out of a tailored shirt."

He pouted. "You make it sound like my body is a negative."

"Not to me, sweetheart. But we're going to have to find stores that sell larger sizes."

He looked down at the menu and I couldn't tell if he was angry I'd pointed out his size, or pleased that I noticed how big and smoking hot he was.

I needed to shift the discussion and I remembered Miriam asking me to get Lester to talk to me about Cuban art. So I asked.

"There's this one guy I really like," Lester said. "Carlos Estévez. He's a painter, sculptor and photographer. You know the pointillists like Seurat, right?"

I nodded.

"Estévez is like that. He connects these star-like dots with lines to make these pictures of mechanical stuff like gears and telephones.

He's got this one painting of a turtle, and all the points of its shell are connected like a constellation. It's totally mesmerizing."

"Miriam mentioned him. He's one of the artists whose work has been stolen recently."

"That's wicked. People should be able to see these pieces in museums and galleries."

It was so cool to see Lester get engaged by something, whether it was the latest small-batch whiskey he was promoting or some random Cuban artist. We talked through our meal about art, and then over dessert we shifted to apartments. He agreed that if we got a place with a good gym, we could work out there together and avoid monthly memberships. "A pool, too," he said. "I'd love to live in a place with a lap pool."

"That might be harder to find. Every place will have a pool so you might have to make do. Do you play tennis? A lot of these places have courts."

"Not since I was in high school. You?"

"Same." We kept talking over our salads. He agreed we'd need a second bedroom for an office we could share, and that we should start our search close to the highway. "If we can minimize our commutes even by a few minutes that will add up over time," he said.

As the server was writing down my order of lemon chicken piccata, Lester said, "That's a high-calorie dish, G-man. I'm getting the grilled grouper. Why don't you try that?"

"I'll stick to my order," I said to the server and smiled. He raised his eyebrows but wrote everything down.

"Did you notice the bands across his chest?" Lester asked after the server had left. "He's trans."

"I was more focused on the way you interrupted me," I said. "I'm a grownup, Lester. I can order what I want."

"I'm just looking out for you."

"I know. So I can be the best G-Man I can be. I appreciate it, but sometimes you can be bossy. Remember, I'm not a client."

Since he didn't look happy about that comment, I shifted gears to

Jesse Venable. "Once the transfer to his checking account went through, I went online and paid all his bills," I said. "I figured out a couple of ways to simplify things for him, too. I arranged for his car insurance, his cell phone and his cable bills to be paid automatically by one of his credit cards and filled out the paperwork to have his monthly homeowner's association payment withdrawn directly from his bank account."

"You may be a G-Man but you're an accountant at heart," Lester said, laughing. "I love it when you get so excited about business stuff."

"And I love it when you geek out about art." That reminded me of my worry that I was following Lester's lead too often. But so far it was working out for me.

I told him about the idea Miriam and I had to get Yulirus Diaz out of Krome and into Jesse Venable's place. "The two of them can talk about art until the cows come home, and Diaz can help with groceries and cleaning."

"Have you talked to either of them about this arrangement yet?"

"Miriam's setting up an appointment with the immigration judge."

"These aren't pawns on a chessboard you're moving around, Angus. These are real people. Suppose this Diaz guy says he's too educated to wipe some old guy's behind."

"Venable can still wipe his own behind," I said. "And wouldn't you do that if it got you out of that detention center?"

"You and I aren't this guy. If I were you I'd make sure both of them agree to your plan before you push it much further."

"You're right. I just assumed it was a good deal for both of them, so they'd both agree."

He smirked. "What was it your stepfather said about assume?"

I frowned. "Roger is my mother's second husband, not my stepfather, and you know that. But you're right, he always said that when you assume something it makes an ass of you and me."

It was an odd dinner, both of us on edge, probably about the whole moving in thing. But I kept reminding myself that he was a good guy, that we fit together well, and that I was lucky to have landed him when so many of the other nibbles on my line had turned out to be jerks.

Lester and I both had early mornings the next day, so we said goodnight after we left the restaurant, though we did find an isolated corner behind a secondhand store where we could indulge ourselves in a few minutes of deep kissing. On my way back to my car I thought about living with Lester, being able to hug and kiss and whatever else whenever the mood struck us because we'd be together.

I had to focus on the positive, I reminded myself. Lester was kind and smart and sexy, and if there were going to be difficulties we'd work through them.

As I drove home, I realized that I hadn't spoken with my mother in a while, so after I was settled in my bedroom I called her. "How's everything, Mom?"

"Not so good. You know Roger's been in poor health lately."

"Something about his heart, right? Blood not circulating properly?"

"His heart isn't pumping strong enough to get the blood down to his fingers and toes, and he's getting worse. He's going in for a cardiac catheterization on Friday to see if he needs bypass surgery."

"He's a tough old bird," I said. "I'm sure he'll be fine."

"He's not so young anymore, Angus. And all those years he smoked didn't help."

My mom had had me when she was twenty, which made her just a bit shy of fifty years old. Roger was ten or twelve years older than she was. He had been a chain smoker when he married my mom, when I was fifteen and Danny was ten, and I remember learning in school how damaging second-hand smoke was. When I'd brought it up Roger had reminded me that I was living in his house and if I didn't like it I could move out.

I managed to do that soon after my eighteenth birthday, when I went to Penn State, and I never lived with my mom and Roger after that. I worked extra hard at school to maintain my scholarship, and at

La Scuola, an Italian restaurant. I bussed tables, waited on customers, then moved up to bartender as soon as I was old enough.

I put away as much money as I could so that Danny could get through school without doing what I had to, and he had followed me to State College just after I graduated with my master's in accounting and moved to Philadelphia.

"I hope everything comes out okay," I said, more for my mother's sake than for Roger's.

"Thank you, sweetheart. I'll let you know what the doctors say after the procedure on Friday."

I was restless after that conversation. My mother had already lived through the death of one husband, and regardless of how I felt about Roger I didn't want her to have to go through that again.

I got up, opened my laptop, and went back to Jesse Venable's affairs. Because he was over sixty-nine and a half, he needed to take mandatory distributions from each of his retirement accounts. He had six different ones, a couple of them with only a few thousand dollars apiece. I was able to close two of them by withdrawing his RMD, and to consolidate two more with the same broker.

He was supposed to be receiving monthly payments from the company that had bought out his gold buyer stores, and he wasn't. I sent an email to his attorney introducing myself, and asking him to look into that payment situation.

I was glad I was able to get his financial affairs in order, and make things easier for him to handle in the future.

Wednesday morning Miriam called. "I've been doing more snooping," she said. "I was wondering why Alvaro Vela Romero would be interested in someone like Yulirus Diaz. I did some digging and discovered that both he and his son, Alvaro Vela Blanco, have significant art collections. The father focuses on artists from the first half of the 20th century, who introduced Modernism to Cuba, like Wilfredo Lam."

The name meant nothing to me, but I wrote it down.

"The son collects more contemporary artists like the Yuana

Valdés, Dalton Gata, and the late Ana Mendieta, among others. I discovered that while his father has been very open about his art collection, Alvaro Vela Blanco hasn't said much, and has never had anyone to his home to photograph it."

"Is that unusual?"

"Collectors like to show off their collections," she said. "Look at the Rubells. They set up their own museum in Miami to share what they own."

I'd been to the Rubell Museum in Miami's Design District with Lester, and knew that it was one of the biggest private contemporary art collections in North America. "OK. But it's not evidence of criminality, is it?"

"He slipped up once and bragged to someone that he has a statue of a cat by Fernando Botero, which he bought because it reminded him of his own pet. Those are very rare, and I couldn't find any provenance that shows he purchased it legitimately."

She paused. "Of course, it could have been a private transaction. It's another small piece of the puzzle we're assembling. But the real reason I called was to let you know that I've arranged an appointment before the immigration judge at Krome on Thursday."

"We should talk to Diaz before that, shouldn't we?" I asked. "Make sure he's willing to go along with our plans?"

"I can't get down there today. Can you?"

I checked my online calendar. "Pretty clear. I'll call and make an appointment for this afternoon."

I didn't relish the idea of making the trek to Krome two days in a row, but I wanted to give Diaz overnight to think about our offer and make sure he would go along with it.

It took a couple of conversations with different individuals at Krome, but I got someone to agree I could speak with Yulirus Diaz at three o'clock. I left in plenty of time because dark clouds hovered over the Everglades. Rain spattered the windshield as I drove down I-75, and by the time I turned onto Krome Avenue I was in a full-on downpour.

I had my lights on and the wipers on high but neither of them mattered. I was on an unfamiliar two-lane road with only the taillights of the SUV ahead of me, and the oncoming headlights in the other lane, to guide me. I felt so vulnerable in my little car. Why hadn't I chosen to buy a big SUV, like the ones that bracketed me front and back? What if I hit a deep puddle and swamped my car?

I wanted to check the weather forecast on my cell phone but I kept my hands on the wheel and my focus on the road ahead of me. Finally the rain let up a bit and I saw the Miccosukee casino rising out of the mist, and knew I was close.

The sun was shining by the time I reached Krome, as if it had never rained there at all. I found my way back to the interview room easily, and Yulirus Diaz came in through the other door a moment later.

"I have an idea." I explained about the possibility of living with Jesse Venable, an art collector in poor health. "He'd need someone to drive him around, fix his dinner and so on. And you could help him catalog his artwork."

"Why would he do this for me?"

"He's lonely, and the home health aides can't talk to him about art the way you can." I hesitated. "There's one more thing you should know. He's gay, and his collection is focused on male nudes. Is that okay with you?"

He smiled. "I am gay also, so that does not bother me. But this is only for work, right? No sex?"

"Not at all." I explained about Venable's surgery, and Diaz shuddered. "I know. I can't imagine not being able to have sex with my boyfriend again. But Venable's a lot older than we are."

I could tell from Diaz's body language that he'd caught the way I outed myself as well. He wanted to know what kind of art Venable collected—paintings? Sculptures? I explained as well as I could what I'd seen at Venable's house, and Diaz was excited.

"You do know how to drive, don't you?"

"I learned on my uncle's farm. I can drive trucks, tractors, cars. Anything." He smiled broadly. "When do I go?"

"We have to meet the immigration judge tomorrow and convince him," I said. "There's one more part, though."

"There is always something," he said. "What else?"

I took a deep breath. "In order to justify releasing you to the FBI, you have to work with us," I said. "You would have to get in touch with your friend Elpidio and find out how he is selling these paintings."

"You want me to offer to help him."

"We have to be very careful." I explained the concept of entrapment, but it seemed that didn't exist in Cuban policing.

"What if he try to kill me again? You will protect me?"

"He's in Cuba, and you're here. He has to get here before he can hurt you. Venable lives in a big house with a burglar alarm. And if you are careful, you will be safe."

I said it but I couldn't be sure of it. We didn't know what kind of connections Elpidio López had in the United States. But if he took the bait, we'd set up safeguards.

Finally he shrugged and said, *"A grandes males, grandes remedios.* It means for big diseases there are big remedies. I will do what I can."

"Excellent." I promised to see him the next afternoon for the immigration hearing, and drove back to Miramar. I went immediately to Miriam's office, where she was on the phone, speaking in fluent French to someone. I could only catch a few words.

"Another art case?" I asked, when she hung up.

She shook her head. "I do some pro bono work for an organization that helps Haitian immigrants. That was one of the women I'm helping."

She sat back in her seat. "Mr. Diaz willing to help us out?"

"Yes, though he's worried about his safety. How easy will it be to convince the immigration judge?"

"No idea. I've never done something like this before. But we need a complete plan in place because I'm sure we will only get one shot at this."

We brainstormed for the next hour, figuring out exactly how to phrase what we wanted. We agreed that Miriam would do the talking because she had more experience, and because, as she put it delicately, enthusiasm was not always welcomed in a court of law.

I understood that, and promised to keep my mouth shut. Then we researched the judge we'd be arguing before. His name was Harold Steiner, and he had been a public defender, then spent a dozen years in private practice before being appointed to the 16th Judicial Circuit Court of Florida, Monroe County, where had served for twenty years. After his retirement, he had become an immigration judge at Krome.

"What exactly is the judicial circuit court?" I asked Miriam.

"County judges handle all basic court matters," she said. "Misdemeanors, low-value civil suits and so on. The circuit court gets the bigger cases—felonies, juvenile cases, probate, domestic disputes, and higher value civil suits."

"So Steiner must be a sharp guy, if they put him on the bigger cases."

"Not necessarily. There is such a thing as an old-boy network in Florida, you know. However, the fact that he's moved into immigration after a full career may mean that he cares about people."

Miriam picked up a card from her desk. "There's one more thing. There's an opening night party at a gallery on Las Olas Friday evening celebrating a young Cuban American artist named Silvia Bernal. It's the kind of event Alvaro Vela Blanco, Alvaro Vela Romero's son, might attend. Do you think you could get there and look around at the crowd?"

"Sure. I'll see if Lester's free to go with me."

By the time we came up with a full strategy, it was long past quitting time, and it was full dark. Instead of driving north on I-75 as I normally would have, I drove south toward Doral. The traffic was just as bad, and there was a backlog of folks getting off at the Dolphin

Mall. But it was easy to get off at the next exit, and there were several new rental communities with fancy names right off 74th Street.

At home that night, I spent a lot of time poring over Google maps, comparing travel time to apartment locations, and coming up pleasantly surprised. Lester had made a good choice for both of us.

That is, if we both decided to move in together. I was excited but nervous, annoyed with Jonas for leaving me, and worried about how Lester's new job, and the travel it required, would affect our relationship. I guess that meant I was growing up.

Chapter 8

With Both Feet

Lester was at a demo that night so I couldn't talk to him about my findings, but I did text him a couple of apartment listings in Doral. I didn't hear anything back that night, but those events got busy, and he was always tired when they were finished. I did text him about the gallery opening on Las Olas, though.

The next morning dawned gloriously sunny, and I hoped that was a good omen for my trip to Krome with Miriam to meet with the immigration judge. It was a real tourist office kind of day, the sky a light blue without a single cloud. A gentle breeze ruffled the tops of the palm trees as I went for a quick run, dodging garbage trucks and old men walking tiny dogs.

My T-shirt was drenched with sweat by the time I got back to the house, and I tossed it into the washer with the rest of the dirty clothes in my room. I dressed with care, in a navy suit, white shirt and light blue tie. I wanted to look as professional as possible in front of the judge, especially because my red hair and pale skin tended to make me look younger than I was.

The weather held as Miriam and I drove to Krome that morning.

"What else are you working on these days?" I asked her as we zoomed down the highway.

"I've been drafted to join the new international corruption squad," she said. "I have some experience with South America, and of course I speak Spanish. It's possible there may be some art connections there, too."

Of course, I thought. I wondered how many languages Miriam spoke. "That's so cool. I've heard people say that South Florida is the corruption capital of Latin America."

"That's a useful summary," Miriam said. "We're working with the Treasury Department's Financial Crimes Enforcement Network. Title insurers have to report the identities of people who buy residential real estate valued at $300,000 or more to them. And you know how much foreign capital flows into real estate here."

"Some of it is legitimate flight capital, isn't it?"

"Absolutely. And there's nothing illegal about that. But if there's money laundering going on, people trying to wash dirty money by filtering it through a real estate transaction, that's where we come in."

I watched a long-legged great blue heron pick at grubs in the canal beside us. What would it be like to have that kind of money, to be able to drop a million or two on a condo I might only visit once or twice a year?

Not going to be a problem for me, though. There was no way I'd ever make that kind of money, and though I experienced the occasional pang of regret that I hadn't chosen a higher-paying way to use my degree, I comforted myself with the thought that I was doing good in the world, and often enjoying my job. One of our neighbors in Wilton Manors had a bumper sticker on the back of his truck that read "My real life is better than your vacation," and I had to agree.

South Florida was not only beautiful, but it was a hotbed of interesting and weird crimes, some of which I'd been able to investigate. I loved the meme on social media that suggested you Google "Florida man" with your birthday, and see what came up.

My result was a young black man bicycling down I-95 wearing

only a neon-pink thong. Lester's came up with a white guy in the panhandle, the area I'd heard referred to as FLA—Fucking Lower Alabama. He had beaten his ex-wife's new boyfriend with a fraternity paddle, stripped him naked and hogtied him to the back of his pickup. Fortunately the cops had intervened before he could take off and drag the poor guy down the road.

"South Florida is one of eight regions subjected to a geographic targeting order designed to flag money laundering through real-estate deals," Miriam said. "We're working with legats all over Central and South America to identify shady officials and follow the money."

Legats, or legal attachés, were FBI employees who worked out of U.S. embassies around the world. When I joined the Bureau I hoped to work my way into one of those jobs—but now that I was getting more serious with Lester, I wasn't sure if that would be possible.

We parked in the same place at Krome but after we showed our badges and were checked in, we were directed to wait in chairs near the entrance. After a few minutes, a young woman in a colorful headscarf fetched us and took us to the judge's chambers.

Judge Steiner had a bald pate and a fringe of white hair that made him look like a medieval monk. Instead of judicial robes, he wore a dark suit like mine, and while his tie was a darker blue than mine, a bright yellow image of Tweety Bird rested at the bottom. I hoped that was a good sign, that the judge had a sense of humor.

Not that we were going to joke about Yulirus Diaz's situation. But I find that people with a sense of humor are often easier to reason with as well.

The young woman settled in the corner with a strange-looking typewriter. "For the record, I am Judge Harold Steiner," the judge said, and he gave the date and time.

Miriam jumped in, introducing herself and me. She gave Diaz's name and his registration number.

Then the judge took over. "What's the Bureau's interest in Mr. Diaz?"

Miriam explained what we knew. "Based on conversations with

Mr. Diaz, we believe that his friend, Elpidio López, is stealing valuable works of art from poorly guarded churches and museums in the Cuban countryside." She went over López's authentication request from Diaz, Diaz's opinion about the Murillo, and the ensuing attempt on Diaz's life.

"Are you making a case for asylum based on that?" Judge Steiner interrupted. "Because I still don't understand the Bureau connection."

I could sense Miriam choosing her words carefully. "We would like to use Mr. Diaz's relationship with Mr. López to explore where the stolen art is being sold. Is it coming into the United States? Or going to another country we share information with?"

"In other words, a fishing expedition."

"A legitimate investigation into the theft of Cuban art patrimony," Miriam said primly. "Using Mr. Diaz's expertise as an art historian. Another case in California has already established a chain of theft from Cuba. And Mr. López has mentioned to Mr. Diaz that he works with a collector of Cuban art in Miami."

The judge still looked skeptical, so I couldn't help myself; I had to jump in. "There is also a humanitarian aspect to this situation. If Mr. Diaz is returned to Cuba, he will be in danger of further attack from Mr. López or his associates unless we can bring the criminals involved to justice. Mr. Diaz will certainly be unable to pursue his livelihood if he returns to Cuba because of his attempt to defect. We have already secured a temporary home and work situation for Mr. Diaz which will keep him from being a burden on the state while we investigate."

Judge Steiner looked at me. "Your enthusiasm is clear, Special Agent Green. And I appreciate that in a public servant. Too many of us would rather go through the motions than jump in with both feet. However, I am concerned that beyond the speculative nature of this investigation, you may be setting up a lure that could be considered entrapment."

"Our plan is to get Mr. López to admit to Mr. Diaz details of previous exports. And then let Mr. López make the offer himself, to ask Mr. Diaz for help disposing of the Murillo painting in the United States."

"If it is a Murillo," Judge Steiner said. "You have only Mr. Diaz's word on that."

Miriam leaned forward. "He is a trained art historian, so he is capable of making an initial judgment."

"Your honor, this is a win-win situation," I added. "If we can arrest Elpidio López we can retrieve this painting and return it to Cuba. Any positive steps we can take may improve our relations with our close neighbor. If López doesn't bite, then there is less threat for Yulirus Diaz, and he can return home safely."

"Or he can disappear into Miami," the judge said.

"The situation we have arranged for him is so appropriate that he would have no motive to leave," I said. "He would move in with an elderly art collector who needs help cataloging his collection, particularly because he is disabled and has a rotating crew of aides coming in and out of the house, who could easily steal from him. Mr. Diaz would be a companion to this man, and also act as a protector of his collection."

The judge was silent for what seemed like a long time, but was probably only a minute or two. "During the last years of her life, my mother was in a similar situation," he said. "She needed the help of aides for her activities of daily living, and they were always changing. She wasn't a wealthy woman, but she did have a few prized possessions, including a diamond engagement ring, and that ring, along with a few other items, disappeared before we noticed."

Miriam and I both listened intently.

"So I sympathize with this art collector. But at the same time, I am reluctant to issue a blanket amnesty. I will allow Mr. Yulirus Diaz to be released to FBI custody for a period of two weeks. At the end of that time we will convene again to discuss your progress and the ultimate resolution of Mr. Diaz's situation. That concludes our interview."

He nodded to the stenographer, who stopped typing. "This is not an open-ended invitation to explore whatever you choose," he said to us. "I expect a full report in two weeks." He stood up. "You can wait in the lobby. I'll call down and have Mr. Diaz brought up."

We thanked him and walked out. "This is great!" I said to Miriam as soon as we reached the lobby.

"It's a start. Why don't you call Mr. Venable and see if you can drop Mr. Diaz off there this afternoon?"

"Where am I going to go?" Venable asked, when I asked if he'd be home that afternoon.

I assumed it was a rhetorical question, so I didn't answer. "We're going to bring Yulirus up to Weston, and I'll have some paperwork for you to sign, just that you agree to keep Yulirus with you until you notify us otherwise."

He grumbled and complained about his aides for a few minutes, and I finally got him off the phone. Miriam was getting increasingly impatient, spending most of her time on the phone. She had a great talent for speaking softly, with her head slightly turned, so I couldn't hear most of what she said, but I gathered something was exploding in her money laundering task force case. I was worried that she was going to have to get back to the office and I didn't know what I'd do. Would I go back with her, and then return for Diaz? Did Uber come all the way out to the Krome Detention Center?

It took more than an hour for them to finish processing Diaz for release, and my nerves were on edge. He wore a pair of cheap jeans and a short-sleeved polo shirt and carried a small backpack, and if I didn't know better I'd think he was just another of the guys I saw at Wilton Manors bars.

"Thank you for help me," he said, and his eyes teared up.

Miriam was still on the phone so I hugged him and said, "We're going to work to keep you safe and get you a shot at staying here."

Lester texted me that he was busy that night and couldn't go with me to the gallery party on Las Olas because he had to sub for one of the other reps at a demo. I wasn't comfortable going to such a gathering by myself, but there was someone else I could call.

Tom Laughlin was an older gay man who lived in a wealthy neighborhood of Fort Lauderdale and he had money, and taste. We'd met in the course of another case, and we'd become friends, and he'd be the perfect companion to take to the gallery.

I called him and was delighted when he answered right away. I explained what I wanted to do, and he said that he was happy to lend a hand. We arranged to meet on Las Olas for dinner, then walk over to the gallery together.

I drove Miriam's car back to the FBI office, with her riding shotgun, still on the phone, and Yulirus in the back seat, his arms wrapped around his pack. I felt awkward; I wanted to talk to him, reassure him and get him on board with our plan, but I didn't want to talk over Miriam. The sun was so bright that it made me squint, and I had to focus on driving.

It was with a great sense of relief that I pulled into the FBI garage and Miriam got out. She turned her phone aside and said, "Keep me in the loop," and then she was gone.

"You okay if we continue up to the place where you're going to stay?" I asked as Yulirus and I got out of the car. "You need the bathroom or anything?"

"I am fine."

"Good. That's my ride over there, the green Mini."

"Like your name," he said.

"You got it." The garage was hot and humid, and I wiped a bit of sweat from my brow as we walked to my car. "Does your name mean something?"

He shook his head. "I come from *Generación* Y," he said. "Some say it is from Russian names like Yuri and Yevgeny. For a time, everyone want to give their child a name that begins with Y, and like my parents, they make many of them up. Your first name, it means what?"

"Angus?" I laughed. "It's a breed of cattle. It's from Irish and Scottish Gaelic, and it means either one strength or one choice."

"I am glad you choose to help me."

I didn't know what to say to that. Yes, I had chosen to help Yulirus Diaz. Why? Because my gaydar had told me he was part of my tribe? Because my spidey senses told me there was a case there, and I might be able to use it to further my career at the Bureau? I was tired of just doing analysis for other agents, and wanted to show that I could run cases myself.

Or maybe I was a gullible fool, too quick to jump in with both feet. That had been a problem for me in the past. Only time would tell if it would happen again.

Chapter 9

Transitions

Yulirus kept fussing in the seat next to me. And since the Mini Cooper is a small car, his nerves were catching. "What's the matter?" I asked, though I was sure there were many answers to that question.

"What if this man don't like me?" He was tapping his fingers on the glove compartment in front of him. "What if I don't like him? Do I have to stay there?"

"You're a nice guy, and you're good-looking," I said. "Don't worry, he'll like you. If you don't like him? You'll have to suffer. It's only for two weeks. And yes, you have to stay there, at least until your next hearing. I guarantee you it will be better than being at Krome."

He wasn't comforted.

I sighed. "Look, I've known Jesse Venable for a while, and he's definitely an unusual guy." I tried to avoid any clichés that Yulirus wouldn't know, like Jesse was a piece of work. "He's sick and he's lonely. As long as you can understand that, and talk to him about art, I think you two will get along fine."

As we got closer to Weston, Yulirus became entranced by the landscaping. "Is so beautiful," he said. "Many rich people live here?"

I shrugged. "Yes and no. A lot of them are ordinary working people."

"In Cuba, only the rich live like this."

"Welcome to the United States," I said. "Where an awful lot of people live beyond their means."

He didn't understand that colloquialism. "They borrow money for mortgages they can't afford. They spend more than they earn and put the rest on credit cards. It's the American way."

I turned into the long, well-landscaped drive that led to the guard house for Venable's community. I showed my ID to the guard, and as we drove through the well-manicured streets, I could see Yulirus perk up. "This man, he must be rich to live in a place like this."

I had seen all of Jesse's financial statements, and I knew how much he had in the bank and the value of his house, but it wasn't my place to decide if he was rich or not. "He's had some setbacks. He was breaking the law, and he spent some time in prison and had to sell his businesses. But I'm sure he can afford to feed you and pay you."

I saw Jesse Venable's house through Yulirus's eyes as I pulled into the driveway. Though it was only a single-story property, to a poor immigrant it was probably a mansion. The yard was trimmed neatly, with several palm trees and flowering pink and purple hibiscus.

Yulirus slung his pack on his back and followed me up the cobblestone walkway. Jesse opened the door as he had to me and Lester a few days before, and I introduced him to Yulirus. His oversized black T-shirt and sweatpants hung on him like a shroud, but there was more life in his eyes.

He held out a hand to Yulirus, who grasped it with both of his. "Thank you for have me in your home."

"I haven't agreed to anything yet." Jesse turned and pushed his walker into the living room, where a different, younger Haitian aide sat on the sofa, earphones in her ears, watching a program on her phone.

Jesse shooed her away. "You can go to your room. I have guests."

She frowned, but stood up and walked away.

"She live here?" Yulirus asked.

"They come and go," Jesse said, settling his bulk into an easy chair. He motioned me to the sofa, then turned his attention to Yulirus. "Angus says you're an art historian. Look around. Tell me what your favorite piece is."

It was as if Yulirus finally noticed that the living room was crowded with art. It reminded me of photos I had seen of Gertrude Stein's salon in Paris, with paintings and photographs covering nearly every piece of wall. A huge armoire with glass doors held shelves of sculptures and other small art works. Jesse grabbed a remote from a pocket on the side of the chair and turned on tiny pinpoint lights that shone down on certain works.

"Go on, walk around," Jesse said. "Angus has some papers for me to sign."

I pulled them out of my messenger bag and stood up. I brought one of the black lacquer dining chairs over next to Jesse and walked him through the paperwork. He had to sign that he would keep Yulirus Diaz at his home until the next immigration hearing, and that he would notify me or Miriam immediately if Diaz left.

As Jesse read, I watched Yulirus walk around the room, looking at the art. When he came to sit on the sofa again, his eyes were starry. "There are many works here I only see in books or on Internet," he said. "The Hockney of the man in the pool, is it original?"

Jesse nodded. His black clothes reflected dark shadows onto his face. "One of my favorite pieces, too," he said.

They started talking about art, and I wished Lester had been there with us. He would have known more of the artists, been able to understand the jargon. I had no idea what a giclée print was, or what chromogenic color meant, but Jesse and Yulirus spoke the same language.

I stood up. "If you two are all right together, I'll head out."

Jesse waved his hand at me. "Okay, thanks."

I looked at Yulirus, whose broad smile told me he was going to be fine with Jesse.

I started my car, and while I waited for the air conditioning to kick in I called Lester. "I just delivered the Cuban guy to Jesse Venable."

"So you're in Weston? Want to meet at Sawgrass Mills and help me shop for clothes?"

Lester was at his place in Fort Lauderdale, so I agreed to meet him at the Paul bakery at Sawgrass. I got a coffee and a raisin pastry, and hooked up my laptop to a VPN, and then to the FBI intranet. I emailed Miriam that I had settled Yulirus in Weston, and then read a bunch of administrative messages. By the time I had caught up, Lester arrived.

He looked more formally dressed than I'd ever seen before, in a white oxford cloth shirt, black dress slacks and black loafers. "Had a meeting this afternoon," he said, after we had hugged and kissed hello. "I figured I'd stay dressed up since this is the kind of stuff I'm looking for."

Lester's was a body to reckon with. The shirt was baggy, because he had a broad neck and a narrow waist. The slacks were tight over his massive thighs and calves. I hated to say it but he didn't look good. Whatever we bought was going to need some massive tailoring.

He had a list of stores he wanted to check out, many of them in the outdoor section called the Colonnade, but none of the fancy brands catered to his size, at least not at the outlet level. By the time we finished at the sixth store he was looking depressed.

"There's one of those larger-size men's stores on the outside, along the circle," I said. "We can go over there."

"I wanted some snazzy brands," Lester said, frowning. "I want to look like you."

I laughed. "You'd have to lose about fifty pounds of muscle for that." I put my arm around his shoulders. "Come on, let's see what we can find that will make you look even more handsome than you are when you're naked."

He couldn't help smiling. We left my car where it was parked and he drove us out to the ring road, where we found the store. There were a couple of brands I recognized in the window, and Lester perked up when the clerk, a Jamaican guy with dreads who radiated gaydar, fawned all over him.

By the time we were finished, Lester had racked up significant debt on his credit card. He and I did have to talk about money. But that wasn't the time or place.

He bought two suits, one a charcoal gray pinstripe and the other in taupe. A pair of sport coats in navy and dark green, and a half-dozen slacks in colors coordinated with the sport coats. Six white dress shirts and two in light blue.

The store had an in-house tailor, an older Cuban man. For the first half hour, I watched as he worked, nipping here, opening up there, until each garment looked like it had been made specially for Lester. Then I turned to my phone.

I knew Danny's shifts at La Scuola, because they had been my own, before I moved to Philadelphia and passed them to him. He had started at Penn State as a freshman at 18, but because the owners already knew him from his visits to me, he'd been able to skip being a busboy and then a server and move immediately to work as a bartender. Even though he couldn't legally drink anything alcoholic he served, he was able to take the job under the state statutes. La Scuola had replaced one Green with another, with hardly a speed bump.

Danny even looked a lot like me, though his hair was more gold than red. We had the same square face, slim nose and dimpled cheeks. Most customers hardly noticed the change.

By my reckoning, Danny would be at home getting ready for his shift. When he answered he even said, "Hey, bro, just about to leave for work. What's up?"

"You spoken to Mom recently?"

"Yeah, she called me Sunday morning. Woke me up out of a sound sleep."

That wasn't unusual. My brother was one of the soundest sleepers I knew, able to drop off in the middle of a conversation, sleep through loud cracks of thunder and torrents of rain. He told me once, when we were both drunk, that he thought it was because he knew I would always be there to protect him, so loud noises never bothered him.

It was sweet but also worrisome. His life and mine had veered apart when I left Scranton for State College, and I had no idea where he would end up after he graduated.

Or who would protect him.

"So she told you about Roger?"

"Yeah, something about his heart. I resisted the urge to say I was surprised that he had one."

"Good call on your part."

"What's new with you?"

"Lester got a promotion," I said. "He's going to work out of the main office, by the Miami airport. So he's looking to move down there to minimize his commute."

I hesitated for a couple of seconds, then added, "He asked me to move down there with him."

"Is that closer to your work?"

"A lot."

"And you two are both still slamming the sausage, right?"

"Danny. Where did you learn language like that?"

"From you."

"Oh. Yeah, Lester and I are still engaged in a mutually rewarding physical relationship."

Danny cackled. "Then good for you, bro. Hold on to him and keep that big boner close."

"I never told you anything about the size of his boner," I said.

"I met the dude, remember? I may be straight but I can still size up a guy's package by how he fills his shorts."

"This conversation is on a vertical slide," I said. "Have a good shift, bro. Catch you on the flip side."

"You too," he said. "And send my brotherly love to your stud muffin."

I agreed that I would do that, and looked over at Lester, who was trying on the first of the shirts that had been altered. He was looking at himself in the three-way mirror and glowing.

I thought about the way Yulirus's eyes had lit up when he surveyed the paintings and sculptures at Jesse's house. I felt the same way – my boyfriend was a work of art.

Lester had his share of body image issues, though. Gay men often looked at his body as something to be worshipped or conquered, giving no thought to the brain behind his handsome face. He had been categorized and commodified since his late teens, when he first began to work out seriously, and he was suspicious of anyone who complimented him. Not because he didn't know he was handsome, but he preferred less superficial comments.

I often had to balance telling him he was smoking hot with other compliments, which wasn't hard. He wasn't a genius, but he was smart, and he had great instincts for people. He had a superficial charm and an inner goodness. All those traits had served him well as a personal trainer, and then doing liquor demos. I worried that he might not be so comfortable calculating budgets or writing personnel evaluations. But he was smart enough to learn all that, and I was there to help if he needed.

We ended up at an American-style grill and restaurant at the far end of the Colonnade shops. We ordered craft beers and personal pizzas, and then sat back to talk. "I was looking at apartments in Doral," I said. "It'll be easy for you to get to your office, and if you have to travel, it's a straight shot from there to the airport in Miami."

"What about you, though? You don't want somewhere halfway?"

"The highways just don't work that way. I drove out there last night. Halfway between my office in Miramar and yours in Doral would put us somewhere in either Miami Lakes or Hialeah. I looked up the demographics, and Miami Lakes skews older than we are and with a larger family size. The prices there are higher than Doral, too. And while I like living in a multicultural community, neither of us speaks fluent enough Spanish to settle someplace where every transaction is going to be in Spanglish."

He looked at me and laughed. "You do analyze everything, don't you?"

"So do you." Lester and I both shared a logical approach to life, which generally made decision-making between us pretty simple. He agreed with my points about Miami Lakes and Hialeah, and that we ought to focus on Doral, where it was more likely we'd live near other English-speaking younger people, perhaps with some gays thrown in.

We were in agreement on the things were looking for—a gym, a pool, a second bedroom for an office, easy highway access.

I was still nervous, but I was moving toward acceptance. "There's one thing, though," I said. "We've never talked about money."

He shrugged. "What's there to say? You earn it, you spend it."

"I'm an accountant, remember? And one of my electives at Penn State was a sociology course where we looked at how peoples' attitudes toward money differ."

"How is yours different from mine? I see you pop out your credit card all the time."

"I live on a budget. Do you?"

He shook his head. "At the end of the month I pay my bills and if there's something left, that's gravy."

I gulped. But I couldn't let that go unnoticed. "That kind of attitude scares me," I said. "I saw how my mother struggled when my father died, before she met Roger. She literally picked up pennies on the street, and sometimes I saw her counting them out to pay for things. I remember once she found a ten-dollar bill, and it was like Christmas and a birthday together. She bought the three of us ice cream sundaes at Dairy Queen."

"My family wasn't rich, but my father did okay," Lester said. He'd grown up in Kentucky and his father worked for a man who trained racehorses. "We always had money for whatever we needed. I think I'll be able to earn whatever money I need, just like my father."

"But what about when you were doing personal training. Didn't your income go up and down?"

"Yeah, and I built up balances on my credit cards. But I always paid them off."

The server returned with our beers, and he held up his glass to me. "Come on, let's toast to moving in together. We're going to be a real couple."

That struck me as weird. We were already a couple, weren't we? But Lester had suffered a couple of broken hearts before he met me, guys walking out on him, so maybe for him getting me to sign a lease with him was a sign that I wasn't going to leave him.

"I'm going to be making more money than you," Lester said. "So I think we ought to split the expenses based on that. I'll pay more of the rent, more of the utilities and so on."

There was that take-charge attitude toward money again. I worried that he'd end up building up his credit card balances again without telling me.

"I don't want to nickel and dime everything, Lester. We'll split everything fifty-fifty."

"That's not fair."

"You don't know how long you'll have this job. Mine is a lot steadier. And what if I get transferred, and it takes you a while to find something in the new place?"

"Hold on. You think you're going to leave Florida?"

I shrugged. "The Bureau moves people around as they need to," I said. "Sometimes if you want a promotion you have to change offices to get it."

"And you'd just pick up and go? Carry me along like luggage?"

The pizzas arrived. "Lester. I've only been in this job for a couple of years. Nobody's going to talk about moving me for a while."

"Yet you're already thinking about it. Here we are, ready to move in together, and you're thinking about moving on."

"I didn't say that."

"I don't want to talk about this anymore." He picked up his pizza and started to eat.

How had we dropped into an argument so quickly? We had been so excited about moving in together. But the truth was that agents rarely stayed in one office for more than a few years. Either there were opportunities for advancement, or a particular agent's skill set was needed somewhere else. Miriam had started her career in Boston, then moved to Chicago, spent a year in San Diego, and ended up in Miami. Vito had been recruited at the New York office, spent five years in Houston, and had been in Miami for four years.

The only agent I knew who had started in Miami and remained there was one of my other mentors, Roly Gutierrez, who had passed up several promotion opportunities and fought to stay in Miami, where his and his wife's family were.

My mom was back in Scranton, and Danny was still at Penn State, so I didn't have family ties anywhere in particular. But if Lester and I became a long-time couple, I'd have to include him in my plans. If I was offered a promotion, or a job on an exciting task force, and it meant relocating, how would he feel about it? Clearly he wasn't thrilled now at the idea that I might need to move on, but surely there were opportunities for guys with his skills elsewhere.

We finished our pizzas in a sullen silence, and I started to wonder if moving in with Lester was such a good idea. Were we going too fast? I had faith in what I felt for him, but living together would add a new level of stress to our relationship. Could we handle it?

I could stay where I was in Wilton Manors, find a new roommate to take Jonas's place. Or cut my commute sharply by simply moving to Miramar.

Suddenly there was a lot more to think about.

Chapter 10

New Beginnings

Since we had two cars with us, we'd have to drive separately wherever we were going. I'd assumed I would be going home with Lester, but he said he was feeling tired and wanted to head back to his place and chill.

He drove me to where I had left my car, and I turned to kiss him. He offered me his cheek. I wanted to push him—why was he upset? Was he having second thoughts about moving in with me? I am an organized person—I needed to know how he felt before I could make plans.

But I swallowed all that and kissed his cheek. "Take care, Lester. I'll talk to you soon, all right?"

He nodded. "I'm going to be busy. I'm doing Larry's job as well as my own, so I'm in the office all day tomorrow, learning the ropes and reviewing my old job description so HR can start looking for someone to replace me. And I have bar demos all weekend—Friday night, Saturday lunch, Saturday night, Sunday brunch."

"Sounds like you're going to be swamped," I said carefully. "Let me know if you want me to come to any of the demos and help out with social media stuff."

There was an implicit request in there to see him sometime, but he said, "Sure. I'll let you know."

Driving home, I analyzed everything Lester had said. Sure, he was going to be busy, but we'd always found time to be together. That was why I went to his damn demos anyway—not for the free drinks or the experience in social media marketing, but to spend time with him.

Was he angry about something? Scared about moving in together? I wished he'd just come right out and say whatever it was he had to say. But maybe he was being kind and sparing my feelings. Was he practicing that tenet of "if you don't have anything nice to say, don't say anything?"

What did it mean that he didn't have anything nice to say to me, when we were about to move in together?

By the time I got back to Wilton Manors I was in a fugue state. I ate a whole chocolate bar with hazelnuts, even though I'd bought it for Lester because that was his favorite. Then I tossed and turned in bed before I finally got off to sleep.

Now that we had a suspect for the barbershop robberies, there was a new set of data to analyze for me to analyze the next morning. He'd come up with some bullshit alibis, and the police had been busy knocking them down. I was in charge of coordinating all the master data which was shared with each of the local departments, and I worked diligently at it all day.

I was entering data when Miriam called me. "I don't know if this is good news or bad news," she said.

"When you start a conversation like that it's most likely to be bad news. What's up?"

"I spoke to my contact at the governor's office about Yulirus Diaz. There's definitely a buzz around Yulirus. My contact told me she had to report back to Alvaro Vela Romero about anything that happens to him."

"Remind me who that is?"

"The wealthy donor who kicked all this off," she said. "He's a bigwig in the Cuban exile community."

"And why does he care about Yulirus?"

"He's an art collector, specializing in Cuban art. He may have read something about the museum in Havana that mentioned Yulirus's name."

"What does that mean for Yulirus, and for us?"

"I don't know, Angus. We're treading a very fine line with what we're doing, and we could all get in trouble if anyone looks too closely."

That was definitely bad news. "What does the governor want? Or Vela Romero?"

"Right now, just an update. I spoke to a woman I know at Immigration and Customs Enforcement, and she's gotten inquiries about a couple of refugees she's working with. So it could be nothing major."

I sat back in my chair and thought for a moment. "You said this Romero guy is interested in modern Cuban art? From 1900-1950?"

Miriam corrected me. "Technically his last name is Vela. According to Cuban custom he tacks his mother's name on the end, after his father's. But yes, that's his particular interest."

"So as part of your next update to the governor's office," I said, "You mention that even though Yulirus is Cuban, and he's an art historian, he doesn't know much about the period that Vela Romero collects. Maybe that will be enough to make Vela Romero lose interest and lay off the governor."

"I like that idea. I don't want the governor to know we've got a convicted felon helping us out."

"Remember, you asked me to go to that gallery opening tonight," I said. "I'll keep my eyes out for either Vela Blanco or his father."

Miriam hung up, but before I went back to my spreadsheets I thought about what she'd said. If the governor's office paid too much attention to Yulirus and what was going on with him, we might get blowback for placing him with a convicted felon. Jesse didn't qualify as a great supervisor, especially given his ill health. Yulirus could walk out at any moment and disappear into the Cuban community in Miami, and we might never see him again.

I called Jesse. "How are things working out with Yulirus?"

"Right now he's too interested in every goddamn piece of art I own to make much progress on listing them all," he said. "But at least I was able to get rid of the aides."

"So it's just you and Yulirus there?" I'd hoped that Jesse would keep the aides around for a while. Even if they didn't speak much English, they'd be a witness if Yulirus took off.

"Just us two," Jesse said. He didn't say anything more for a minute, but I waited. "You sure I can trust him, Angus?"

"What's the matter?"

"I don't know. Maybe it's that I associated with crooks for so long. But I keep thinking that while he's cataloguing everything he could be slipping something off on his own. Fund his life after you get him amnesty."

I sighed deeply. That was a complication I hadn't considered. "Keep your eye on him, then. And as soon as you think he's behaving badly, let me know."

"All right. I gotta get back to him. He was handling one of my stone phalluses like he was ready to stick it up his ass."

"TMI," I said. "And ouch." I hung up.

I went back to work, and didn't finish everything until nearly five o'clock. I didn't hear from Jesse again, so I hoped that was a good sign. I left Miramar and drove north and east to downtown Fort Lauderdale, where I was to meet Tom Laughlin at the gallery party.

Tom Laughlin and I were unlikely friends. He was in his late fifties, some thirty years older than I was. He had retired after a lucrative banking career in Boston, and I was a low-paid government minion starting my career. He was about four inches shorter than my six feet, and his hair was dark and thinning, while mine was red and thick.

He was standing by the front window of the gallery admiring a pen and ink sketch of Havana's Malecon when I walked in. I hugged him and smelled his lime after shave. As usual, he looked elegantly dressed, though his inner gay man came out in a rainbow-colored handkerchief in the breast pocket of his jacket.

"Don't look now, but someone seems to disapprove of our show of affection," he said. "The grim-looking fellow in the Tom Ford suit."

"I'm afraid I don't know enough about designers to recognize what you're describing," I said.

"His suits are tightly tailored," Tom said. "Wide shoulders, heavyweight materials and nipped waist."

"Sounds like something Lester could wear." Tom had met Lester a couple of times and I knew he appreciated my boyfriend's physique.

"If he has a spare four thousand dollars," Tom said.

"Wow." I turned halfway and spotted the man in question, who appeared to be glaring at us. I smiled and gave him a fey wave, and he turned away quickly.

The gallery was one big room, separated by free-standing walls that created a path for visitors to follow. Tom and I looked at the sketches as we walked and caught up. We'd only been there about fifteen minutes when a thirty-something dude with a man bun tapped on his champagne glass to get our attention.

"I won't take much of your time, because I know you want to admire Silvia's wonderful work," he said. "But I wanted to introduce her to you."

The artist herself stood beside him—she was a short woman with long black hair shaded with green, in a tight-fitting floor-length dress that Morticia Addams would have liked. The gallerist spoke briefly about her education and accomplishments. Then he said, "And I'd like to introduce the man whose patronage has allowed Silvia to come here. Alvaro Vela Blanco."

Vela Blanco was the man in the Tom Ford suit, the son who according to Miriam collected contemporary Cuban art. He smiled at the crowd and nodded, and the gallerist encouraged us all to look at the artwork and then open our wallets.

"That's the guy I was supposed to look out for," I whispered to Tom. "Doesn't look very friendly, does he?"

"Not to our sort, certainly," Tom said. "Though he does appear to be charming that woman with the over-plump lips and the Judith Leiber purse."

"I learn so much every time I see you," I said. The purse in question was shaped like a small hippo and studded with tiny crystals.

"What are you looking for?" Tom asked.

I shrugged. "Miriam wasn't clear. Just get a sense of him, I guess."

We completed a circuit of the gallery, and Tom said, "I've seen many paintings of Cuba, particularly Havana, but Ms. Bernal has a unique ability to render a very colorful country in dismal shades of gray and black."

"She's probably making a statement about how the Castro regime has stripped all the life from her country."

Tom looked at me. "That's very perceptive of you, Angus."

"Well, between my brother and my boyfriend I've picked up some of the lingo. And now, shall we get something to eat?"

We walked down the block to an Italian restaurant where we continued our conversation. As usual, Tom insisted on paying. "You risked your life to get Frank's painting back from Italy," he said when he'd handed over his black American Express card. "We'll never be able to thank you enough."

Frank Sena had sent me to Italy to pick up a painting that once belonged to his uncle—where I'd stabbed a man with an antique sword. "How is Frank these days? I assume you're still seeing each other?"

"We are. Though he likes the opera a great deal more than I do. You rescued me from having to accompany him to a performance this evening."

As we walked back to the garage, we passed the gallery, where a black Bentley was idling on the street before it. The door opened and Alvaro Vela Blanco exited, accompanied by the artist and the gallerist.

"Two hundred grand on the hoof, easily," Tom said as the three of them got into the Bentley. "Nice to have money, isn't it?"

I was pretty sure Tom could afford a Bentley if he wanted one but I simply agreed, and then drove home in my Mini Cooper, which was worth approximately a tenth of that luxury car.

When I got back to Wilton Manors, I checked out Lester's Instagram account. He must have recruited someone at the bar to photograph him because he already had a couple of pictures up.

Good for him, I thought sourly. I imagined him flirting with the customers and them flirting back. At least he was at a straight bar in Fort Lauderdale, not a gay one, but hey, gay guys go to straight bars.

Saturday morning, after a long, sweaty run around the neighborhood, I showered and sat down at the dining room table with my laptop to finish the work I had promised Jesse. Before I did I called him. "How's everything going today?" I asked.

"He's pestering me about eating," Jesse said. "At least with the aides, they didn't care if I ate the crap they fixed. But he watches me like a hawk. He soaked a couple of slices of bread in café con leche and then fried up a couple of slices of ham and he made me eat every bite."

"That's good. You've got to get your strength back."

"And he makes me walk back and forth across the damn living room," he said. "He even took my walker away and made me hold his arm."

"All this sounds good," I said. "He's showing you that he appreciates what you're doing for him." And maybe tiring him out so he could pocket some of those small items Jesse had on display. But I didn't say that.

"I'm close to having all your accounts reconciled and your major bills on auto-pay," I said. "My goal is to turn it all over to you with clear steps that you can manage on a monthly basis."

"I may not sound like it, but I appreciate everything you're doing for me," he said. "Hell, even if the kid robs me blind I know you'll figure it out."

That wasn't very reassuring, but I thanked him and hung up, and went back to his paperwork.

Jonas's door was closed, but his car was in the driveway, so I assumed he was sleeping late. Around eleven o'clock, the doorbell rang, and I opened it to see a shapely blonde with big round sunglasses propped on her head. "You must be Angus," she said, sticking her hand out. "I'm Camilla."

"Pleased to meet you. Come on in. I think Jonas is still asleep, though."

"Don't worry, I'll wake him." Her British accent was lovely and musical. She breezed past me, obviously familiar with the house's layout because she walked right to Jonas's door and pushed inside without knocking.

Well, that was interesting, but I still had work to do. I was plowing through Jesse's next estimated tax payment when I heard Jonas's door open. He went into the bathroom, and Camilla passed me on her way to the kitchen. "Want a cappuccino?" she asked.

"We don't have a machine for that. Just plain coffee."

"I had to clear a lot of stuff out of my place so I'm lending you mine until Jonas and I can get into the apartments above the store."

"I'd love one. We have chocolate syrup in the cabinet above the stove."

"Know it." She busied herself in the kitchen while I finished calculating what Jesse owed. I had just initiated a payment from his account to the IRS when Camilla brought two steaming mugs out to the dining room.

"I figured you'd want whipped cream and a chocolate drizzle on yours," she said. "That's the way Jonas likes his."

"I'm delighted. Chocolate is my favorite food group."

She looked me up and down. "You couldn't tell from your figure."

Camilla's obvious familiarity with a lot of things in my life made me uncomfortable. "Jonas hasn't told me much about you," I said. "What's your story?"

"Born and raised in this nowhere town in the Cotswolds called

Little Billing. My father made a few million pounds in the City, dumped his first wife and married my mum, twenty years younger. Very stereotypical story, sadly. I was so jealous of my step-siblings who lived glam lives in London, and all I wanted to do was get out of Little Billing."

She paused and sipped her cappuccino. "I convinced my dad to send me to school in Switzerland, where I got my international baccalaureate, focusing on expressive and performing arts, smoking, and eating pussy."

Fortunately I wasn't drinking at the moment so I didn't have to worry about choking.

"Followed a girlfriend to Miami, where we broke up within minutes after landing at the airport. I needed something to do so I registered for courses at the school where I met Jonas."

"And the obsession with Provence?"

She shrugged. "Spent too much time on the Riviera during the winter when I was supposed to be in school. Fell in love with the lifestyle and the linens. If I hadn't met Juliette I'd probably be in St. Tropez now."

Jonas joined us then in a T-shirt and shorts, his hair still wet from his shower. He looked at Camilla "You ask him yet?"

"I thought I'd leave that up to you. Him being your mate, after all."

"Ask me what?"

Jonas slipped into the third chair at the dining table. "Can I get one of those cappuccinos, love?" he asked Camilla.

She smooched at him. "As you wish, master."

She went into the kitchen and I looked at Jonas.

"Seeing as how you're such an ace accountant, Camilla and I were hoping you could help us with our business plan," he said. "We did a preliminary version for our class, but it needs a bit of fine-tuning."

"What grade did you get?"

Jonas's face reddened and he looked down at the table. "C."

"Sounds like you need more than just fine-tuning, Jonas. I can take a look and give you an estimate of how much time it would take me and how much I'd charge."

"You'd charge?" he squawked. "Even though we're friends?"

I put on my best sad face. "And you're leaving me." I lowered my voice. "For a woman."

Jonas's eyes opened wide. In the kitchen I heard the milk being frothed.

"Because you're moving out, I don't know where I'm going to be living next month," I said. "I don't want to pay the full rent here and you haven't given me a lot of time to find somewhere else to go."

"Can you move in with Lester? You spend enough time with him."

Was Jonas jealous of my relationship? We'd never been best friends, but we had spent a lot of time together at Wilton Manors bars, and in intense late-night conversations when he was high and I was drunk. He and I hadn't gone out bar-hopping in a while, because I was so busy with Lester.

Had I driven him to Camilla because I'd abandoned him for Lester?

"Lester and I are considering getting an apartment together," I admitted. "But nothing is certain yet."

Looking at Jonas's hangdog face, I realized that in the time I'd been in Miami I hadn't made many friends my own age. I knew a disproportionate number of older gay men like Tom and Frank and Jesse. Most of the younger guys I met in Wilton Manors were there to dance or tend bar and collect big tips from the older crowd. Not my kind of guys.

"I suppose I could cut you a deal." I let out a big breath. "Because of our friendship."

"It better be a good deal," Camilla said, as she returned to the dining room with Jonas's cappuccino. "Most of our working capital is already tied up in orders to wholesalers."

"Email me what you have," I said. "I'll look it over."

They left a few minutes later, and I checked my email, where I found their business plan. It didn't take me long to figure out why they got a C. They had made a lot of wild assumptions about price points and inventory turnover, none of which were based on real statistics.

The plan was going to need a lot more than tweaking, and explaining why might mean the end of my friendship with Jonas, especially if they resisted my advice and ended up in bankruptcy. Then Lester might be the only friend my age I had in town. It wasn't a good idea to put that kind of pressure on our relationship, especially as we were considering moving in together.

Chapter 11

The Man

My phone rang then with Lester's custom ring tone, "The Man," by The Killers. "Hey," I said. "Listen, I didn't mean anything about the Bureau moving me. I'm settled where I am and I have no interest in going anywhere else."

"I know. I overreacted. It's my bad record popping up."

Lester had endured his share of heartache, crushing on other jocks who either weren't gay, or weren't willing to come out of the closet, and he was sensitive to anything that might lead to us breaking up.

"You still want to look at apartments today?" he asked. "I've got a demo tonight but I have a few hours free."

We agreed that he'd pick me up in half an hour, and we'd drive to Doral. I assumed that we'd have dinner together, and I'd help him at his demo. Then I remembered what Roger always said about assuming.

I dressed and put together my overnight bag, and I was on my phone making a list of properties when Lester texted he was turning down my street.

I slid into the seat beside him and pecked him on the cheek. "I've got a couple of places we can look at," I said, as he backed out of the driveway.

I kept tapping away at my phone as we drove. We looked at apartments in three different complexes, and Lester had something to complain about at each one. At the first, the rooms were too small, at the second the gym not up to his standards, and the third was too close to the highway and too noisy.

None of those mattered to me, but I let Lester take the lead. There was still an undercurrent between us, and I didn't want to rock the boat.

"Maybe we should look at renting a house," he said, after we left the third place.

"But a house wouldn't have a pool or a gym," I said.

He shrugged. "That isn't a deal breaker. We could still get memberships."

Even though it might set us off again, I asked, "Are you sure you want to do this? We don't have to move in together if you aren't ready."

He stiffened for a moment, then relaxed. "I'm being a prima donna, aren't I?"

"No. You seem nervous. That's okay, I am too."

"What if we move in together and start to piss each other off? Then we're trapped by a lease."

"Leases can be broken. Or one of us can stay and get another roommate."

"But I don't want to lose you."

"Lester. You're not losing me, and I'm not losing you. If we move in together and it doesn't work out, then we'll work from there. It doesn't do either of us any good to imagine the worst."

"You're right as always, G-Man." He reached over with his right hand and grabbed my left. "I'm lucky I found you."

"Back at you."

It was nice to have the air clearer between us, but I knew that there would be more arguments before we closed the deal.

We had an easygoing dinner. I told him about how Yulirus had reacted to all the art at Jesse Venable's house, and we speculated about how things would work out for them. Then we drove to a bar on South Beach where Lester had a demo scheduled, and we both worked our asses off for the next couple of hours. I had to drive his SUV back to Fort Lauderdale because he was so exhausted from hauling cases of whiskey, making drinks and talking until his throat was dry.

Sunday morning we slept in, then went to the gym together, where all Lester's exhaustion of the night before disappeared, and he put me through a punishing workout.

I was ready to collapse by the time we were finished. "Jesus, if you're going to work me this hard I don't know that I want to live with you," I said. "You'll kill me within a month."

"Just want you to be the best damn G-Man you can be. Besides, if we're both working nine-to-fives we won't have that much time to work out."

There was that phrase again. Wanting me to be the best G-Man I could be. Was that all he saw of me—a government agent who had to be in good physical shape? And what did he mean about less time to work out? Exercising was one of the few things we did together on a regular basis. Well, that and sex. If we lost that "us time" what did it mean for our relationship?

Chapter 12

Roger That

He dropped me at my place and then headed to his brunch demo. Jonas's car was gone and I had no idea where he was, so that meant I'd have to dive into the problems with his business plan.

I'd just finished reading through the business description and structure when my phone rang, showing my mother's cell number. It wasn't often that I was glad to get a call from her, but that felt like a reprieve.

"Hey, Mom. How did Roger's surgery go on Friday?"

"He came through that but he was very weak, and they had him hooked up to all kinds of machines." She gulped out a sob. "He passed away this morning."

"Oh, Mom. I'm so sorry. I know how much Roger meant to you."

"It wasn't supposed to happen like this. To lose three husbands. I was supposed to marry for life like my parents did."

And there in a nutshell was my mother. Don't get me wrong, she had always been good to Danny and me, but she was the center of her world, not my father or Roger or her sons. "Can you come up here,

Angus?" she asked. "There's so much to do and I can't manage on my own."

Danny was in his senior year at Penn State, and I couldn't expect him to take too much time off from class to babysit our mother. Fortunately I hadn't taken most of the vacation time the FBI gave me, and I had a few days of compassionate leave coming to me, too, if I was willing to call Roger my stepfather.

I'd have to man up about that. "Sure, Mom. Let me see when I can get a flight."

The quickest flight from Miami to Wilkes-Barre, the closest airport to Scranton, took eight hours, with stops in Atlanta and Charlotte. I could fly to Philadelphia in two and a half hours, rent a car, and drive to Scranton. I had a choice of an 8:30 flight that evening that would get me to Philly at eleven, and I'd face a two-hour drive home.

Or I could take a Monday morning flight, and get to Scranton by early afternoon. My mother would prefer the one that would get me there quickest. But I booked the flight the next morning.

Then I called my brother. I knew he'd be at work, and that he kept his cell phone in the locker at the back of the restaurant where he stored his outer coat and whatever school stuff he was carrying. So I called the restaurant number, which I was sure my mother didn't have, and asked to speak with him.

"This is Dan."

His voice sounded deeper than it had when we'd last seen each other, on that vacation-slash-work deal in Italy. My baby brother was growing up and I had to deal with it.

"You spoken to Mom today?"

"Hey, Angus. No. What's up? Roger OK?"

"Nope. He didn't make it."

"Crap. Poor guy. He didn't do much for us, but he did keep Mom off our backs for a decade or so."

"I'm flying up to Philly tomorrow morning and then renting a car. I'll let you know when the funeral is."

"You want me to drive out there tomorrow and meet you?"

"You've got class, don't you? If I can make the funeral for Friday, you can stay the weekend."

"Deal. You always make things so easy for me, Angus."

"It's my job. And my calling."

He snorted with laughter, and after a bit more banter we hung up. That was the silver lining of this cloud—I'd get to spend some time with my bro.

I called my mother back and told her I'd be there Monday afternoon. She couldn't talk much because several of the neighbors had come over to comfort her, and that was fine with me.

I figured Lester would have a break between his afternoon and evening demos, and I called him. "Hey, G-Man. Can we make this quick? I was just about to take a nap."

"My mom's husband had heart surgery on Friday, and he passed away this morning. I have to go up to Scranton tomorrow for the week."

"Whoa, you didn't have to make it that quick. This is Roger, right? How long were he and your mom together?"

"Nearly fifteen years."

"That seems like a lot, but it's not," Lester said. "My parents have been married thirty-one years and they're still going."

"My mom's going to be a wreck. Fortunately she's got some neighbors with her now. I'm going to make the funeral on Friday so my brother doesn't miss too much school. I should be back here next Sunday."

"Call me whenever you need me, G-Man. I know you and Roger weren't that close, but he was still in your life for all those years."

"Roger that." It was a silly expression Danny and I had picked up when we were kids, and used it at home when we wanted to say we understood. It was also a way at poking fun at Roger, who was dull, and obsessed with his used-car business and our mother. Us, not so much.

My hands were shaking, and I had to put the phone down on the table and take a couple of deep breaths. Why was I so upset? I hadn't even liked Roger that much, and it wasn't like he'd been a father figure. We'd never tossed a baseball around, or bonded over a couple of beers once I was old enough to drink. Hell, he'd only come to my Penn State graduation because my mother wasn't willing to drive so far by herself.

But there was a strange symbolism going on, that I was solidifying my relationship with Lester just as my mother lost hers with Roger. Was I concerned about him dying? I couldn't be. He was the picture of health.

Or was I still worrying that the stress of moving in together would cause us to fall out of love with each other, and I'd end up with a broken heart?

I had hidden a pint of Ben and Jerry's Chunky Monkey behind a package of frozen broccoli in the freezer, hoping Jonas wouldn't find it, and I was glad to see it was still there.

I wasn't like my mother, I reminded myself as I shoveled the banana ice cream into my mouth. I didn't need a man's love to make my life complete. I wasn't going to defer every decision to Lester the way she had with Roger.

Shit, was I doing that? I'd always considered myself strong, knowing that I had to look out for myself and Danny in the face of my mother's self-centeredness. Was I so glad to find someone who'd take over that I'd settled for Lester's attitude?

I bit down on a chunk of chocolate. No. I loved Lester for many reasons. It didn't make me less of a man, or less strong, because I deferred some things to him. At work I was still the take-charge guy I'd always been. Look at the way I'd figured out the key to the barbershop robberies. And how I'd manipulated the situation with Yulirus, convincing Miriam we had to work for him. I'd done the same thing with the judge.

I was strong. I could take care of myself and Danny without Lester's help, if it came down to that. Hell, I could even shoulder some of my mother's burdens if I had to.

By the time I had demolished the pint of ice cream, I was ready to face the world again. I composed an email to Vito, explaining about Roger's death and asking to take a week off, a mix of compassionate leave and vacation days. I probably went into more detail than necessary, explaining my progress with the barbershop robberies and offering to make myself available by phone or email if he had questions.

Then I added that I was determined to prove I could handle anything the Bureau wanted of me, even if my personal life intruded sometimes.

That sounded wrong. I knew other agents who had gone on sick leave, or taken time off for family matters. No one had ever criticized them for having a life outside of work.

I deleted the last sentence. And I forced myself to remember everything I'd accomplished since coming to Miami. That was good enough.

I was good enough.

Then I smiled. Lester believed in me, and knowing that made me feel better.

I typed out another email to Miriam, with the same explanation. "I know I'm leaving you in the lurch, because of the pressure from the governor's office," I wrote.

I promised to keep in touch with Jesse and Yulirus by phone, and that I would keep up the pressure on Jesse to dig up information through his criminal contacts. "Right now Yulirus is busy helping Jesse catalog his art. I saw how curious he was when I was at Jesse's house, and I believe that curiosity will keep him there. He's a smart guy and he understands the importance of sticking to our deal."

At least I hoped he did. And that Jesse would want to avoid going back to the aide agency so he'd keep Yulirus on a short leash. Plus he'd signed a form promising he'd keep Yulirus, and he wouldn't want to do anything to damage his parole status.

"When I get back to Miami, I'll meet with Yulirus and work out how he can approach Elpidio," I continued. "I'm confident we can develop an anti-smuggling case and keep Yulirus safe at the same time."

Before I could over think it, I sent the email, even though I knew I was making a lot of promises that might be difficult to keep.

I shut down my laptop and looked across the room, where I had a photo of myself, my mom and Danny at his high school graduation. My mom looked happy then, and I hoped that she could hold on to some of those good memories in what was going to be a difficult time.

Then I remembered what she'd said on the phone. She wasn't supposed to lose three husbands.

Hold on. My dad had been number one, and Roger number two. Where did the third one come in? She couldn't have married someone between them without Danny or me knowing. And the way she spoke, it sounded like all three had died.

I'd been so caught up in carrying my own secrets when I was a kid, the knowledge I had deep in my heart that I wasn't like other boys, that I wanted to play with their cocks and balls more than I wanted to play ball with them. Had I missed some big secret my mother was holding?

And would I discover that during my week in Scranton?

Chapter 13

Baggage

I was at MIA waiting for my plane when Vito called. "Sorry to hear about your stepfather, rookie."

I usually corrected anyone who called Roger that – he was my mother's second husband, not my stepfather. But the Bureau's compassionate leave guidelines extended to grandparents, parents, siblings, and step-parents—not necessarily to my relationship with Roger. And I wanted those three days, so I said, "Thanks, Vito. When I get settled in Scranton I can log in to the VPN and catch up on any work you need."

"Don't worry about that. I can get Zolin to add any new information to the files."

Zolin was another junior agent, a moon-faced guy of Tex-Mex origin who had been at the office only a few months longer than I had, and was already lobbying for a transfer back to Texas. I didn't like the idea of him getting his fingers into my project, but I couldn't protest. And it felt weird that I could be replaced on a moment's notice.

I'd have to work harder when I returned to make sure Vito felt I was indispensable.

Miriam was just as kind, though not quite as tolerant, when she called me as I was in the boarding line. "What are we going to do about Yulirus?" she asked, after we'd gone through the formalities.

"We leave him with Jesse," I said. "They can get to know each other, Yulirus can settle down, and I can talk to him over the phone about how he's going to approach Elpidio."

"I'd rather you do that kind of thing in person," she said. "There's a lot of body language you miss on a phone call."

I didn't know how to answer that. I was about to get on a plane. What did she want me to do? Jump out of line and drive to Weston?

"We'll have to make it work," she said eventually. "I'll be out of town myself—I have meetings in New York and Boston. Next Monday morning you and I will meet first thing. We'll only have one week left before we have to go back to Judge Steiner."

"Actually four days," I said. "We met with the judge last Thursday."

"Accountants," she said. Then she had to go and hung up.

What was that dig about accountants, I wondered, as I settled into my seat. So I didn't have a PhD in art history. I could still follow this case. It reminded me of that fable about the scorpion and the frog, which ended with the scorpion stinging the frog and both of them dying in the river. The tag line for the story was something like 'you knew who I was when you agreed to this trip.'

Although that fable ended badly, so perhaps it wasn't a good way to think about my relationship with Miriam.

Instead, once the plane took off, I opened my laptop and got to work on Jonas's business plan, marking it up with a million questions and comments. I skipped past the executive summary—that would all have to change once I ripped through the underlying numbers.

Their first objective was unreasonable—to end their first year in business with a substantial cash balance. According to the Small Business Association, 90% of startups fail during that year, due to poor planning, lack of capital, lack of research and inadequate marketing. Jonas and Camilla would be lucky to survive their first year, and not even think about ending with money in the bank.

This was exactly the kind of project I had worked on during my master's in accounting at Penn State, and all those old skills, underutilized in pursuing criminals at the Bureau, came back to me.

I took a break when the flight attendant brought us our snacks. That's when the guy in the seat next to me asked, "College student?"

I got that question all the time, because of my red hair and fair skin, and according to Lester because I had such a happy attitude.

I shook my head. "I'm older than I look. I already have a master's in accounting and I work for the government."

That combination usually shut people up. Accountants have a reputation as boring number-crunchers, and who wants to chat up a bureaucrat, unless it's to complain?

"I used to work for the government, too, until they screwed me over."

That was an opening salvo I couldn't resist. "What happened? Whistleblower?"

He sniggered. "There was blowing involved, but no whistles."

Then I got a good look at him. He was about fifty but looked haggard, his face creased and the red lines that told me he had an alcohol problem crisscrossing his bulbous nose. There was something about the way he made direct eye contact with me that told me he was gay, and knew I was, too. So he was blowing cocks, not whistles.

"Chuck," he said, and he stuck out his hand for me to shake.

"Angus."

We shook. "Cute name for a cute guy."

I smiled tightly. "My boyfriend thinks so too."

He laughed, and for a moment I could see that once upon a time he'd been a handsome guy. "You're damned lucky you can say that kind of thing out loud now," he said. "That's what got me kicked out of the service, long before Don't Ask, Don't Tell. Well, that and getting caught with my pants down."

"What branch?"

"The Marines. The few, the proud, the intolerant."

Ouch. He had to have been kicked out years before, and yet he was still bitter.

"Sorry, I shouldn't say shit like that. I loved being a Leatherneck, and I was damn good at it, too." He shook his head. "Then they kicked me out and I discovered I wasn't good at anything else."

"You must have found something," Angus said.

"I found the bottle and the needle," Chuck said. "My only decent skill was marksmanship, and nobody other than the military hires you for that. Plus I had a dishonorable discharge so I hid my service years for a long time." He shrugged. "Eventually I sobered up and went to X-ray school. Been taking pictures ever since. But getting kicked out of the Marines did a number on my head. Thought I wasn't good enough for anything for a long time."

He took a long swig from his water bottle. "But enough about me. What's your story, Angus? Which branch of our austere government do you work for?"

"I'm an accountant with the FBI," I said, with more than a little trepidation, afraid I'd send him into another rant. Before he could, I continued, "I loved numbers, always calculating how much cash I had and how many more lawns I'd have to mow to buy something I wanted. I decided to be an accountant, just like my father."

But that didn't distract Chuck. "No shit? They let faggots in there now?"

I didn't like the word faggot—I'd been called that enough times in high school that it still hurt. "I prefer queer, actually," I said. "Or gay. And yes, they do."

He shook his head. "And here I am still fighting against my discharge to be able to get VA benefits." He leered at me. "Tell me about your boyfriend." Then he leaned in close, and I smelled his morning coffee on his breath. "He got a big dick?"

I motioned toward my laptop. "Sorry, I'm on my way to my stepfather's funeral, and I have to get a head start on some work."

He straightened up. "I'm the one who's sorry. That was an inappropriate question. Let me just say you're a lucky man, Angus. You must be smart to get into the FBI, you're cute and you've got a boyfriend. Don't ever take any of those blessings for granted."

He pulled the airline magazine from the seat pocket and paged to the crossword as I went back to my laptop. Yes, I had a lot of blessings in my life. I knew that. I'd been lucky to be born when I was, to come into manhood as opportunities opened for gay men. And I had good genes—intelligence and the looks he'd complimented. But I also worked damn hard to keep those looks and excel at my job.

We all had baggage. Despite his rocking body, Lester had self-image issues. I was willing to admit that losing my father so young had a big effect on me, turning me into Mommy's best boy and Danny's protector. It also probably attracted me to a big, take-charge guy like Lester, who'd look after me when I was tired of carrying my loads.

Now I'd taken on the responsibility for Jesse Venable and Yulirus Diaz. They were counting on me. And so were Jonas and Camilla, who desperately needed help to avoid losing Jonas's father's investment and to keep the chance they both had to remake their lives.

I got back to work.

Chapter 14

Canned Potatoes

I spent the next hour working on Jonas and Camilla's business proposal and avoiding thinking about my mother, Roger, and Yulirus Diaz. I counted all that as a plus.

Chuck had finished his crossword, and he was eager for conversation again. "You from Philly?" Chuck asked. "Only you said you're going for a funeral."

"Scranton," I said. "My dad studied bookkeeping at a trade school, and he'd been ready to go to college when my mom got pregnant. By the time he died of a heart attack at twenty-eight, he was an accountant for a coal mining company."

"That sucks."

My parents had married soon after high school, and I came along about seven months into the marriage. Yes, I did the math, though it wasn't until a couple of years after my father died. It wasn't something I could bring up with my mother, though.

"He was a great dad," I said. "I used to sit on his lap and we'd page through the atlas together and he'd tell me about all the places in the world he wanted to visit." I was sure that I'd inherited that wanderlust. One of the things that attracted me to the FBI was the chance to travel.

"He did everything a responsible guy could to look after his family. He took out a big life-insurance policy at ten times his salary, which was $25,000 back then. A quarter of a million was a nice windfall, and he left my mom detailed instructions: pay off the mortgage and invest the rest in long-term municipal bonds, which were paying over eight percent. That would have given her between fifteen and twenty thousand a year to live on and raise Danny and me."

"Something tells me she didn't do that," Chuck said.

I shook my head. "She listened to a man from our church who charged her big fees and eventually lost most of her principal in risky investments. She was a beauty when she was young, but she had no real skills. She took a job as a clerk at a discount store, which she hated, but at least she had access to everything in the cosmetics aisle for skin creams, makeup and hair color."

"I've known a few women like that," Chuck said. "I work the MRI now, and we have to make them take out all their earrings and nose rings and belly button piercings. We had one gal who refused to take off her steel-toed boots, and I wasn't going to argue. I let her get into the machine and as soon as the magnet turned on, whomp! Her legs went straight up."

I laughed. "As soon as I could, I got Danny into an afterschool program that kept him busy for a few hours while I cut lawns, shoveled snow, and did everything I could to make a few bucks. I used to take him with me while I walked the Collie that belonged to the old lady down the street."

"An enterprising kid."

"I had to be. Most Friday and Saturday nights she would leave me in charge of Danny, 'put her face on,' and go out to the all-night happy hour at the American Legion Hall in search of a man to look after her. Ironically, she met Roger at the discount store when he came in one day looking for duct tape."

"Wish it was so easy for guys like us," Chuck said. "But go on."

"After they married, Roger sold his house and moved in with us—because the one instruction my mother had followed was to pay off the mortgage. My mother quit her job, but I was encouraged to keep mine, for 'pocket money.' At least I didn't have to give any money to her, and we had the kind of treats we'd never been able to afford before, like ice cream sundaes once a week, tickets to the Lackawanna County Heritage Fair in the summer, a Christmas tree as tall as our ceiling decorated with hand-blown glass ornaments my mother ordered by mail from Czechoslovakia."

"I'm glad that worked out."

I shrugged. "Roger made it clear to Danny and me that we weren't his kids, so we couldn't expect much from him. We'd always have a home, food, and decent clothes. Anything else, like sports equipment, fancy sneakers, or movie tickets, was up to us. And college? Roger had strong opinions about higher education."

I put on his working-class accent. "The higher you go, the deeper you end up in shit, he said. There's plenty of work for mechanics, salesmen and delivery drivers—good jobs, with union pay."

Even years later I could hear him say that, over and over again. "There was no need to waste four years of your life to get a stupid piece of paper, unless you were a rich kid intent on drinking and screwing. And we weren't rich kids."

Then the flight attendant came on the public address system, telling us to put away our devices in preparation for landing. Just like Chuck, I'd overshared with a complete stranger. To get the conversation back on neutral ground, I asked, "What brings you to Philadelphia? Or brought you to Miami?"

"Rad tech convention in Miami," he said. "I'm the supervisor of my department at a hospital in Chester County, and we're looking to upgrade equipment." He smiled. "And I wanted to see what South Beach was like."

"No offense, but if you come back down you want to head to Wilton Manors," I said. "South Beach is pretty straight and touristy these days, and there's a great selection of good-looking guys, young and old, in my neighborhood." I looked down. "I actually met my boyfriend when he was a bouncer at a bar and he helped me out with a case."

"Good for you," he said. "Wilton Manors, huh? I'll keep that in mind. Never too late, you know?"

"I agree." Though as we stood up to depart, I hoped that I wouldn't end up like Chuck. I had a lot of thinking to do about what I was willing to do to hold onto Lester.

It wasn't until I had picked up a rental car and gotten on the highway that I started to think about what waited for me in Scranton.

My mother was, and always had been, a drama queen. I thought that was probably what had attracted Roger to her—she was a damsel in distress when they met, a widow with two young boys who desperately needed help.

I turned on the radio and found a station that played 80s pop, the kind of music Cameron and Annette Green had grown up with, which they danced to in the living room sometimes on a Saturday night. Bruce Springsteen was born to run as I was growing up in Scranton. Bonnie Tyler mourned a total eclipse of the heart, and Culture Club sung about a karma chameleon. I'd been a bit of that myself, drawing on different identities until I was ready to assume my own.

I sung along with them, remembering the lyrics to "99 Red Balloons" and Starship's "Nothing's Gonna Stop Us Now." I didn't focus on where I was going, or why, until I arrived in Moosic, on the south side of Scranton.

As I switched over to I-81, which would drop me off a few blocks from home, I remembered. Roger was dead and my mother was a mess, and it was up to Mommy's Best Boy to clean things up.

I pulled up in the driveway of our single-story house, turned the car off and rested my hands on the steering wheel. Roger had kept the place up, you had to give him that. He'd put in aluminum siding years before, then new gutters and drains, and a new row of azaleas under the front windows. The big maple in the front yard was stark and leafless.

Who would rake the leaves for my mother in the fall? Who would drag the heavy garbage can out every week, shovel the snow in winter and mow the lawn in summer?

My body sagged with the enormity of it. Then my phone rang, Elton John singing about brother Daniel, and I straightened up. I had to work things out for Danny's sake. He needed to finish his bachelor's and then be able to decide what to do with his life without the extra burden of our mother.

"I looked up the flight I thought you'd take and calculated your travel time," he said. "Are you there yet?"

"Just pulled in the driveway."

"I'm walking out of my Introduction to Security and Risk Analysis class and I don't have anything else until Contemporary Political Ideologies tomorrow afternoon. I'm leaving State College now and I should be in Scran-town in about two hours."

"Hold on, I thought you were majoring in Italian and minoring in Art History."

"That was my original plan. Then an advisor told me that if I wanted a job in Italy I should switch my minor to teaching ESL. Then I switched to Global Security. I'll tell you about it when I see you."

"Danny, you don't need to come until the funeral."

"It's going to take two of us to handle mom, bro. Let me share the load."

I looked up at the house. My mom was probably inside, crying. I doubted that she'd made any of the funeral arrangements yet, or even knew where Roger kept his important paperwork. "All right, I'll see you soon. Love you, bro."

"Back at you."

I kept a key to the front door, though I'd had to dig it out of my jewelry box before leaving Florida. I unlocked the door and called, "Mom?" as I walked in.

She was in the living room, which was surprising, because we almost never used that room. Soon after she and Roger married, she had bought a new suite of French Provincial furniture, all twirled legs and tufted seats, and covered it with plastic.

Sometime in the last few years the plastic disappeared, though the room still looked more like a furniture showroom. My mother sat on one of the cream-colored sofas, staring into space.

"Mom?" I dropped my duffel bag in the foyer and moved in, and she looked up.

"Angus." There was no welcome in her voice, just resignation.

I sat next to her and took her hand in mine. It was cold and so skinny I could see the veins. "I'm so sorry, Mom."

"Roger said he would never leave me. He even promised me as they were wheeling him into the operating room. That he'd right as rain very fast, nothing to worry about."

"He wanted to take care of you, Mom. He tried his best."

"Well, his best wasn't quite good enough, was it? I told him to stop smoking, and eventually I wouldn't let him smoke in the house or the car. He had to go outside in the shelter of the carport if he wanted a cigarette." She shook her head. "He was out there in all kinds of weather, the fool."

I didn't know what to say to that, so I kept holding her hand, hoping that was enough.

"I got him down to one martini at dinner," she said. "And no beer." She looked at me. "You don't drink, do you, Angus?"

I shook my head. "Only socially."

"You need to stop that. Alcohol does terrible things to your body. High blood pressure, heart disease, stroke. If Roger had listened to me and taken better care of himself, he'd still be here."

"Have you eaten anything today, Mom?"

She looked at me and frowned. "I don't know."

"How about if I fix you something? Scrambled eggs, a cheese omelet? A sandwich?"

"Roger taught you how to scramble eggs, didn't he?" she asked. "I remember that. Keep the heat to medium, take your time. Pretend the eggs are a woman you're making love to."

God, that had embarrassed me. And being a redhead with fair skin, it always showed, and Roger would laugh. But he was patient, too, and I learned to make eggs that were luscious and pillowy. Use the right pan, enough butter, a flexible spatula to fold the eggs. If he was in a fancy mood, he'd add some chopped chives or goat cheese.

He also had a weird fondness for canned sliced potatoes. He'd keep a second pan going with the potatoes, sprinkling them with paprika and getting a light char on each slice.

I stood up. "Scrambled eggs and potatoes?"

"Eggs, yes. There's some of that goat cheese Roger liked in the refrigerator, too. But no more of those awful canned potatoes."

"I thought you liked them."

"There are things you do when you love someone," my mother said. "Someday you'll figure that out."

Chapter 15

Global Security

I wanted to talk to my mother about funeral arrangements, but she wasn't ready. "He's dead less than twenty-four hours," she said. "I can't think about burying him yet."

Cameron Green had been buried in a single plot in the cemetery where his parents were. Both his parents were alive when I was a kid, and I had the impression, even at ten years old, that they took care of his funeral and all the arrangements. All my mother had to do was put me and Danny in black pants and white shirts and get us to the church.

I couldn't even ask her to hunt through Roger's paperwork for any instructions he might have left. The accountant in me wanted to put everything in order, and knowing that there was disorder ahead made me itchy.

But I took deep breaths and realized the most important thing was to be there with her. At least until Danny came. He was right; it was going to take two of us to manage Mom.

I sat in the kitchen with her and we shared a plate of eggs scrambled with goat cheese. "I guess I won't need to buy this cheese anymore," my mother said.

"You don't like it?"

She shrugged. "I don't taste anything these days. I put Roger on a low-calorie no-salt diet last year and I got accustomed to the blandness."

Oh my God, shoot me now, I thought.

"Is there anything you've always wanted to do?" I asked. "Travel? Start a hobby?"

She looked at me like I was out of my mind. "My whole life was Roger, Angus. You can't expect me to start all over again so quickly."

It had taken her three years between my father's death and meeting Roger, and then she'd had more financial urgency.

We talked aimlessly, mostly about Roger and her. I cleaned up the kitchen and we went back to the living room. "Would you like some music?" I asked. Maybe I could get her to dance again, the way she had with Cameron. Get her mind off the present and remember how she'd survived in the past.

She shook her head. "I just want to sit here."

Okay, then, we'd sit.

I let my mind wander. I had a funeral to plan, and a wake, if my mother wanted one. There had to be people to notify. "You called the car dealership, didn't you?" I asked.

My mother cocked her head. "Why would I do that?"

"To tell them about Roger," I said gently.

"They knew he was going into the hospital. They aren't expecting him back for at least two weeks."

Something else for me to do. And there was my Bureau work, too. My fingers itched to check my email on my phone. What if Zolin was so good at taking over the barbershop robberies that Vito recommended him to help Miriam?

I swallowed. If either of them needed me, they had my phone number. I wasn't indispensable. They'd all believe my place was with my mother.

After what seemed like an eternity, I heard Danny's used Suzuki

SUV pull up in the driveway. "That's Danny," I said as I stood up. "I'll go let him in."

"He has a key," my mother said, but I was so itchy to get off that couch I didn't listen.

Instead I bolted out the front door as my brother was getting out of the car. "Dude," he said, as I grabbed him in a big hug.

"Mom's being mom, huh?" he asked, when I finally let him go.

"Yup. You think you can handle her for a while? I want to look through Roger's paperwork and get started on a funeral."

"Will do. I'm her baby boy, after all."

I always had the sense, growing up, that I was my father's favorite, though maybe that was because I was an only child for my first five years of life. Then when Danny was born, my mother fussed over him and my dad managed to spend a lot of time with me. As I had told Chuck, often we'd sit in the ratty spare room Cameron called his den, with an atlas open on his lap, pointing out all the places he dreamed of traveling.

Then he died, and at ten years old, I had to be the man of the family, while Danny was still her baby. I followed him inside, carrying his backpack for him, and he went right over to her and she started crying.

And then, it was as if I wasn't even there. Which was fine with me. I carried both our bags upstairs to discover that my old room had been converted into Roger's office. Fortunately Danny had always had twin beds in his room—he was a much friendlier kid than I was and always had pals for sleepovers. I put both my bag and his in there and then sat down at Roger's desk.

Roger had teased me about my accounting major, but fortunately he was pretty organized himself. I looked over the desk, discovering that he had paid all the recent bills and left the photocopies of the stubs and checks in a neat pile.

He had already picked out a rehab center where he was to go after his surgery and the information about it, now unnecessary, sat in another pile. It didn't look like he'd considered his death, though.

I hunted through his file cabinet and drawers for the next couple of hours. I found a will, leaving everything to my mother. The deed to the house had been transferred to both their names soon after their marriage—a detail no one had ever mentioned to me. At least her name there meant she wouldn't have to go into probate to hold onto it. I found the title to both their cars, both in his name. Something else to change.

But nothing about a funeral or burial. I went downstairs. "Mom, what religion was Roger?"

"I don't believe he had a religion. We went to St. Andrew's sometimes for Christmas mass."

"Good enough. So Holy Trinity Cemetery would work for him?"

"I don't want to talk about it."

"Mother." I sat down beside her on the couch. "Sadly, this is not all about you. This is about taking care of the man who took care of you, and Danny and me, for thirteen years. He deserves a funeral that offers people a chance to express their sadness to you, and one that celebrates his life. I'm going to make sure he gets that."

She pinched her lips tight. "Fine. Holy Trinity. He wanted a double plot for the two of us, with a joint headstone." Her face softened. "He said he wanted to be able to turn to me in the afterlife and see my beautiful face."

I stood up. "I will make that happen, for you and Roger."

Then I went upstairs before she could change her mind. I called the funeral home and used a credit card I found in my mother's purse to secure the arrangements. We would still have to pick out a coffin, but I set up everything else. Roger was a salesman, and he died relatively young, so I expected there would be a good turnout, and I booked a chapel at the funeral home, and the services of a priest to say the last rites.

"Angus," I heard my brother call from downstairs. I looked at the clock. It was nearly six, and he'd been with my mother for two hours while I worked. "Come down for dinner."

Friends and neighbors had been bringing casseroles—macaroni

and cheese, lasagna, beef stew, a pan of home-baked rolls. I recognized our neighbor Mrs. Wallach's signature carrot cake by the elaborately piped carrots on the frosting, but there were many other dishes, filling the refrigerator.

"Mom, you have to eat something," I heard Danny say as I browsed the offerings. "How about some mac and cheese? You always used to make that for me when I was sick."

"All right. A little."

We sat through an excruciating dinner, as both Danny and I tried to engage our mother, asking about friends and relatives. The only person she'd told was Mrs. Wallach, who she called a nosy cow. She was the one who had spread the word around the neighborhood, arranging for all those covered dishes. It was going to be up to Danny and me to take care of everyone else.

Fortunately my mother took a couple of pills after dinner and went to sleep. Danny and I raided her address book and split up calling family members, friends, and Roger's boss at the dealership.

People were sad, but no one was surprised. "The way he smoked I'm surprised he lasted that long," said one man he went bowling with. "He told your mother he stopped years ago but he didn't."

And that one martini he had at home? That was often following a couple of beers after work. He always brought a twelve-pack to picnics and parties, usually drinking a lot of the cans himself. And I found several notes from his doctor encouraging him to take pills for his blood pressure and sugar. No prescriptions for them, though.

What an odd marriage, I thought between calls. Lester was already pushing me to exercise more, be more flexible. He knew the kind of danger I had faced and wanted me to be in the best possible shape for any in the future.

I felt the same way about him. If a doctor told him to take pills for something, I would make sure he did.

Or at least I hoped I would. I got caught up in cases sometimes, working late and then collapsing into bed, only to rise early, run, then start all over again. If we lived together, how would I fit a relationship with Lester into that schedule? Would there be plenty of space between us to keep secrets?

By ten o'clock it was too late to make any more calls, and Danny and I ended up in his room, lying on the twin beds. "Roger, huh," Danny said. "I thought I knew all about him, living with him for years. But he was an enigma wrapped in a mystery."

"No, he was just an ordinary guy who kept a couple of things to himself."

"Like smoking and drinking."

"I've been going through his papers and dreading finding a secret stash of porn," I said.

Danny held up his fingers in the shape of a cross. "TMI."

"Exactly."

We sat in silence for a few minutes, and then I asked, "What do you think Mom is going to do now?"

Danny shrugged. "What she did before. Muddle through. Look for another husband. She's still pretty, you know. And she's only what, forty-nine? She'll find some sixty-year-old." He leaned back against his headboard. "It sucks being her. Losing two husbands."

That reminded me of what she'd said, and I told Danny.

"Three? Who was the third one? Someone between Dad and Roger?"

"I don't see how she could have married someone and had him die while we were both living with her."

"She must have gotten confused. Maybe she considered herself a bride of Christ before she married Dad."

"Mom? A nun? I don't think so. Remember, I was conceived before they got married."

"Again, TMI."

"I know. So tell me about this switch in minors. You don't want to go to Italy and teach English anymore?"

He shook his head. "For the ESL minor you have to take a bunch of classes in applied linguistics. I took my first one last spring and it was OK. Introduction to Language, Culture, and Social Interaction.

How different cultures communicate. But then I started the second level class, a seminar in applied linguistics, and literally, it was like they were teaching it in another language. All this stuff about anthropology, sociology, philosophy—I just couldn't get into it. So I went to my advisor and we talked about my trip to Italy in the summer, and what I liked about it, and I guess I went on and on about you."

I pretended to fan myself. "Yeah, I'm so fabulous. I'm an accountant, remember?"

"But you do cool stuff, too. So she suggested I combine Italian with Global Security, and I switched into a political science class in contemporary political ideologies. And I'm totally digging it. Did you know that the Middle East was broken up by Europeans like they were carving up some dude's birthday cake? Without paying attention to the people who live there, what their tribal and religious affiliations are?"

"I did know that," I said. "We studied some of that in the FBI Academy. But I never thought it was something you'd be interested in."

"I'm not the teacher type. And while I love speaking Italian, that's pretty much what you do with my degree. You go on for a PhD and get a university job, of which by the way there are none, according to my professors, or you go the ESL route. With this combination I can go work in national security, for example."

"Yeah, in case the Italians invade."

"Dude. Mussolini was no accident. Fascism is on the rise again in Italy and all over Europe. I could work in corporate security for a company that trades with Italy." He looked down, like he didn't want to face me. "Or I could work for the CIA."

"Oh, no, Danny. Nothing dangerous. It would kill mom to have two of us working in jobs where we could get hurt."

"Oh, I'm an accountant," he mimicked me. "Nothing dangerous there. Except getting shot in Miami and disarming guys with swords in Venice!"

"Those were flukes." I had to admit I'd had more than my share of dangerous assignments. I was worried that Danny was attracted to the glamor, such as it was, of working in jobs like mine.

"Besides, most of the CIA work is analysis, anyway," Danny said. "I spoke to a recruiter last week and he thinks there's a real opportunity for someone with the combination of skills I'll have when I graduate."

"Hold on. You already spoke to a recruiter for the CIA? And you didn't tell me?"

"You're busy, dude. I'm not going to call you about every little thing."

I stood up to go the bathroom. "Danny, this is your life we're talking about. Not every little thing. I'm beat. I'll talk to you more in the morning."

"This isn't over, bro," Danny called to my back. "I'm living my life."

Chapter 16

Once a User

Tuesday morning Danny drove back to State College, and I picked out a suit for Roger to wear and took my mother to the funeral home. She was surprisingly animated, debating the different casket finishes and linings with the "advisor."

Danny had no class on Friday, so we had decided on a Friday afternoon service for Roger. Working folks who wanted to come could duck out of their jobs early, then go somewhere and have a beer in memory of him. And I could head back to Miami on Saturday. Danny agreed to stay through until Monday morning.

I hated to put a burden on him, when it was so important for him to do well in his last year in school, but I was worried about all my responsibilities back home. I talked to Lester regularly, answered emails from the Bureau, and even called Jesse Venable.

"How are things going?"

"Great. He's adorable, Yulirus. And he agreed to do everything the lousy aides were, so I fired their asses." He laughed. "Yuli's ass is much better to look at."

"Remember, Jesse, he's there to help you catalogue your artwork, not prance around naked for your enjoyment."

"He's not naked," Jesse protested. "We went to Sawgrass yesterday and bought him some clothes."

I could just imagine what Jesse had bought him. "But the art, Jesse. We need to have a list of your artworks to take to the immigration judge. Preferably something that looks professional, with the details of how you acquired each piece and its current value."

"That could be difficult," Jesse said.

I groaned. We had originally met when he was trying to buy some gold coins that had been smuggled out of Turkey. "Is there anything in your collection that's legitimate?"

"Of course there is. You don't pick up Hockneys like the one I have off the back of a truck."

"Then start there. If the immigration judge doesn't think there's value in keeping Yulirus here, then he'll be sent back to Cuba stat. He has to prove that he's doing something he's uniquely qualified for."

"Got the message. I've become very fond of the lad and I wouldn't want him to be sent away."

I hung up worrying about the mess I'd set up at Jesse's house in Weston. Yulirus was young and vulnerable. Suppose Jesse started demanding more—naked housework, erotic dancing... I wouldn't put any of it past Jesse Venable. Once a user, always a user. But in this case I hoped he was smart enough, and empathetic enough, to be responsible and help Yulirus stay in this country.

My mother spent most of her time in the living room, receiving visitors. I was called downstairs occasionally to say hello to neighbors and long-time friends of the family, but for the most part I stayed in my old bedroom, Roger's office. He had been a commissioned salesman all his life and his income had gone up and down, but he had a small investment account and enough in his checking account to cover the burial.

After that? My mother would have to get a job again.

She didn't need much; the mortgage was paid off, the taxes and insurance were low, and she wasn't an extravagant spender, on food or travel or anything else. If I had to, I could send her money, especially if Lester and I chose an inexpensive apartment. But the woman was only forty-nine; there was no way I was going to support her until she was old enough for Social Security.

I broached that question Wednesday night at dinner. We were working our way through casseroles—that night's was baked chicken with pineapple and a crust of crushed potato chips. "Can we talk about money, Mom?"

"Do we have to?"

"Eventually you'll have to. When you turn sixty-five you'll be able to access Dad's pension from the mine, but that's a long time away."

"They closed the mine years ago, Angus."

I nodded. "But before that, it was bought by a big conglomerate, who assumed all the pension liability. It doesn't look like Roger had a pension through the dealership, but he has been putting money into an IRA account. You can start withdrawing from that without penalty when you turn fifty-nine and a half."

"That's a long time from now."

She stood up and began clearing the table, and I helped her. When we had put the food back in the fridge and the dishes in the dishwasher, we sat beside each other at the kitchen table, and I went through the rest of her finances with her. "So it looks like you'll have to get a job," I said at last.

"Oh, that's all taken care of."

I cocked my head. "Really?"

She nodded. "Delia McQuiston works in the medical center billing office, and the woman who handles Medicare claims is retiring next month. Delia's in charge of hiring her replacement and she's already promised to help me get up to speed with the computer system there and give the job to me."

"Wow."

She must have seen something in my face. "I'm not an idiot, Angus. I know how to type and how to use the Google and Delia says everything that comes into her office already has diagnostic codes. It's just a matter of transferring information from one system to another. I'll be covered for life and health insurance and we get a ten percent discount in the hospital cafeteria."

"I'm impressed, Mom. It sounds like a good job, and you'll be working with a friend."

"You don't have to worry about me. I'll be just fine."

I wasn't sure of that, but I wasn't going to argue.

"There is something I need to tell you," she said. "Roger's death, it reminded me that we don't live forever, and that I want you to know something I've kept to myself all these years."

She frowned. "No one else knows, Angus. Not even my sister."

I looked over at her. This sounded serious. "What's up, Mom?"

"I'm sure you did the math at some point. I was not married when I got pregnant."

"I know, and once you told Dad, you got married. That's old news."

"There's a part you don't know." She inhaled deeply. "Cameron Green was not your biological father."

I pushed my chair back and turned to look at her. "What do you mean?"

She curled her lip and stared at me.

"So if Dad's not my father, who is?"

"His name was Arthur Tanner. Artie. He worked at the mine, too, but he was a miner, not in the office. We dated for a few months—it was a summer romance. And then he announced that he was going into to the Navy. There was nothing in Scranton for him, he said."

She took a deep breath. "And I said, 'What about me?'"

Of course. As I'd known all my life, Annette Green's primary focus was herself.

"He promised to write me from boot camp, and we'd see how well our romance survived while he was away. Then he was home for a week at Christmas before shipping out, and … well, we committed ourselves to each other."

"Which is your coy way of saying you had sex."

"Angus. This is hard enough for me."

I took a deep breath. My world had come unglued, and the only way to piece it together again was to keep my mother talking.

"He was being deployed to a ship in the Persian Gulf. He was very brave, you know. He didn't even know I was pregnant then—neither did I. But he wanted to take care of me. So we got married at the Lackawanna Government Center in Scranton, and we didn't tell anyone, and he shipped out."

She began picking at one of her manicured nails where the polish had begun to peel away. "I didn't know things like this happen, but sailors die on those ships even when there's no war. Artie was assigned to the boiler room, and one day there was a fire, and he was killed."

She reached for a tissue and dabbed her eyes. "I was just destroyed. It was such a stupid thing to have happen. And I had to hear it second-hand, from someone who heard it from Artie's mom. He hadn't even told the Navy we were married."

I put my hand on her arm. "That must have been hard for you."

She nodded. "And then a few weeks later I was pregnant." She paused. "With you."

"Did you go to the Navy?"

"I didn't know what to do. I was just a silly girl from Scranton who'd gotten herself into a pickle. As a good Catholic I had to bring you into the world, but I had no idea how I would manage a baby."

She picked up a glass of water from the table and drank. "I eventually confided in my best friend, Delores Kowizki. She said that she was dating a smart guy who worked in the office at the mine, and he'd help me figure out all the paperwork."

"Was that Dad?"

She nodded. "Delores wasn't happy that I stole her boyfriend. She left Scranton three months later, before you were even born, and I never heard from her again."

Get back to Dad, I wanted to yell. But I held my temper.

"Cameron was so sweet, and he helped me register with the Navy. They had already given his death benefit to Artie's parents. But there was money for a surviving wife and children, and I registered for that. It wasn't very much, because Artie had the lowest rank and he'd only been in the service for a few months."

I thought of my parents then, at a kitchen table much like the one where we sat, going over paperwork. My dad being compassionate to a woman carrying another man's child.

"We talked a lot. There was a terrible stigma, you know, on unwed mothers. Would I go out of town to have the baby, would I give you up for adoption."

It felt like a knife was twisting in my heart, to hear my future discussed so blandly.

"I wanted to keep you so much, Angus. You have no idea. It wasn't about Artie. I could feel you growing inside me, already a part of me. I couldn't give you up."

Well, that was nice to hear, even if it was all focused on Annette, as usual. What she felt, what she wanted.

"And one day we were sitting at the table, and I was crying, and Cameron came over and moved my bangs over my face. And that gesture was just so kind and caring that... well, I kissed him."

One the one hand, I felt this conversation was TMI. But on the other hand, I desperately had to know how the man I had known as my dad had come to that position.

"He hesitated for a moment, but then he kissed me back. And he told me that he loved me and wanted to take care of me. He asked if I would marry him."

"Right then?"

She nodded. "It had been brewing inside him for a while, and he looked so sweet and hopeful. And I had been developing feelings for him, too. I knew he would be a good father to you, Angus. So I said yes."

Wow. I sat back in my chair. Lester and I had been dithering about moving in together, after two years of dating. Yet my parents had decided to marry after a single kiss.

"It was embarrassing, of course, and I fudged the dates for my parents and my friends. But the story was that Cameron and I had fallen in love, that we'd gotten careless one night and gone too far, but that we were committed to each other and to you."

"And everyone accepted that?"

She nodded. "We went back to the Lackawanna Government Center, and the same judge married me a second time. I had to explain about Artie, though. And he could tell that I was pregnant, so he knew we were doing the right thing."

She stood up and picked up her water glass. "And that's the secret I've been hiding from you all these years. I'm sorry I didn't have the courage to tell you earlier."

Well, that explained how she had lost three husbands, when I'd only ever heard about two.

I stood and hugged her. "It's okay, mom. Dad was the best guy you could have picked for me. He loved me and Danny."

I pulled back. "Wait. Danny..."

"Danny is Cameron's son. I was lucky that you both took after me when you were babies." She put her hand up to my chin. "And both handsome young men. You won't... hold this against me, will you, Angus?"

"Oh, Mom. You know I love you, and I appreciate everything you did to give me and Danny a good start on life. That'll never change."

"I'm glad." She stuffed her issue in her pocket. "I think I'll go up to bed now."

"Okay." I sat at the table again and began cleaning up the paperwork. I had to talk to Danny, but I needed to process everything myself first.

Artie Tanner. Arthur Tanner. I might have been Angus Tanner. Then again, it was Cameron Green who felt so strongly about his Scots heritage that he gave me the historic name of Angus, after Angus of Moray, a long-dead leader. Though sometimes he'd teased my mother that I was named after Angus Young, the lead singer of the Australian band AC/DC, because my mother liked the way he played with his shirt off.

I grabbed my laptop and looked for information on Arthur Tanner. All I could find was a single mention, in the Scranton *Times*, of his death. He had been an only child, and when I cross-checked, both his parents had passed away since then.

I pushed the laptop aside. I was Angus Green, son of Cameron and Annette, brother of Danny. They were all the family I needed.

Chapter 17

17: My Father, My Apple

I looked at my watch. It was still about a half hour before Danny started his shift. I could call him then, or wait until his shift was over at midnight.

Annette might have held this secret for decades, but I couldn't wait a few hours. I didn't want my mother to overhear my conversation, so I went outside and dialed his number.

"Hey bro," he said. "Everything copacetic in Scran-town?"

I heard his labored breath, which meant he was on his bicycle on his way to work. "You might want to pull over for this one, bro. Annette told me tonight about her first boyfriend, a guy named Artie Tanner, who joined the Navy and died." I paused. "Turns out he's my real dad."

"Holy shit, Angus." I heard his bicycle brakes squeal and the rattle of gravel. "Is she sure?"

"From the way she described it, I'd say sure." I gave him the brief version of Annette and her two men. I had begun calling her by her first name instead of Mom, the way Danny and I did when we were frustrated with her. Somehow, the distance made the situation more understandable.

"Dad's still your dad," Danny said. "Like totally. I may not remember much of him, but I always had the sense that he was your favorite, and I was Mom's."

I agreed with him. All that time we'd spent together, me on his lap, him showing me the atlas and all the places he wanted to travel. And me another man's son.

I had to stop thinking that. Artie Tanner may have been the sperm donor, but Cameron Green was my father.

"So wow," Danny said eventually. "This doesn't change anything between us, though. You're still my brother."

"Half-brother. Like the hobbits in *The Lord of the Rings*, who they called halflings."

"Dude. Are you calling me a hobbit?"

"You do have hair on your feet.'"

"You watch, I'm gonna grow another couple of inches just to show you how tall I can get. I'll be taller than you before you know it."

I doubted that. Cameron Green had been at best five-six or five-seven, while Annette was a petite five-three. She and Roger had been surprised in my teens when I had a growth spurt. Now I wondered how tall Artie had been.

But I couldn't keep obsessing so I told Danny, "In other news, Annette already has a new job lined up. A friend of hers works at the hospital and is going to hire her to do medical billing."

"I didn't think Annette Green had that much gumption," he said.

"It's probably her friend Delia who's behind it," I said. "But good for her anyway."

We promised to talk again soon, after we'd both had the chance to let the news settle in. I went back inside, and in one of Roger's file folders called "Annette," I found the Navy paperwork for Artie Tanner. My mother had briefly collected the Military's Survivor Benefit Plan after Artie's death, but as soon as she married Cameron it stopped. Though it started again after Cameron's death and she was able to collect again until she married Roger.

When he joined the Navy, Arthur Tanner was five feet, eleven inches and weighed a hundred forty pounds. He had brown hair and brown eyes. His blood type was O positive, the most common in the United States, and so was mine. I couldn't find a picture of him, but I had seen enough photos of my mother as a child to know that I resembled her. She didn't have red hair, but I had learned in high school biology class that gene could skip a generation or two, hiding out behind a dominant trait. Artie must have had that recessive gene, too, in order for me to be born a ginger.

If Cameron didn't have that recessive gene, it explained why Danny's hair was a light brown, though as kids we'd always assumed there were red streaks in it because we were brothers, right?

Oh crap. Annette's announcement not only changed my relationship with Cameron, but with Danny, too. He was, as we'd said on the phone, only my half-brother. Did that matter?

From the deepest part of my body, the answer was an emphatic no. I loved Danny more fiercely than anyone else in the world, and I could never consider him anything less than my dearest family member.

Wednesday morning, my aunt Jenny, Annette's older sister, took her shopping for a dress for the funeral. Her friend Delia brought her a manual for the medical office computer system and went over it with her.

From upstairs, I heard a lot of muffled cursing. "I thought you said you knew how to type," Delia said once.

"I can pick at the keys," my mother said.

"You'll have to get better."

I couldn't hear my mother's response to that, but I guessed it was accompanied by a frown.

"Why do they need so many different codes?" my mother complained later. "It's all surgery, isn't it?"

"Do you want to learn this or not, Annette?" Delia demanded. "Because I'm sure I can hire someone else if you don't want the job."

"Fine. I'll study the manual. Angus can help me. He's smart."

"He must take after his father, then," Delia said.

That sent me off on another tangent. Had Artie Tanner been smart? He was certainly sharp enough to realize there was nothing ahead of him in Scranton. I went back to the folder with Artie's enlistment information. His combined subtest scores on the ASVAB, the IQ test for the military, was 230, which qualified him for a wide range of jobs.

Though there was nothing about where he'd ended up after basic training, it was clear that he was smart. What if he'd never gone near that boiler? If he'd come home to Annette? I might have grown up in a different place, with different siblings. Maybe Artie would have encouraged me to study and to aim high when it came to college.

I had great test scores and grades in school, but I applied to Penn State, where the tuition was low and I qualified for scholarships. If Artie had been around, I might have tried for a better school, maybe even the Ivy League.

I shook my head and closed the folder. That kind of thinking wouldn't get me anywhere.

A steady stream of women, occasionally with husbands, came by with more food and condolences. For the most part, I stayed up in Roger's office answering Bureau emails and doing research on art thefts. I was sure Miriam knew more than I could learn on my own, but I wanted to prove my diligence. I began compiling spreadsheets of thefts cross-referenced by country, state, artist, period and materials. Every time I found information, I added it painstakingly to my sheets.

Lester called late on Wednesday morning to check in with me. I told him she was managing, then added, "But she had a piece of news that shocked me."

"What's that?"

"The guy I thought was my dad wasn't my birth father. I knew that my dad married her when she was pregnant, but I didn't know she'd been secretly married to someone else, a guy who died in the Navy."

"Does that make a difference?"

I was stuck for a moment. "Now I know who my real father is. And that I wasn't born out of wedlock."

"You know who your real father is," Lester said. "This other dude is just the sperm donor, even if he and your mom were married for a hot minute. Your dad is the one who took responsibility for you, took care of you. Held you on his lap and showed you the world. At least that's what you've always told me."

"That's true, but..."

"I know a lot of gay people who've been rejected by their families of origin," Lester said. "You're lucky to have your mom and your brother on your side. Genetics is highly overrated when it comes to who you connect with as a family."

"You compare yourself to your dad."

"I do. He's big and strong like I am. And my mom has a lot of good qualities I think I've inherited. But a lot of the time growing up I felt like I didn't belong to them. They were good people, educated, but they had narrow views about homosexuality. They're changing, the more I am open with them, but I think you're lucky you had that relationship with Mr. Green. What was his first name?"

"Cameron. It's a Scots clan."

"And what does clan mean? Family, right?"

"You're right. How did I get lucky enough to land with a smart guy like you?"

"Be honest, it's the muscles that attracted you. The brain just holds you here."

"I wish I could hold you now."

"Soon, G-Man. Soon."

Miriam called me a couple of hours later. We made small talk for a moment, and she reminded me that the clock was ticking on our next visit to the immigration judge. I told her I'd been assembling a database of stolen art. "Is it true that more than 50,000 pieces of artwork are stolen each year?"

"That's a good number. And the black market for stolen art is valued at between $6 billion and $8 billion annually. But I need you to focus more closely on our case. I checked the National Stolen Art File, the Interpol records, and the Art Loss Register, and there's no record in any of them of a painting like the one Yulirus says he saw, either by Murillo or any of his students."

The FBI maintained the Stolen Art File, while the Register was a due diligence provider for the art market. If a museum had noticed the Murillo's loss, it would have been reported to one or both of them.

"What does that mean? That it's not real?"

"Not necessarily. An Old Master like Murillo could go through dozens of owners in its life span, and not all of them might be legitimate. What I'd like you to do is comb through the records of paintings by Murillo or his school and see if we can narrow down the name or the time frame for the painting."

"Without actually seeing it ourselves."

"That makes it tougher, certainly. But you have the photos from Yulirus's phone. Didn't you say your brother studied art history?"

"A couple of classes," I said.

"Have him look at the painting with you and come up with some search terms. I'll send you a few that come to my mind. Look for auction results, anecdotal information about the painting or similar ones. Let's see if we can crack this puzzle before we go back to the judge."

I agreed, and began to compile a list of places I could search and terms I could use. But I needed Danny's help. I checked his schedule and he was between classes. I texted him, "Got a minute to help me?"

Almost immediately he responded, "In the library. Call u in 5."

"What's up? Mom acting up?" he asked when he called.

"No, I'm working on this art theft case and I need some help from you. Got a minute?"

"Sure. What was stolen?"

I explained the circumstances and texted him the photo of the Murillo we'd gotten from Yulirus's phone. He suggested a couple of additional keywords based on what he had seen in descriptions of paintings. "'Husband of Mary,' 'Father of Jesus,' 'True Spouse' and 'Putative father."

"What does that mean?"

"Essentially a man who claims to be a child's father, but isn't married to her at the time of either conception or birth. It's a term used a lot for Saint Joseph in artwork."

"So like Cameron Green and me."

"No. Cameron was married to Annette when you were born, and I've seen your birth certificate and I know he's named there. That makes him your father no matter what. If anything, that Tanner guy is your putative father, because he wasn't married to Annette when you were conceived, or when you were born."

"Life is complicated, isn't it?"

Danny moved on. "You should also try St. Joseph's feast day. The painting could be connected to that."

I thanked him, and spent the next couple of hours hunting through various databases without result. I couldn't find a painting by Murillo titled any version of these.

Did that mean the painting Yulirus had seen was a fake? Maybe Elpidio had recruited someone in Cuba to reproduce famous paintings, or create works in the style of famous artists? Miriam wasn't good enough to recognize a fake from a phone image. What if we went to all this trouble to get Elpidio to smuggle the painting to the US and discovered that it was a fake? Was there a crime there?

Probably not one that the FBI could prosecute, which would leave Miriam embarrassed, and wouldn't help me either.

My mother was coming out of her shock by Wednesday evening. We had dinner together, a beef stew with carrots prepared by Mrs. Gurewich, a woman down the block I'd never spoken to. My mother knew her and they often shared tips about their gardens.

"Does she know someone you can hire to clean the driveway when it snows?"

"I'm not an invalid, Angus. I can shovel a path to the car if I need to. I'm the one who climbed up and cleaned the gutters. I wouldn't let Roger up on a ladder."

She started to cry. "I thought I was protecting him. But it didn't matter."

I reached out and took her hand. It was still thin and bony but at least there was some warmth there, probably thanks to the stew. "Roger knew what he was doing wrong, Mom. He made a conscious choice to smoke and drink when you, and the doctors, said he shouldn't. You have to accept that he made his own decisions."

"Deciding to leave me?" She looked at me with a tear-stained face.

"Not that," I said. "Roger loved you. But he was bull-headed and determined to do things his own way."

She used her napkin to wipe her tears away. "You're right. And if he were here today he'd agree with you."

As I cleared the dishes, I thought about Lester and me. We both had a stubborn streak. Mine usually took the form of perseverance. That had allowed me to be successful in college, to land my first accounting job, then become an analyst for the FBI. I'd pushed hard through the Academy and since my arrival in Miami.

Lester was determined, too. He'd taken a long time to find his path, and his current job might not be the right one. But I had faith that he'd figure out what he wanted eventually.

I hoped that included me.

After dinner, my mother asked me to sit with her in the living room while she read the medical billing manual. I brought my laptop downstairs and did some mindless work on Jonas's business plan, running different scenarios through Excel spreadsheets.

"I've been reading this over and over again, and I don't understand the difference between 'allowable' and 'allowed amount,'" she said after a while.

I shuddered to think about the bills that would come in after Roger's surgery and hospitalization. I moved over next to her on the sofa and she showed me the manual.

I read over the material, which wasn't very clear, and then I struggled to explain it to her. Eventually she got the distinction. "Delia says that all those numbers are already coded in the computer, so all I have to do is enter the data. But I want to understand what I'm doing."

She went back to reading, and asked me a few more questions during the evening. By bedtime, she was very pleased with her progress, and so was I. She didn't have the determination that I did, though. She'd gotten through life so far on her looks and the kindness of others. I hoped Delia would be patient with her.

Danny was working the late shift at La Scuola, and Lester was doing a bar demo, so I couldn't talk to either of them before I went to sleep.

Thursday I woke up feeling angsty about working on Jonas's faulty business plan. I couldn't tell him it was bound to fail—he'd get angry and I'd lose one of the few friends I had made since moving to South Florida. And I didn't want him to fail.

I had to let the numbers speak for themselves. I looked for similar business plans and compared their start-up capital. The same for first-year cash flows. I researched the cheapest business loan rates and calculated that to get the lowest interest, they'd need an additional infusion of capital from Camilla's father, and perhaps Jonas's father as well.

It was in both their interests, after all, that the business succeed. I didn't pay attention to any of their marketing ideas—I trusted that Camilla had a handle on that.

By the time Danny returned on Thursday night I had marked up the plan with notes and web links and enough calculations to make an MBA's head spin. I hoped Jonas and Camilla had the patience to read through it all with me and then act on it.

After dinner, our mom once again went to bed with a couple of sleeping pills, and I sat down with Danny. "Let me see that picture again," he said. I opened a large version on my laptop screen and he pointed. "See that apple there, in Jesus's hand? That's symbolic."

"Adam and Eve and the apple of desire?"

He shook his head. "There's a place somewhere in the Scriptures where Jesus says something about the apple of his eye. Hold on. Let me search."

I shifted the keyboard and he typed, and quickly came up with the reference he was looking for. He read out, "I conversed with Joseph in all things as if I had been his child. He called Me son, and I called him father; and I loved him as the apple of My eye."

I felt a pang of memory. Cameron Green had loved me the same way, even though he knew I was not his biological child.

"Interesting," I said, swallowing hard. "But how does that help us?"

"Because that might be the title of the painting, or someone might have used that phrase in referencing it." He typed some more. "In Spanish the idiom translates to *"la luz de mi ojos,"* or the light of my eyes. But the apple also has connotations of health and well-being. See, there's a tree in the background, in the literal center of the painting, and it's loaded with ripe apples."

We started searching for apples, or *manzanas*, and very quickly we found a painting attributed to Murillo called "Mi Padre, Mi Manzana" – My Father, My Apple. Painted in 1659, while he was living in Madrid, it was bought by Luis de Haro, a childhood playmate of King Philip IV. The painting remained in the family, and in 1848 a Carlos de Haro moved to Cuba to take ownership of a sugar plantation, and brought the painting with him among his household goods.

That's where the provenance stopped. De Haro and his entire family were killed in a failed rebellion in 1875, but there was no mention of what happened to his household and goods.

"We've got a painting that resembles a known Murillo, lost in Cuba sometime between 1875 and today," Danny said. "That's got to be something you can take to this immigration judge."

"It's only part of the picture, if you'll pardon the pun," I said. "It's still a painting owned by the descendants of foreign nationals, in a foreign country. It's a step forward, certainly. But now we need Yulirus to contact his friend in Cuba and offer his services to sell it if his friend can get it here."

"And then you catch the friend smuggling, and your guy gets to stay here?"

"Supposedly. But it's close to entrapment, and I'm worried the judge won't go for it."

"Then you'll have to convince him, won't you?" Danny asked.

Chapter 18

A Good Son

I was surprised at how many people showed up for Roger's funeral. But most of his contemporaries were still alive, and he'd been a friendly guy, the life of his bowling team, always joking with his colleagues and car buyers.

I wished we'd seen that side of him. But by the time he got home from a day of glad-handing, he was tired and cranky. And maybe because he knew Danny and I would never buy a car from him he had no reason to be nice to us.

A number of people spoke, anecdotes about how Roger had helped them, either with a lent tool, a kind word, or a deal on a used car. My mother's demeanor changed from sadness to a kind of glow, as she realized how many people he had affected.

Danny and I had both decided we would not speak. "I come to bury Caesar, not to praise him," he said, when I asked if he wanted to.

I was sorry Roger had died, of course. He had been good to my mother, and she would miss him, and that was quite enough to be sorry about, despite any personal feelings I had about the man.

After the ceremony, mourners came over to our house in pairs or small groups to pay their respects to my mother. Even a couple of old friends of Danny's and mine showed up toward evening. Danny was closer to the young man he'd been when he graduated from high school, both in age and temperament, so he was happy to see his friends.

I had come a long way since graduating from Scranton High—come out of the closet, gotten two college degrees, joined the FBI. The people I had known in high school were virtual strangers to me, though I thanked them for coming and spent some time on the back porch catching up with them.

Jack Boland had been my debate partner; he went to Lehigh and then Penn State Dickinson Law, and had returned to Scranton to start his own practice—and, he confided, run for office one day. Sue Kay Greene, who sat next to me in years of homeroom, had gone to Luzerne County Community College but never finished; she had married and had two small children.

There were a few others and while it was very kind of them to reach out, I felt distanced from the whole process, and them as well. I told them about finding accounting dull and joining the Bureau, mentioned I was "seeing someone" in Miami, and expressed surprise at how the old hometown had changed.

After everyone left, Danny and I put on our coats and sat on the screened-in porch in the gathering twilight. "I'm going to come back next weekend to check on Mom," he said.

"Don't give up your life for Annette Green," I said. "She didn't do that for us."

"What do you mean, Angus? She gave birth to us, she raised us, she made sure we had food on the table and a roof over our heads."

I remembered again that Danny had been her favorite, and tried not to begrudge him that. "I mean you've got a tough last semester until you graduate, jamming in all the courses for your minor. I looked up the program online. You're smart enough to excel in all of them, but they're going to be tough."

"I know. Risk Analysis is kicking my butt. It's a whole different way of looking at the world. But I'm digging it, and I'm going to make sure I have enough time to do all the homework."

"If you need to cut back at La Scuola…"

"I already have. My advisor helped me get a fellowship in global security for the spring that will pay all my tuition, and cover a conference in DC. So I'm only working three nights a week now."

I was impressed. My little brother was figuring things out on his own. At the same time I hoped he'd always come to me for advice.

Saturday morning I said goodbye to my mother, promised I'd call when I got home, and then drove to Philadelphia, where I returned my rental car and caught an afternoon flight to Miami.

Lester had found a guy to replace him, and he was training him that night at a bar in Boca. I texted him that I got in, and he replied that he'd call me when he had a chance. It was still early in the afternoon, so I drove out to Weston to see Jesse and Yulirus. I was struck by how much the young man who answered the door had changed. He no longer looked frightened, and he'd traded his cheap Cuban clothes for skinny jeans and a tank top that clung to his body like a second skin, revealing muscles I hadn't known he had.

"Come in, Angus," he said. "Is good to see you."

Jesse's house looked better, too. The glass on the display cabinets shone in the lights centered above them, and the house smelled slightly of Windex. Jesse moved more smoothly with his walker, too, more like he was using it for balance than a lifeline.

"I got rid of the aides," Jesse proclaimed. "Yuli is doing everything they did, and a whole lot more. He even got me in the pool this morning. Just walking in the water for now, but I'm going to start to swim again."

"Good for you. How about cataloging the art, though? I'm going to need something to take to the immigration judge."

"This isn't enough?" Jesse waved his arm. "My life is a thousand percent better since Yuli got here."

Yulirus looked down at the ground. "He's not an aide, Jesse. He's got a master's degree in art history. He's supposed to be doing something few other people can do, reviewing and organizing the records on your art. That's a reason he can stay in the States."

"I work," Yuli said. "I show you."

"Get the man a drink," Jesse said. "I'll take one of those raspberry waters."

The three of us sat at Jesse's shining mahogany dining table a few minutes later, with Jesse's laptop open in front of us. Well, it was actually Yulirus's, another gift from his benefactor. I was surprised to see that between cleaning the house and looking after Jesse, he'd already done a lot of work.

He had photographed the front and back of each piece, scanned the bill of sale (where there was one) and referenced recent auction sales for comparable works. "Wow, you've made terrific progress," I said, after I scanned through page after page of spreadsheets, photos and data. "How far have you gotten?"

Yulirus looked sad. "Jesse has many art works," he said. "I only catalogue maybe one fourth."

"We took your advice to start small," Jesse said. "Anything an aide could have walked off with. One good thing about the lousy cleaning job they did—it was easy to see if something had been moved. Only a couple of little pieces missing, crap I didn't care about. A couple of Lalique ashtrays, a Baccarat cigarette jar."

"Small items of high value," I said. "The kind of thing someone can slip into a pocket. Anonymous enough to sell to an antique store easily and impossible to trace."

I turned to Yulirus. "Make sure you include that information in your reports. That shows that Jesse needs your help before something bigger gets stolen."

"We've been talking," Jesse said. "About Yuli's situation, and what I can do to help. What do you know about adoption?"

I sat back in my chair and looked at him. "Adoption?"

"Suppose I adopt Yuli. Does that help him stay here?"

"You're jumping the gun, Jesse. Right now we're making a case that Yulirus needs to stay here because of his skill set, and because he's helping us with an investigation. Let's see how that plays out."

I turned to Yulirus. "Have you contacted your friend Elpidio?"

He nodded. "I tell him I land safe in America, that already I know collectors who want art."

"Be very careful. You don't want to create a situation that puts you in trouble." I turned to Jesse. "You've got to watch him, too. You already went to prison once for receiving stolen goods. You go back? I don't see you getting out again."

"I know," Jesse said. "I was reckless before. Only thinking about me and what I wanted. Now I'm looking after this one. I won't let him make any wrong moves."

The word of a convicted felon didn't encourage me very much. "You have email between you and Elpidio?" I asked Yuli.

He nodded.

"Forward it to me. And blind copy me on everything from now on. You know what that means?"

"I'll show him," Jesse said.

"We are scheduled before the judge on Friday. I'll be in touch once I'm back in the office to coordinate."

I turned to Jesse. "Any luck finding collectors who are willing to look the other way when it comes to Cuban art?"

"I asked around and got a couple of names. Ernesto Montes de Oca, Pio Garcia, Harvey Pearlman, and Alvaro Blanco."

I wrote the names down in my pocket notebook. I wondered if Alvaro Blanco was any relation to Alvaro Vela Blanco, the nasty guy I'd met at the art gallery. A cousin, perhaps? One who collected Old Masters? "Do you know any of these guys personally?"

He shook his head. "Nope. And I had to call in a few favors to get them."

"Thanks, Jesse. I'll dig into these guys when I get to the office."

"How was your stepfather's funeral?" he asked.

I took a breath. I had made peace with that title during the week. Yes,

Roger was my mother's second husband, but he had done what he could to be a stepfather to Danny and me. "It was tough," I said. "Like you, my mom has to start over again. Roger left her some insurance and the house is paid off, but she's going to have to get a job, and she'll be on her own."

I thought for a moment about what my mother had told me, about Artie Tanner and Cameron Green. I still had a lot of processing to do with that information.

"I bet you're a good son," Jesse said.

"Not as good as I could be." I stood up. "I've got to get home. You guys are making great progress on the collection. I'll look over your emails on Monday and see where we stand."

Chapter 19

Trust

When I got home, Jonas and Camilla were in the living room comparing samples of tablecloths. "I've been waiting for your seal of approval on our business plan," Jonas said.

He had lost some weight and he looked happy—not as much of a sad sack as he had been. Good for him. Now I could tell him how much his business plan sucked.

"Well, you got a C from your professor," I said. "That should tell you something."

"He hated the products," Camilla said. "His office is very Zen. Like only one picture on the wall, of some temple in Japan, and one of those little sand pits you can rake when you're stressed."

"He had some valid points," I said. "You guys want to take a look now?"

Jonas looked at Camilla, who shrugged. "Why not?" she said.

I got my laptop and brought up the document and started walking them through it. Within the first page I could see eyes glazed over, shoulders sagging.

I went back to everything I had learned at the FBI Academy about interrogating witnesses. Gain their trust, start with good news.

"OK, let me regroup. I like the products you've chosen, and I think there's a market for them." I had done a bit of research they hadn't, and brought up charts of ages and income levels in the area near their store. "Who's your customer?" I asked Camilla.

She crossed her arms over her chest. "Anyone who appreciates good design."

I shook my head. "Too broad. Lots of poor people appreciate good design, but they can't afford a hundred bucks for a tablecloth."

I gradually talked them through the characteristics I believed identified their customers, starting with young marrieds, furnishing a home together. "That means you need a bridal registry," I said. "Aunt Betty can afford the tablecloth. The members of the bridal party can each buy a place setting of the china."

Camilla grabbed a pad and a pen and started writing.

"This is also an area where a lot of wealthy older people buy second homes," I said. "You want to target them through affiliate programs with Realtors, ads in home design magazines, maybe direct mail postcards anytime a property changes hands above a certain price point. If you bring them into the store they'll have the money to redo all their kitchen stuff at once."

They were both pleased, and it was easier to approach the difficult topics of operating capital and reserves. When I finished, Camilla said, "That's what my father said, too. He offered us more money."

Jonas looked at her in surprise.

"Well, he didn't quite offer it. I told him that if more capital was necessary to keep me from failing, well, he didn't want me to fail, did he?"

"You need to use that same strategy on my father," Jonas said.

I was struck then how different our family backgrounds were. I was struggling to make sure my mother could pay her own bills, glad she'd been able to get a slightly better than low-wage job with little work experience. I couldn't expect her to be funding a business of mine.

Lester called that evening as he was driving to Boca to meet the new guy. "How'd you leave things with your mom?"

"Danny's there. I went over the manual for her new job with her a couple of times, and she starts on Monday."

"She wasn't too flipped out after the funeral?"

"No, I think she's had the chance to get accustomed to the fact that Roger's dead and she's on her own again. I might go up and see her again in a few weeks. I wish she could come down here, but she probably won't get vacation for a year."

I heard a siren in the background and hoped Lester was driving carefully. "How about you? How's the new guy look?"

"He knows how to mix drinks and how to schmooze customers," Lester said. "Straight, cute blond, twenty-five. Degree in business management so he understands how to write reports and handle spreadsheets."

I liked the fact that the guy was straight. Not that I didn't trust Lester, but.

"You free tomorrow?" he asked. "I found an apartment I want you to look at."

"Doral?"

"Yup, right off the expressway."

He'd be home too late that night to see me, but he agreed to pick me up on Sunday morning. "We'll do gym and brunch and then house hunt," he said. "Very heterosexual."

"There is nothing heterosexual about how I feel about you."

He laughed. "Back at you, G-Man."

I Face-Timed Danny around ten, hoping our mother would already be asleep. "How's she doing?"

"Good. Not great, but good. We went to the farmer's market this afternoon, bought cider and some Indian corn for the front door. I heard all about the Halloween costumes she made for you and me when we were kids."

"I never had a real costume," I said. "I had a pair of fake six-shooters on a belt, and Mom would put some black powder on my cheeks and I'd go as a bank robber."

"I guess she was mostly talking about costumes for me when I was little. You know, before Dad died. One year I was a rabbit, one year an alligator. She said she used to buy the patterns in the summer and then sew them off and on until October."

I tried to remember trick or treating with Danny. I must have gone with him—he was too young to go on his own. But I couldn't remember any of those costumes.

"She's still looking forward to starting work?"

"Oh, yeah, it's been Delia this and Delia that."

"You focus on your classes when you get back to Penn State," I said. "If there's any mama drama, you let me handle it."

"Yes, sir, Special Agent Green."

I held up the middle finger of my right hand and pretended to scratch my nose, and Danny laughed. "You do that at the FBI you'll get yourself fired."

"Believe me, I'm on better behavior with them than with you. You bring it out in me."

We laughed and teased for a while, and then ended the call.

I went to bed pleased at the way everything was falling into place, though I knew that Lester and I still had a lot to work out before we signed a lease together.

Lester picked me up the next morning and we went to the gym, where he kicked my ass, as usual. It seemed like he had extra energy, because he'd tasked the new guy with carrying all the bottles and setting up the demo, and he'd spent most of the evening lounging in a chair by the bar, doing the social media stuff I had done for him.

Then we showered and dressed at his place, and drove down to Doral, where we had brunch at a brand-new Southern restaurant, where every dish came with biscuits and the staff beamed with hospitality.

"I could get used to this," I said, as I dug into my eggs Benedict, the perfectly poached egg contrasting nicely with the warm English muffin beneath it. "Tell me about this apartment."

"Two bedrooms, one smaller than the other. We could put a desk in there with two chairs, use it as an office when we work from home. Modern appliances, two dedicated parking spaces." He smiled. "And a gym."

I could tell that was the best part. "Explain."

"I just took a quick look at it online. I was hoping we could get a tour today."

We found the complex easily, and because it was new there was a staffed rental office. A young woman showed us a couple of different layouts, and we decided that we liked the one Lester had picked out the best. The bonus was that the available unit in that line had a view of a small lake.

The gym was smaller than Lester had hoped, but it had most of the right machines. "We can always get a day pass to one of the big gyms if there's something special we want to work on," he said to me as we walked back to the office. "Is this all okay?"

"Better than okay." My heart was thumping in my chest, a combination of fear and excitement. I was going to yoke my life to Lester financially, at least for the year of our lease. But it felt like the right thing to do. I had to trust Lester, just as I trusted the men and women I worked with at the Bureau.

Chapter 20

Worms

This being the era of the internet, we were able to email the rental rep all the paperwork she needed. We signed the lease that afternoon, to start a week later, on February 1.

I felt an adrenaline rush that overwhelmed any last-minute jitters I had. I was moving in with Lester!

"You're going to be able to get out of your deal with Jonas okay?" Lester asked.

"His is the only name on the lease. So I can walk away. He's already been talking to the landlord about getting out, and it's going to be easy. Rents are on the rise in our neighborhood so it's better for the landlord to move someone else in at more money."

We drove around the area for a while, ducking into the huge Dolphin Mall to window shop, and Lester bought a couple of ties that caught his attention. Then we went back to his apartment and fooled around, and I slept over there and went running with him early on Monday morning.

I was at my desk reviewing emails when Vito stopped by. "Everything all right at home?" he asked.

I nodded. "My mom starts her new job today. Working with a friend, in an all-female medical billing office."

"That's good. Women, they look after each other better than us guys do. What are you working on now?"

"I kept up with the barbershop robberies while I was away. I have some emails to look at for Miriam, and we're meeting with the immigration judge again on Friday about this stolen artwork case."

"I have some small stuff you can help me with, but I can spare you for Miriam for the next week or two."

I thanked him and kept working. The emails between Yulirus and Elpidio were in Spanish, of course, and my command of that language was limited to ordering beer and food and a few epithets to throw out at bad drivers. The material was too sensitive to throw out into the world via Google Translate, so I copied everything into a proprietary translation program the Bureau had developed.

It was clunky, and sometimes the sentences didn't make sense because of colloquial terms, but I printed everything out and read though the English, jumping back to the translation program to fiddle with it. When I came upon a phrase that made no sense, I went back to the words before it, trying to determine context.

I realized, for example, that Elpidio did not intend to have sex with his car, the way the verb "joder" was translated. Instead, it meant "fool around" or "screw around." From the context, I understood he was having engine trouble. That meant he couldn't get out to the country to get the Murillo until the car was fixed.

Once I had a good handle on the text, I sat back and tried to pull back my perspective. Elpidio had laid out, in vague and colloquial terms, that he had a thriving business going, discovering valuable artwork in poorly guarded museums and private homes around the island, then "*liberando,*" or rescuing, them.

A few of those pieces went to prominent government officials – unnamed, in the emails. But their patronage enabled him to make arrangements to sell the other works to overseas buyers. He had one buyer, a "*gusano,*" in Miami, who bought anything by a Cuban artist.

That translated as "worm," and was also a pejorative term used by Fidel Castro towards Cuban counter-revolutionaries.

Elpidio apologized, in vague terms, for treating Yulirus badly, and offered to make it up to him by pulling him into a deal he had going to sell the Murillo. He needed someone to meet the boat bringing the painting to the US and then deliver it to the buyer.

When I had finally done as much as I could, I called Miriam to fill her in. She told me to email the documents to her, and then come to her office in an hour.

Then I turned to the names Jesse had found. Harvey Pearlman was a prominent cardiologist in Miami. He was a Juban—a Jewish Cuban. His grandparents had fled Poland during World War II, and because they'd been denied entry into the United States, they'd landed in Cuba. His parents were born there, and so was he. When Castro came to power, his family had moved to Miami, where he'd gone to college and medical school.

I found very little online about his art collection. If he was buying pieces through illegal channels, he probably didn't want to boast about it. Could he be Elpidio's contact in the US?

Ernesto Montes de Oca owned a chain of Cuban restaurants in Little Havana, Coral Gables, and Westchester, Miami neighborhoods with a large concentration of Cuban emigres and their descendants. He was a patron of an organization that sponsored artist fellowships, and his restaurants were filled with work created by the painters he knew through the organization.

But if Jesse had heard his name mentioned, he must have other works that he'd gained through illicit means, perhaps a private collection.

The final name on the list was much harder to find. There were an awful lot of men named "Alvaro Blanco" in the Miami area, and I couldn't find any of them connected to art. I finally gave up and looked at the finances involved in Elpidio's art smuggling.

Elpidio told Yulirus he had a bank account in the Cayman Islands to receive international funds, and he offered to open one for

Yulirus, too. When the buyer saw the painting, he would transfer half the payment to Elpidio's account, and then Elpidio would send ten percent of that to Yulirus. Once the buyer had the painting verified by his expert, he'd pay the rest to Elpidio. Elpidio would then send another ten percent of that amount to Yulirus.

The buyer had agreed to pay fifty thousand dollars to Elpidio – a bargain, considering the last verified Murillo had sold at auction for over four hundred thousand. But without provenance, the painting was worth what the buyer wanted to pay for the privilege of hanging it in his home.

It was a big score for Elpidio, considering the average Cuban made about $30 US per month. And he hinted that he had leads on other works of art, so there would be more opportunity for Yulirus to make money.

As I walked to Miriam's office, I thought that perhaps Elpidio didn't realize how little five thousand dollars was, for the risk that he was asking Yulirus to take, and that there might be some bargaining room there that would clarify the terms of the illegal enterprise.

Even though I wore a suit and tie to work every day, Miriam always made me feel underdressed. Her suits were as well-tailored as the ones we'd bought for Lester, and I thought perhaps it was time to up my game.

I slid into the chair across from her. "What do you think of the emails?" I asked. "Is there enough to convince the immigration judge to let Yulirus stay?"

"It's a start."

"There's one thing I didn't understand, no matter how I tried to translate," I said. "Elpidio calls his buyer in the US a worm. Do you think that's code for his real name?"

"Castro used that term, *gusanos*, to describe the first waves of wealthy white former landowners who fled Cuba back in the 1960s. So yes, it might be relevant, or López could simply be using it to refer to any exile."

"Yulirus is doing good work for Jesse Venable, too." I explained what I'd seen at Jesse's house, and the careful way Yulirus had been cataloging Jesse's art.

"It's another piece of our argument, but I can't ask the judge to let Yulirus stay in the United States just because he's cheering up a convicted felon."

Having it laid out so clearly made me squirm in my seat. "What else can we do?"

"I'd prefer to have a definite arrival time for the painting before we meet the judge," Miriam said. "That way he won't feel like he's signing something open-ended."

"But we want an open-ended release, don't we? I mean, if Yulirus had arrived here when the wet foot, dry foot policy was still in force, he would have qualified to stay. He was already on U.S. soil when the police apprehended him."

"That's true. But that was then and this is now. A lot of immigration officials didn't approve of that policy, which was more political than humanitarian. So we may face a backlash—Cubans got special treatment for years, so now let's push them to the back of the immigration line."

She must have seen something in my face, because she continued, "What we want, or what I should say the appropriate, humanitarian policy, would be to examine each individual case on its merits."

"I agree. And I understand that we don't have proof that Elpidio tried to run Yulirus down in Havana."

Miriam nodded. "And this exchange of emails weakens that case. Elpidio doesn't admit to the accident."

"But what about the government? Wouldn't they punish Yulirus for trying to escape?"

"Because the Cuban government hasn't been willing to take refugees back in large numbers, we don't have much evidence of what happens to the ones who are sent back. And since he wasn't a political agitator, the government probably wouldn't care."

"But he gave up his apartment and his job," I protested. "We'd be sending him back to a life of poverty."

"Thus the humanitarian angle. The only bright spot here is that Cuba may simply refuse to take him back. They paid for his education and he betrayed them by leaving. So his case could sit in limbo for months, maybe years."

"Could he keep working for Jesse while it drags out?"

"I don't have all the answers, Angus. All I can do is speculate based on what I've seen in the past. Jesse Venable is not a blood relative of Yulirus, so the government doesn't care if he's doing a good job cataloging artwork."

I remembered what Jesse had suggested. "What if Jesse adopts him?"

"Angus. Be realistic."

"No, that's something Jesse suggested. That would establish the family relationship."

"But in a way that makes it clear they're trying to subvert policy. Not a good idea."

"What if they got married? Obergefell v. Hodges makes that a possibility, right?"

"Did Venable suggest that, too?"

I shook my head. "But it's the logical next step, if adoption doesn't work."

She blew out a big sigh. "I knew Jesse Venable was a loose cannon when I agreed to this deal. Let's not suggest anything to him right now. Keep preparing the data to back up our appeal to the judge. Research anything you can find about what would happen to Yulirus if he went home. Does he have family to take him in? Friends? How did he leave his last job—on good terms? Would they take him back? And see if you can get Elpidio to confirm how and when he's going to get this painting out of Cuba."

"Let me call Yulirus right now and see if there's any update." When Yulirus came on the phone, I said, "You need to lock down Elpidio on the details of this delivery. We need that to persuade the judge to extend your stay."

"I try," Yulirus said. "Depend on his car. If he get it fixed. But he give me phone number of the man in Miami who will buy painting."

He read the number out to me, with a 786 area code, the secondary one for Miami-Dade County. I copied it out and swiveled the paper around so Miriam could read it.

"Keep me informed," I told Yulirus, and hung up.

Meanwhile, Miriam was searching for the owner of the phone number.

"Good news and bad news," she said, when she looked up at me. "The good news is that I found the owner of that number."

"And?"

"The bad news is that he's the subject of an ongoing Federal investigation."

Chapter 21

Alvaro Vela Blanco

I groaned. I had been down that road before. Crooks rarely confined themselves to one crime these days. They had their hands in all kinds of dirty pots.

"Tell me," I said.

"Alvaro Vela Blanco. Son of Alvaro Vela Romero. Vela Romero is the governor's pal and major donor. The father is the one who put in the initial query about Yulirus Diaz to the governor."

"Jesse gave me a bunch of names of men known to buy Cuban art without caring about provenance," I said. "One of them was Alvaro Blanco. But there are so many men with that name I didn't get to him."

"The father is one of the last surviving organizers of the Bay of Pigs fiasco, owner of a successful appliance chain known for benevolence toward immigrants. You must have seen their ads – dishwasher, dollar down?"

I nodded.

"The father, Vela Romero, is a patron of the arts, a major donor toward the new art museum. He employs a lobbyist in Washington to push his agenda of sanctions against the Castro government and relief for Cuban refugees."

"Sounds like a saint."

Miriam leaned back in her chair. "Many in the community consider him that way. His son, however, is another story."

"He's the one who's the subject of the investigation?"

"I'm not that familiar with the case, but I can sketch out the background."

Miriam usually moved her hands as she spoke, which I knew from my study of body language was a sign of thinking as well as anxiety. Right then she had them clasped together. "There have been rumors for quite a while that once Vela Blanco took over the family firm, suppliers were being pressured to lower prices, to enter into anti-competitive deals."

The clasped hands became steepled. "In addition, because Vela Appliances is so generous toward Cuban immigrants, other ethnic groups have begun to bring discrimination lawsuits."

"Do they have proof?"

Miriam began to worry her right index finger with her left hand. This was getting more serious.

"The U.S. Attorney's office sent married couples in to get price quotes on appliances. In each case the couples' backgrounds were the same—roughly the same age, number of years married, education and income levels. The Cuban couple was offered a significantly lower price than the Dominicans or the Argentines. The Haitians got the highest price and highest interest rates."

"Why haven't they arrested him yet?"

"An ongoing investigation," Miriam said. "My intuition says they're looking for the smoking gun that points at Vela Romero. Getting something on tape or in writing that establishes this is a company policy that comes from the top."

She frowned. "Otherwise he'll blame it on the individual store managers, and all the politicians his father has donated to over the years will jump to his defense."

"If we can catch him accepting this painting, we could snare him on receiving stolen goods."

She steepled her fingers again. "We have to be very, very careful. The phone number López gave Yulirus is the direct line to the son's private office, but it's also answered by his secretary, and occasionally by someone else in the senior management area, if Vela Romero is out of town. We need to be sure that Yulirus speaks directly to him, not a go-between, and that Yulirus delivers the painting to him."

That had been the plan for the last art case I'd worked with Miriam, until things went wrong and I ended up on a boat with a gal with a gun. A very strong, smart woman who was determined to get away from FBI custody.

But that's another story.

I went back to my office and spent the rest of the day searching for information about refugees who were returned to Cuba. There wasn't much to find, and I couldn't tell if that was because those people disappeared into the system, or were sent to prisons or work farms, or because they had to lie low and stay away from journalists and social media.

I called Yulirus to answer some of the questions Miriam had posed. "I don't want to frighten you, but I have to ask you some questions for our presentation to the judge," I said. "Do you have any family back in Cuba?"

"My parents, they not married, and my father, he leave when I am very young. My mother's family don't approve of her, so I never know them. And my mother, she die two years ago."

"No brothers or sisters?"

"No, I am only child."

Well, that eliminated family who might help Yulirus if he went back to Cuba. "How about friends?" I asked. "Someone who could take you in?"

"I don't want to live with Elpidio!" he said.

"I know. Anyone else?"

"My friend Marianela, she live with her parents in La Guinera, very poor neighborhood. She is often in demonstrations against the government. Not very safe for me. Her sister Susana, also my friend, she and her husband have two very small children and they live in one bedroom. No room for me."

"That's it?"

"Maybe if I know I will lose everything I try to make more friends!" Yulirus said, and he began to cry.

"Don't get upset, Yulirus. I told you, I'm just gathering information."

He sniffled. "I know. I sorry."

"How about your job? Would they take you back?"

"The museum depend on government for money," he said. "A job like mine, they probably glad not to have to pay my salary anymore."

I added all that information to my report to Miriam, thanked Yulirus, and told him once again not to get too upset. "We're doing everything we can to keep you here."

There was something very sad and fatalistic in his tone when he said, "I know, Angus."

I picked up a takeout salad on my way home, and after I ate I wanted to collapse into bed. The workout on Sunday, combined with the stress of Yulirus's case, was wearing me down. But I called my mother.

"How was your first day at work?"

"Oh, you know, very ordinary," she said. "I had to sign a lot of papers and watch so many videos. My goodness, I had no idea there were so many employment rules and regulations these days."

"Welcome to my world. Let me guess. Sexual harassment in the workplace? Confidentiality of information? They want you to know that you can't use their equipment for your personal purposes."

"Oh my, all of that. I had to sign up for health insurance and life insurance and then take a test on the material Delia gave me to read."

"How'd you do?"

"I passed. I got a few questions wrong, but Mrs. Giordano, the office manager, said they were tough ones, and I'd learn more on the job. I didn't sit down to start entering data until nearly four o'clock, and then it was time to go home."

"Do they seem like nice people?"

"Oh, yes. Delia suggested that I bring in some of the food people brought after the funeral, and the six of us in the office all ate lunch together."

"Delia's a smart cookie." Bringing food was a sure way to ingratiate yourself with your co-workers.

The next day I wanted to learn more about Alvaro Vela Blanco and his criminal tendencies, but we had a meeting with the immigration judge on Friday and I had to finish the assignments Miriam had given me.

I focused on opportunities for Yulirus in the United States. Were there jobs in galleries, museums, or universities, for someone with his credentials?

Sadly, there wasn't much. The art world was a closed community, and even entry-level gallery assistants needed connections to get their feet in the door. I read a bunch of blogs from eager young women who were recommended by their professors, or wealthy friends of their parents, for jobs that paid barely above minimum wage. And to be successful, they needed degrees from good colleges and an understanding of how wealthy buyers operated.

Yulirus had none of that.

One young woman suggested getting familiar with top shoe brands. Even if rich people dressed down, wearing jeans and T-shirts, they always wore expensive shoes. Jewelry was important too, whether it was heavy gold chains on wealthy rappers or huge diamond rings on pampered second wives.

Most entry-level jobs in museums required technical skills, like experience with archival programs – once again gained through education or connections. And a teaching or research job? Forget that. I only found a few jobs available across the country, and they all wanted a PhD in a narrow field along with publication credits.

The only way for Yulirus to stay employed was going to be to continue to work for Jesse. Through him, he could make contacts with galleries, learn the necessary software.

Or he could become Jesse's boy toy. I doubted that had been Yulirus's goal when he doubled down on his education back in Cuba. I'd looked at Jesse's finances, and he didn't have the funds to continue his lifestyle unless he started selling his art. Which, of course, Yulirus could help with.

I was sure that Jesse owned some very valuable works. I looked back at the spreadsheet Yulirus had begun, and while he had focused on the smaller objects, he had also priced out a couple of very valuable works, including the David Hockney I'd seen on Jesse's wall. A print from the same limited-edition set was appraised at between $30,000 and $50,000. If Jesse managed his portfolio well, he could probably sell a painting or sculpture a year and stay in the house in Weston.

That evening I went to Lester's apartment, and we went to the gym together for a quick mid-week workout. Then he made us a quick stir-fry for dinner.

Was this going to be my new life? Sleeping in the same bed with Lester every night, waking up to him every morning? He'd be traveling some, but sharing an apartment would bring us to a new level of closeness.

I hoped I was ready for that—I'd become accustomed to the casual nature of sharing a house with Jonas. I didn't know where he was all the time, never had to worry about making plans without consulting him. I often got caught up in work, staying until late. I'd have to learn to check in with Lester, make sure I wasn't screwing up any plans he had for exercise or dinner, or anything else.

But I had managed when I lived at home, kowtowing to Roger and my mother, looking after Danny. Then at Penn State I'd learned to manage multiple masters—my professors, my homework, the managers at La Scuola.

For the moment I had to focus on the case in front of me. How was I going to implicate Alvarez Vela Blanco well enough to prosecute him, while leaving no possibility of entrapment?

Chapter 22

Shadows

I spent all day Wednesday putting together the information Miriam and I had for our meeting in front of the immigration judge on Friday. It was very tricky, presenting only what was specifically relevant to keeping Yulirus in the country. I could bring in details of the way the Murillo would arrive in the United States, and how we proposed to manage the handoff, but I couldn't compromise the investigation into Alvaro Vela Blanco on other charges.

All that was relevant was his willingness to accept a painting smuggled out of Cuba for which there was no clear provenance of ownership. We had to establish that he knew the painting was stolen, which was tricky. Suppose it wasn't? What if Elpidio had found that painting at that farm where he took Yulirus, which had been abandoned for years?

If the painting fit the legal definition of abandoned property, "property to which the owner has relinquished all rights," then there was no stolen property and no felony.

In order to prove that, I needed the address of the barn, as well as who owned it. I called Yulirus and asked him for more information on where Elpidio had taken him. "Like I tell you, outside Santa Clara," he said.

"I understand that. Which way outside? North, south, east west?"

"He was drive, all country roads."

I pulled up a map of the city on my computer. "Let's take it step by step. It looks like the best way to get to Santa Clara from Havana is the A1 highway. Does that make sense?"

"Yes, yes, we take *autopista*. I remember."

"There is an exit for Santa Clara that puts you on a ring road." I peered closely at the detail. "A *circumvalacion*. Did you take that?"

"Yes, I remember. We pass exit for Che Guevara Mausoleum, and Elpidio make a joke. I no laugh, though. You must be careful what you say, even among friends."

"Good. You kept on that *circumvalacion*?"

"Yes, I ask him how much longer. He say be patient, my little friend. Then we cross Carretera Central, and he say we are there soon." He took a quick breath. "Ah, then I remember, we take road toward Sagua La Grande and he say almost there."

I traced the route on the map. "That's route 221. The next town north of there is Hatillo. Did you go that far?"

"No, not far. We go past farms, and to our left much empty land. Miles of it. All left barren. That is where barn was. All that is left, just that one building."

I peered at the map and found the big empty space, with a single building. "Excellent," I said. I hung up and switched to a U.S. government map of Cuba I had found in one of our databases, probably from a surveillance aircraft from the early 1960s. At that time there was a large plantation house, and evidence that the ground was being tilled.

Through a combination of luck and the use of latitude and longitude points, I discovered a single reference to that property. Hacienda Maloles.

A quick check at Google Translate showed that Maloles was not a noun, so more likely a family name, though there was a shoe manufacturer called that.

My next step was to establish, if I could, ownership of that property. A Cuban version of the Spanish Registral Law was in effect when Fidel Castro took power in 1959. Had it been owned by the de Haro family? They had allegedly been decimated in a revolution in 1875. What had happened to ownership of the property then? Had it lain fallow all these years? If so, there was an excellent case for abandonment—and then no way to charge anyone with receipt of stolen property.

I started looking through ancestry databases, searching for the de Haro family. I tried a bunch of different searches, hoping to pin them down to Santa Clara. Instead, I found that their plantation had been in Camaguey, much farther east and south of Santa Clara.

How could the Murillo have gotten from Camaguey to Santa Clara?

It was already late, so I called it quits and met Lester for dinner in Doral, near where we were going to be living. Over cocktails I explained my problem to him.

"What if the painting was stolen in Camaguey, and this guy Elpidio carried it to Santa Clara?" he asked.

"Why would he do that?"

Lester shrugged. "If he's stealing art on a regular basis, he has to have a place where he can store it, right? He can't just take it home with him. He probably lives with his extended family in some tight apartment. At least that's what I've heard about the poorer classes in Cuba."

I started to think out loud. "Yulirus says that Elpidio travels all over the island looking for artwork he can steal. Suppose he found this abandoned barn at the edge of nowhere and decided to use it."

"Isn't that what I just said?"

"Yes, dear." I smiled at him. "Sorry, just thinking out loud, trying to process. Then where did the painting come from?"

"You said the family was from Camaguey province, right? Are

there museums out there? Maybe when the plantation was destroyed this painting was saved and put into a museum."

I pulled out my phone and Googled Camaguey museum, and came up with the San Juan de Dios Museum. I read a couple of the reviews, which said it was a nice historic house with some old furniture. An old painting, too?

There was a phone number, with the 53 prefix for Cuba. I copied it onto my phone.

The next morning I was eager for Miriam to come in, haunting the corridor outside her office until I saw her arriving. "Can you make a phone call for me?" I asked.

"Good morning, Angus," she said

"Sorry. Good morning."

"Who am I calling?" she asked, as she walked into her office and deposited her bag on the chair.

"The San Juan de Dios Museum in Camagüey. We want to find out if they had a Murillo painting from the de Haro estate which has been stolen recently."

"Interesting. How did you narrow that down?"

I sat across from her as she turned on her computer and explained my train of thought. "It makes sense that if the de Haro plantation was in Camaguey, and the family owned the painting, that it might have ended up at the local museum."

"Worth a try." She picked up her phone and punched in the digits I read to her. Then she launched into Spanish.

I could only follow a few words of the conversation. It seemed that she spoke to someone, who referred her to someone else, and there was some discussion over whether the painting was a real Murillo, and valuable. Finally Miriam thanked the person and said she'd be back in touch.

"Interesting," she said. "I described the painting, and the curator recognized it, and said yes, it was stolen a few months ago. She didn't think it was valuable so she didn't report it to anyone."

"Why not?"

Miriam shrugged. "Maybe she didn't want to get in trouble. She said that the painting had been in a local church for a hundred years or so, and then when the church was damaged in a hurricane, the painting and some other artifacts were moved there."

"We're continuing the chain of provenance," I said. "Someone in the de Haro family must have donated the painting to the church. Then when the church was damaged the museum took ownership."

"This is all conjecture so far. It's hard to verify anything without having the real painting. And so far we don't have any proof that Vela Blanco knows he is buying a stolen painting."

"How do we get that? Can we have Yulirus call Vela Blanco once he has the painting here, and get Vela Blanco to admit that it's stolen?"

Miriam frowned. "We're talking about a very successful businessman, Angus. He's not likely to admit to a crime over the phone with a stranger."

"Suppose Yulirus calls him and says the deal is off. He says something like, I'm a trained museum professional. Now that I see this painting and realize it's the real thing, I can't turn it over to a buyer who will keep it hidden. It has to go back to the museum it came from."

"And?"

"And then we hope that Vela Blanco's ego kicks in. He wants this painting. He doesn't care if it was stolen from a museum, he made a deal to buy it and if that deal doesn't go through he'll make a lot of trouble."

She nodded. "It's often a good bet to consider a successful man's ego."

"And remember the subject of the painting. It's of Saint Joseph and Jesus, right? Father and son. And Vela Blanco has grown up in the shadow of his successful father. I'll bet you he has an emotional connection to the painting he's not willing to give up."

Miriam sat back in her chair. "Are you talking about yourself?"

I shook my head. There was no way I had a connection to Artie Tanner. And Cameron Green? Yes, but. "My father died when I was ten. Way too early to cast much of a shadow."

"You'd be surprised," Miriam said.

Chapter 23

Good Mood

I spent Thursday putting together the new information. Now that we had established the painting had been stolen from the San Juan de Dios Museum, our job in front of the immigration judge was easier.

We had to convince him that we needed Yulirus's help in retrieving the painting. Miriam had cautioned me again that we could mention we knew the intended buyer, but not that he was the subject of another investigation.

Lester had flown to a small-batch bourbon conference in Kentucky that afternoon and was going to see his parents after that. He called me to let me know he'd landed safely. "I'll be on the ground in Miami by noon Sunday," he said. "I've got my friend Tony lined up with a truck. We'll load my stuff and then come to you."

I agreed. "See you then, sweetheart," I said.

That evening, after I got home, I called Yulirus to go over the details of the appointment with the immigration judge the next day. Jesse answered the phone, and when I asked to speak to Yulirus he said, "You're not going to be happy, but he's not here."

"What do you mean? He went out to the store?"

"I gave him some money and sent him away. Much as I liked having him here, it's better for him to disappear."

My blood pressure zoomed, but I tried to keep things cool. "Oh, well, at least it means I don't have to drive all the way to Krome again tomorrow."

"You're not angry?"

"What good does it do to get angry? I never should have trusted the little shit anyway. Or you."

"He's a good guy, Angus."

"He's an illegal immigrant. He'll get picked up somewhere, someday, and they'll send him back to Cuba. Good riddance to bad rubbish, as my mother says."

Jesse started to argue, but I said, "Don't even think of asking me for any more favors," and hung up.

I knew Yulirus hadn't run away. He was too smart for that. Instead, he'd been listening to Jesse, who was more cunning than intelligent.

I dressed like I was going to a club, in skinny jeans and a tight T-shirt that read "Let me be perfectly queer" in rainbow letters, and I packed up an overnight bag, including the suit I'd wear the next day.

I drove out to Weston. I showed my ID to the guard at the gate and told him I was there on official business, and that he was expressly forbidden by the FBI from calling Jesse to warn him I was arriving.

He looked at my outfit and my ID and then shrugged. Maybe he thought I was there as a surprise stripper, but he let me in.

I pulled up two houses down from Jesse's, parked on the street, and walked the rest of the way. I skulked around the house, looking for a lit window, and spotted Jesse and Yulirus watching TV. Sweet.

Too bad I didn't have the rammer that the Bureau uses when we want to break down a door. It would take two guys to use, and besides, Yulirus was going to answer the door anyway.

He did, to his surprise.

"Guess you haven't left yet, huh?" I asked, as I walked past him.

"Angus," Jesse said, from the living room, as he struggled to get up from the sofa.

"Wait, *Papi*," Yulirus said, hurrying over to him.

"Don't get up on my account," I said, as I sat on the sofa across from Jesse. Then I turned to Yulirus. "I'll have a gin and tonic, please."

"We have fresh limes," Jesse said, but he shut up when I glared at him.

"Did you think you could get away with such a lame story?" I asked.

"I was going to send him to Frank Sena in Wilton Manors," Jesse said. "Until things blew over."

"Even for you that's a stupid move, Jesse. You know that I'm friends with Tom Laughlin. If Yulirus showed up at his boyfriend's house, he'd certainly call me."

I looked at him. "Why didn't you trust me?"

Jesse snarled. "The last time I trusted you I ended up in prison."

"True. But you committed a crime."

"Entering the United States without the right documentation is a crime, too."

Yulirus brought me my drink in a crystal lowball glass and then sat beside Jesse. I took a long sip. The tonic was cold, the lime was fresh, and the gin stung. Good stuff.

"The difference," I said slowly, "is that we have a plan to make Yulirus legal. A plan you very nearly scuttled."

"A plan with no guarantees," Jesse said.

I sipped my drink again. "I agree, no guarantee. But there have been some new developments."

I laid out the plan for them, but I didn't give them Vela Blanco's name. Instead I called him Señor Y—and pronounced it the Spanish way, ee-grieco. He was older than Yulirus and didn't have one of those funny Y names like Yulirus did, so I hoped that might throw them off the track if they tried to identify Vela Blanco on their own.

"Have you heard from Elpidio yet?" I asked.

"He call me this afternoon but I don't answer," Yulirus said.

"My fault," Jesse said. "I told him not to get involved."

"Call him back. Maybe he's ready to deliver the painting. We can take that information to the judge tomorrow, get you another couple of weeks."

"But what about after that?" Jesse said.

"The Bureau has been known to cooperate with other agencies," I said drily. "Like Immigration and Customs Enforcement. You already filed the form I-40, didn't you?"

That was the Petition for Alien Workers, with the goal of getting Yulirus an employment-based immigrant visa. I'd gone over it with Jesse on the phone, and felt that Yulirus fell under category five, an individual with a baccalaureate degree who had special skills that a US person did not.

"If Yulirus helps us put Señor Y behind bars, then Miriam and I can push up the chain for his I-40 to be approved." I looked at Yulirus. "The other option is a life on the run. Always hiding, afraid that someone will give you away, that you'll get picked up for a traffic stop or some other reason, and you'll be on the next plane to Havana."

"I want stay here. Legally."

"And I'm going to do my best to make that happen. But first, you call Elpidio."

Apparently his Cuban Android phone was too old to operate effectively in the US, so Jesse had upgraded him to a shiny new iPhone, fresh on the shelves only a few weeks before. He had texted his new number to Elpidio as soon as he had it, but he was still learning how to operate the phone. All he could do so far, he said, was make calls and take pictures.

"Make the call then. You don't have to put it on speaker—I won't understand the Spanish. You tell me what he says afterward."

As he pressed a series of buttons, I realized that was a tactical mistake. I should have had Miriam there when he called, so she could verify the information. But I was flying by the seat of my skinny jeans at that point.

After a series of odd noises, I heard a man's voice answer the phone. Yulirus launched into what sounded like an apology for not taking his call earlier. I heard him say *"Lo siento, lo siento"* several times.

Then he stopped talking and listened. He picked up a pad and a pen from the coffee table and started to write. He repeated a series of numbers to Elpidio as he wrote. The first number was two digits followed by a period and then six more. The second number began with a minus, then followed the same format.

While he continued to talk, I plugged those numbers into my phone. They were the latitude and longitude for a spot between two uninhabited islands—Saddlehill Key and Pelican Key. Then I heard the words *"no barco,"* and more argument. I took the pad and wrote, "I can get you a boat."

Yulirus was good at thinking on his feet. I heard the words *amigo* and *barco*, and then he wrote down more information. Finally he said *adios*, and ended the call.

"Saturday night, maybe eleven o'clock," he said to me and Jesse. "Boat come from Havana with painting. I need boat to meet at this point." He put a finger to the coordinates. "No radio, no phone. *Completamente silencioso.*"

I nodded, my brain racing. How would I get hold of a boat? The Bureau had various watercraft, but they were all plastered with government identification. That would be okay if we wanted to grab the incoming craft—but would it screw the deal with Vela Blanco? I needed to talk to Miriam.

But first things first. "This is going to require some coordination and I need to talk to my supervisor. Tomorrow morning, I'm going to take you to Krome for your hearing." I looked at what Yulirus was wearing—a skimpy T-shirt like mine, and short shorts. "Jesse buy you anything suitable?"

"He has a suit," Jesse said. "But I can bring him. He can drive my car."

"Jesse. He's an illegal immigrant at this point. There's no way he has a driver's license."

"I have license from Cuba."

"Even so. Based on today, I don't trust Jesse to bring you to Krome tomorrow." I stood up. "I'm sure you have an extra bedroom in this big house, Jesse. I'll stay here overnight."

Jesse started to argue, but Yulirus said, "*Papi*, please."

"I'll be right back." I walked back to where I'd parked, then pulled my Mini Cooper up into the driveway, blocking anyone from pulling out of the garage. Then I carried my bag inside.

Jesse was still looking sour, but Yulirus led me down the hall to a spare bedroom. It was generic, from the queen-sized bed to the chrome-accented furniture. The only thing that distinguished it from a room you'd see in a model home was the artwork on the walls—a collection of male nudes in erotic poses, the kind he might not want to display in his living room.

An oversized penis sculpted from marble held pride of place on the dresser.

"Jesse, he is angry, but he get better, I promise," Yulirus said.

"I know how to put him in a better mood." I opened my bag and pulled out the tiniest bikini I owned. Then I pulled off my T-shirt, my jeans, and my boxer briefs. Yulirus watched as I shimmied into the bikini.

"Jesse like this," Yulirus said, and he followed me back to the living room.

"You don't mind if I take a quick swim, do you, Jesse?" I asked as I walked in.

I watched his eyes pop. All those workouts with Lester had helped define my six-pack, my pecs and my biceps.

Jesse cleared his throat. "No, go ahead."

"It's a nice evening." I looked at Jesse, and at his walker.

Yulirus said, "Come, *Papi*, I help you. We go outside while Angus swims."

And that was how I put Jesse in a good mood, and ensured that Yulirus would be at his hearing the next morning.

Chapter 24

One Year

It was weird trying to sleep in that erotic museum of Jesse's. Shafts of moonlight illuminated pieces on the wall, and I'd think of Lester and want to try the positions in the artwork with him. Thank God the marble penis on the dresser was huge, or I might have tried to sit on it. But there was no way I was jerking off in Jesse's guest bed. I could only imagine Yulirus doing the laundry and giggling with Jesse over what he found.

I called Miriam first thing and let her know I'd meet her at Krome with Yulirus. "You're already at Venable's house?"

"I stayed here last night. Wanted to make sure Yulirus didn't get any ideas of running."

I left out the part about Jesse's lie and my own persuasive techniques. There were some things she didn't need to know. "He spoke to Elpidio last night. A boat is going to deliver the painting to a coordinate in the Keys. I need to go over the details with you and make sure we can manage it."

"We'll talk about it at Krome. We have an eleven o'clock meeting with the judge. Can you get there by 10:30?"

"Absolutely."

Yulirus looked handsome in his new suit. He'd gotten a good haircut, too, and a pair of dress shoes, and he looked a hundred times better than he did in his jumpsuit uniform.

It was a long, straight shot alongside the Everglades from Weston to Krome. Directions said it should take us about forty minutes, but I gave it an hour. As we switched over from Route 27 to 997, Yulirus asked, "What if judge decide to send me home today?"

"He won't," I said, and I believed that. "Miriam and I have gone to a lot of trouble to set up a Bureau operation, and he won't interfere with that."

"But after?"

"Like I said, we'll do our best to involve the Director of the FBI and have him make a plea to the judge." I looked over at Yulirus, who was watching a flock of white egrets rise from the marsh and flap off in synch. "You know about politics in Cuba. Well, politics is the same all over the world. Judges and law enforcement and politicians all need to work together."

He nodded, but his gaze remained on that flock of egrets.

We pulled up at Krome fifteen minutes before my scheduled meeting with Miriam, but her car was already in the parking lot. She sat behind the wheel, a folder in front of her and her earpiece in. She noticed me and Yulirus approach and held up a finger.

It was a beautiful late January day, almost like spring back home in Scranton. Yulirus and I walked once around the parking lot, until Miriam got out of her car and approached us. "You're looking very handsome," she said to Yulirus, as she shook his hand. "Good job. Let's show the judge you're prospering here in Florida."

She turned to me. "You and I need to talk before we go inside."

I'd already thought of that. "Can Yulirus sit on that bench over there?"

"Good idea." She nodded, and he set off toward the bench. "Now, fill me in."

We circled the parking lot ourselves as I told her what I'd learned the night before. "Do we have access to an unmarked boat, and someone to drive it?" I asked when I'd finished.

"Yes, and yes. The only question is if we can get everything in place by tomorrow night. Not much wiggle room."

I sat on the bench beside Yulirus as Miriam completed another circuit of the parking lot, talking on her phone. When she joined us, she said, "Wheels are in motion. Yulirus, when we're in this meeting with the judge, please don't speak unless he asks you a direct question. And even then, keep your responses short. Let me do the talking."

I held my hands up, palms out. "I'll be quiet, too."

She looked at me and laughed. "At least you'll try."

This time, instead of going to the judge's chambers, we waited in a queue in the hallway for Yulirus's name to be called. Most of those around us were people of color, both those in jumpsuits and those in business suits. The hallway was crowded and rang with voices in Spanish, Haitian Creole, Portuguese, Russian, and a few others I couldn't recognize. A palpable current of tension ran through the hallway every time the bailiff called a name.

Finally it was time for Yulirus, an hour later than our scheduled appointment. "Remember, let me talk," Miriam murmured. "I want to get in and out of here quickly."

We walked into a small courtroom. Judge Steiner sat on the bench in his judicial robes, with piles of paper to either side of him. The court reporter in the head scarf sat to his right, while the bailiff stood to his left. Because his robe came up to his neck, I couldn't tell if he was wearing a funny tie again.

Miriam presented the situation clearly and eloquently, emphasizing that Yulirus's help was crucial not only in recovering the stolen painting but in assisting with a related ongoing FBI investigation. Yulirus was sweating beneath his fancy suit, and my heart was doing flip-flops.

The judge turned his attention to Yulirus. "I understand the individual in Cuba is a friend of yours. You're willing to betray that friendship to pursue your citizenship?"

Yulirus cleared his throat. "After I identify painting for Elpidio, he try to run me over with his car. He not my friend after."

The judge nodded. "I can see how that would change your opinion. What about this place you are staying? You are cataloging the owner's art?"

"Yes, sir. I match bills to art work and put information into computer. Then I look online for similar works and their auction prices."

"You know how to do this?"

He nodded. "Is what I trained to do, for museum where I work in Cuba."

The judge looked at me. "And this work will continue?"

"I've been to Mr. Venable's home. I'm no expert, but the sheer volume of art on his walls, in display cabinets, even in the bathrooms, has staggered me."

"You think there's a year's worth of work there?"

I nodded. "I'm an accountant by training, so I'm familiar with how much work can go into a single spreadsheet. I've seen how much Yulirus has accomplished in the past two weeks, and it's my considered opinion, based on the meticulous care Yulirus has taken in assembling provenance, photographs, and value, as well as the so-far undocumented works, that he could easily work for a year or more at this project."

I looked at Miriam, who nodded slightly.

"I see from the records that Mr. Venable has filed a form I-40, proposing to offer citizenship to Mr. Diaz through a position that requires his unique ability."

I could sense all three of us holding our breath.

"That's what the form is for, and you've done everything I asked of you so far. I'm granting Mr. Diaz the liberty to remain in the

United States for one year, pending the conclusion of the FBI case and the progress of the I-40 form."

He looked at Miriam. "Will that do it for you?"

"Yes, thank you, your honor."

He banged his gavel. "Next case."

Chapter 25

Additional Focus

Yulirus didn't speak until we were outside, when he stumbled on the pavement and I grabbed his arm. "I no believe it," he said. "Thank you so much."

"That was the easy part," Miriam said when we were all in the parking lot again. "Now we have to carry out tomorrow night."

"Whatever you need, I do," he said. "Back in my country, we hear such mixed stories. For some, America is paradise. Freedom to speak, beautiful home like Jesse has. But for others, is poverty and shame, kept in prison like dogs in a kennel and then sent back. You give me the chance to have first story."

"What do you want me to do next?" I asked Miriam.

"I need you back at the office as soon as possible to coordinate logistics," she said. "There's a whole list of agencies to notify and liaise with. And then I want the two of you down there as early as possible to meet with the agent who'll be driving the boat and rehearse the operation."

I was excited as I drove back up toward Weston, but at the same time I felt overwhelmed by everything that had to be done in such a short period of time. I was lost in my thoughts, and so was Yulirus until we approached the gate to Jesse's community.

"This is all I want, even as young boy," Yulirus said. "To live with art. To fill my soul and spirit every morning with beauty. Thank you again for give this to me."

"I'll call you later to arrange a pick-up time Saturday morning. Don't go anywhere, all right? You have the chance to stay here legally if you carry through this operation tomorrow."

"I understand. You think Cuban police arrest Elpidio?"

I shrugged. "If we're successful, and if the painting stands up to further investigation, then Miriam will probably notify a guy she knows who handles art theft for the Cuban government. But I don't know what they'll do with that information. Maybe they'll arrest him, maybe they'll watch him and try to catch him stealing something in Cuba."

We pulled up in Jesse's driveway, and by the time we reached the door, he had opened it, just one hand on the walker for balance. A lot better than he'd looked two weeks before. "I got it, *Papi!*" Yulirus exclaimed. "I have one year for paperwork to finish."

He hurried up and embraced Jesse, kissing him once on each cheek. "This calls for a celebration," Jesse said. "Let's all go out to lunch."

"I've got to get back to the office. But you two have fun." It was sweet to see them both so happy, which cheered me up for a while. But my doubts began to rise again as I got on the highway. I hadn't slept well in Jesse's guest bedroom, and my emotions had been all over the place that morning.

I was happy we'd convinced the judge, and excited and terrified about the handoff the next day. I'd been shot in the chest on my first major Bureau operation, and I'd had to fire my weapon multiple times, severely wounding one criminal. I didn't want to have to go through any of that again. And then, as my brother had reminded me, I had stabbed an Italian in the chest with an antique sword in Venice.

By the time I got to FBI headquarters in Miramar, Miriam had gotten the name and number of the Fish and Wildlife Commission agent who was going to handle the boat for our rendezvous. His name was Ike Jiskani, and he was an expert at navigating the shallow channels of the area.

I called him to confirm details, and pulled up the navigational chart he had emailed on the screen in front of me. "We have two ways to get to your pickup zone," he said. "The simplest is to head out to the Atlantic, and follow the coast of the Saddlebunch Keys."

He spoke without the hint of an accent. Probably a transplant like I was. "Then we'll come to an inlet next to Pelican Key. Follow Pelican around to your rendezvous point, between there and Saddlehill."

"Sounds simple," I said.

"It is. But anyone offshore will see us coming, and potentially get the drop on us. Are you expecting hostility?"

I shook my head, though I knew he couldn't see. "The captain's motivation should be to hand off this painting, then return to Cuba where he gets paid. If he brings weapons into the picture that jeopardizes his ability to do the job and get back home safely."

Ike directed me back to the nautical chart. "There's another way, through the back of the keys, but some of these channels are shallow and it's not advisable to navigate them in a boat with the draft we have."

"What about if we got there early?" I looked at the channel between Pelican and Saddlehill. "Is there someplace back there we can hide until we see them coming?"

"There's three feet of depth up to the side of Saddlehill," he said. "And then two feet once you get to Bird Key. We could hunker down with our lights off in the shelter of Saddlehill with a good view of Hawk Channel, and we'd see anyone coming."

"Any danger to that?"

He shrugged. "There's always danger in these shallow areas.

Sands shift with the tides. Debris floats down. But if we find our way in by daylight I can identify any potential dangers."

"Let's do that then. What time is sunset?"

"Should be about six tomorrow night. Can you get down to the Sammy Creek Entrance by five? If you look on the chart, it's a few inches to the right, just beyond the bridge over Sugarloaf Creek."

I found it. "I can drive out there from A1A?"

"Sure. Take Sugarloaf Boulevard all the way east to old route 4a. Do you have any fishing clothes?"

"I've got a long-sleeve microfiber shirt and jeans." Because of my fair skin, I preferred long sleeves and long pants outside, at least when I wasn't exercising.

"Good. Wear deck shoes and bring plenty of bug spray. Make sure your phone is charged—we might not get a signal out there, but at least you can play games while we wait."

I checked the directions on the map after I hung up with him. It was about a three-and-a-half-hour trip there from Jesse's house in Weston.

I sat back in my chair and calculated. To get there by five, I'd have to pick Yulirus up at 1:30. We'd spend about seven hours in the boat, waiting for the midnight rendezvous. If all went smoothly, we'd be back at Sammy Creek by 12:30, and I'd have to drive another three and a half hours back to Weston. If I wanted to, I supposed I could crash at Jesse's for the rest of the night, or drive the further half-hour back to my place.

Either way, I'd be dead tired. The adrenaline from an operation would drain off quickly, leaving me exhausted.

I walked down the hall to Miriam's office, and she waved me inside. "I don't want to seem like a wimp," I said. "God knows I pulled a few all-nighters in grad school, and I've worked whatever I had to for the Bureau."

I sat across from her and spelled out the agenda for Saturday night. "Do you think I should pull someone else in as an alternative driver?"

"Why don't you take a motel room somewhere in the lower Keys?" she asked. "Make it somewhere remote so you don't have to worry about Yulirus walking away. Put your car keys under your pillow if you need to."

"You think that would be okay?"

"There are a lot of drunk drivers on A1A in the middle of the night," she said. "Trust me, I've seen the reports. And if you're exhausted and distracted, that puts you, and Yulirus, and the painting, at risk."

Her eyes lit up. "How about this. I'll drive down Saturday evening in my own car and get a room at the same motel. You can transfer custody of the painting to me. Then we'll connect in the morning over breakfast before we all head back up here. That way I get to see this painting up close and personal as soon as possible."

"I like that idea."

"You're going to be close to Sugarloaf Key, aren't you? There's an old fifties style motel on the bay side of the key. I'll get us two rooms there. You don't mind sharing with Yulirus, do you? To keep an eye on him?"

"No problem, though I'd prefer two beds."

"I'll try and make that happen."

I walked back to my office, feeling better about the next two days. Sure, Yulirus and I would both be tired by the time we got back to the motel, but I'd be able to hand off the painting to Miriam, and Yulirus would have no reason to run, because he was looking forward to a year cataloguing art, with a green card at the end.

When I got back to my office I called Yulirus and explained the plan to him. I couldn't get the idea of fishing shirt or microfiber across to him so he put Jesse on the phone. "I'll get him the right clothes," he said after I explained. "I used to fish, when I was younger. You'll bring him back after this is over?"

"Probably going to stay the night in a motel in the Keys," I said, trying to be vague. "I don't want to make such a long drive that late at night. But I'll have Yulirus call you once everything is resolved."

"He's a good kid," Jesse said. "Take care of him."

"I'll do my best."

I spoke to Lester briefly that night. I couldn't get into the specifics of the case with him, even though I trusted him. "We'll get the painting around midnight, and then hand it off to Miriam. I'll stay over at a motel so I don't risk an accident that late."

"What about the Cuban guy?"

"He'll stay with me, then I'll take him back to Weston Sunday morning."

I could almost hear Lester growl. "Tell him to keep his hands off you."

"Lester. Give me a break, will you? In the first place, I'm a professional and I'm not going to cuddle up with a guy in my case. And second, as you well know, I'm totally into you and I don't have eyes for anyone else."

"Keep it that way."

I might have been annoyed with Lester's tone, but he'd been cheated on before and it had broken his heart. I could never do that.

"Are we still going to move on Sunday? Because I already have the truck reserved and Tony to help us."

Oh, crap. In the fuss of figuring out the logistics of the painting retrieval, I had forgotten that I was moving from Wilton Manors to Doral on Sunday.

With Lester.

Moving in together.

Well, at least having something else to focus on had kept me from obsessing. "I can get up early Sunday, drive Yulirus back to Weston, and then be at my place by noon. Is that too late?"

"Will you have a chance to pack up your gear?"

I had been living light during my year with Jonas. I had seven suits, a rack of dress shirts, and casual clothes. Books, computer stuff and athletic gear. "I'll put everything together before I leave for the Keys."

"Stay safe, G-Man. Our lives together start on Sunday, and you don't want to let anything screw that up."

No, I didn't, though a twitchy Cuban refugee, a mangrove rendezvous, and a half-million dollar painting certainly could make for trouble.

Chapter 26

Hawk Channel

Saturday morning I went for a run around my neighborhood at dawn to clear my head. As I ran I noted landmarks, like the electric stump where someone planted a giant menorah each Hanukkah, the palm tree with a bend in its trunk that looked like it was kneeling, the pair of Egyptian geese that quacked nervously when anyone approached, then hurried into the small lake and paddled away.

I'd miss all these, moving to Doral with Lester, but there would be new landmarks to help me navigate my course. When I got home, I took a quick shower and then ran out to the local U-Haul place to buy some boxes. By the time I returned, Jonas was awake and making coffee in the kitchen.

"Boxes," he said, as I walked in, carrying a flattened set under my arm. "So I guess you decided to move out."

"Yeah, I should have told you, but it's been crazy. Lester and I signed a lease last Sunday, and I've been totally swamped with a case at work."

I put the boxes down on a kitchen chair as Jonas poured his

cappuccino into a mug. I noticed he didn't offer me one. "You signed a lease on Sunday?"

I nodded. Well, if he wasn't going to offer me a cappuccino, there was still coffee in the pot and I'd make my own.

"With Lester." He turned to face me, body blocking me from the coffee machine. "And you couldn't find a minute to tell me."

"You didn't exactly give me much notice that you were moving out," I said.

He shrunk a little and moved away from the coffee pot. "I'll give you that. But wow, you and Lester, huh. You think this is the real thing?"

I grabbed a mug and poured some coffee into it. "We'll see." Though I had begun to think of Jonas as a friend—perhaps my only friend of my age other than Lester—I didn't want to spill my guts about my reservations, because the next day I'd be gone, and I wasn't sure our friendship would survive.

But I had to give him a bone, because he had his good points. "Did you and Camilla talk to your fathers about the extra money you need?"

"Yeah. They were both impressed with the financial projections you did." He looked down at the floor. "They kind of made a condition, both of them."

I poured the last of the hot milk into my cup, along with some chocolate syrup. "What condition?" I asked, as I opened the refrigerator to look for whipped cream. Might as well go all the way. It was going to be a long day.

"The condition is that we keep you on as our bookkeeper," Jonas said.

There was no whipped cream. I closed the refrigerator and looked at Jonas. "I didn't make any provisions to pay a bookkeeper when I ran your numbers."

Jonas kept looking at the floor, holding the coffee mug in his hand. In rainbow letters it read, "Dudes taste better."

I picked up my coffee, sipped, and waited for him to respond.

"Both dads kind of think you and I are friends. That you'd do it for free."

"Well, they're wrong. I don't work for free, even for friends."

"You're working for that old guy in Weston."

"For money, Jonas. And because I feel sorry for him."

Jonas's body language froze. I'd hurt his feelings, made him think I felt sorry for him, too. Which I did, but I didn't want to say.

"Look, I'll keep helping you, but you've got to pay me something. I put a thousand dollars into your budget for consulting services when I wrote it up. I'll take half of that now, and half in six months. You know that's dead cheap for all the work I put in."

He nodded. "It is. All right, I'll talk to Camilla and then write you a check."

"I'm leaving tomorrow afternoon," I said. "But I'll give you my forwarding address."

"Thanks, Angus, I appreciate it." He gave me an awkward one-armed hug and I wondered if the dude would ever get comfortable enough in his body to have a real boyfriend. He'd had a few one-night stands during the past two years, but he'd paid for some of those, at least.

I was done being his wingman. Maybe the gorgeous Camilla could do those honors.

I spent the next couple of hours packing boxes. I hadn't realized I had so much sports equipment, for one thing, or how awkward it was to pack roller blades, ice skates, weight belts and ab rollers in standard sized boxes.

Nor had I realized how many books I had. Many of them were still stacked in the closet where I'd put them when I moved in, everything from accounting texts to mystery novels. Lester had a whole bookcase of art books and physical fitness texts, so we'd have to find a way to put everything together.

That's what we were doing. Putting our lives together. I had read somewhere that the choice of a mate was the single most important factor in financial success long-term. You had to be on the same page about saving and spending, about priorities like cars and travel. You had to be willing to talk to each other about money, too.

Lester had tried to talk to me, offering to take on more of our household expenses because he'd make more. And I'd screwed that conversation up by thinking too far in the future. Who knew, maybe it would be Lester who'd be offered a job across the country, and I'd be the one trailing behind, trying to negotiate a transfer to a different field office.

I'd never be like my mother had been, expecting someone else to pay the bills and make the decisions. That would have been a better conversation to have with Lester than the one we had.

But we'd have time. Maybe even the rest of our lives.

I picked up Yulirus at one-thirty, and was pleased to see that Jesse had outfitted him properly. He even had a small duffle bag with his clothes for the next day. "How are you feeling?" I asked.

"Nervous. I no trust Elpidio."

"He's not going to be there, though. Just sending the painting, right?"

"He say he use this captain before. *Viento en popa*, he say. In English is smooth sailing."

"Let's hope for that, then."

It was a long drive, and we talked off and on. I told him I was moving in with my boyfriend the next day. "*Verdad?* Very exciting! How long you have dated?"

"Two years." I told him how I had met Lester when he was a bouncer at a gay bar where I'd been following a witness.

"*Que romántico!*"

"I guess. Did you have a boyfriend, back in Cuba?"

"Is very hard there for gay men. Easy to find sex, but harder to have boyfriend."

"Well, maybe once you're settled here you can start dating."

He looked down shyly at his lap.

"You're not... romantic with Jesse, are you?"

"He so kind to me," Yulirus said.

"I thought from his operation, he couldn't... you know."

"Is not perfect. But if I am naked, and I dance for him first, then he get hard. We go slow."

"And he's so much older than you are!"

"Angus, I learn something in Cuba. When someone is kind to you, accept. Be kind to other people. Jesse is old and sick. He like look at me naked. He like, you know, to do things. To make me feel good. I try be good for him, too."

Well, that was more than I wanted to know about the relationship between Jesse and Yulirus, but I had opened the door. Hell, I'd opened the door, knocked and said hello. So I couldn't blame Yulirus for telling me.

"He want me to have boyfriend," Yulirus said. "After I settle in America. Even when I finish with his art, I am his friend."

After we passed through Key Largo, we had water on both sides of us, and the setting sun sparkled gold on Florida Bay. I was feeling positive about the operation when we approached Sugarloaf Boulevard and Yulirus said, "The police stop me here."

He shivered slightly. "I no realize how alone I am until other people from boat stop and call family and friends. I have no one, and I didn't know the way."

I reached out and put my hand on his knee. "You have friends now."

As I did it, I couldn't help thinking of my conversation earlier in the day with Jonas. He thought of me as a friend, when I thought I was being kind. But wasn't that what friends did—acted kindly toward each other? Jonas and I were knitted together by two years of history and connection, just as Yuli and Jesse were forming similar bonds.

I had considered my relationship with Jonas only one way—what I did for him. I hung out with him at bars and tried to attract guys to him. I helped him with his business plan.

But he'd been kind to me, in his own way. He'd provided me with a place to live—though I paid for that—and he'd ignored my many faults. He'd been a sounding board for me and even helped me with a case once. Maybe he was more my friend than I'd realized.

We took Sugarloaf Boulevard all the way to the Atlantic, then turned south on Old State Road 4a, surrounded by acres of brown and green mangroves on both sides. I remembered a line from a poem by Elizabeth Bishop: "The state with the prettiest name,/

the state that floats in brackish water,/held together by mangrove roots."

As we approached a low bridge over a creek, I turned left and pulled up in front of an orange gate which led into a coral rock parking lot.

A dark-haired young guy in a pale green microfiber fishing shirt pulled up to the car in a modified golf cart, and I showed him my Bureau ID. "Hey, I'm Ike Jiskani," he said, offering his hand to shake. "I'm going to be your pilot tonight."

I shook his hand awkwardly through the window of the Mini Cooper. "I'm Angus, and this is Yulirus."

Ike had large eyes with big whites and narrow pupils, and his deeply tanned skin had a yellowish tinge to it. It struck me as unusual to find a backwater guide of South Asian origin, but then, all of South Florida was one big tossed salad.

"Pleased to meet you all. You can park down by the truck. I'll be right behind you."

He opened the gate and I drove slowly down an incline. Once I'd parked, I got out of the car and looked around. We were on a small offshoot of the mainland, three or four feet above water level, with a broad band of riprap protecting the site from the ocean. A landscaped island sat in the middle of the area, with a few palms and some low ground cover. Additional palms and other trees were spaced along the side of the riprap walls.

At the far end sat a three-paneled display map of the area, under a black sloped roof. A similar roof sheltered a rest area with a couple of benches, tables and trash cans. The view out to the Atlantic was majestic, miles of ocean with nothing to disturb the horizon. Looking back to the west, where the land was so unendingly flat, I saw the occasional roof of a building on Lower Sugarloaf Key.

A launch ramp stood in the shadow of the bridge. A small, unmarked powerboat attached to a trailer and a pickup truck sat there ready to be unhooked. "This is my personal truck. I borrowed this boat from my brother-in-law because you said you didn't want anything with ID."

"It's great. Thank you."

"You have nothing to worry about tonight. I've been patrolling these waters for three years, and I know this boat as well as the patrol I run."

We followed him under one of the small chickee huts and he pointed to a nautical map of the area. It was already getting dark, so he pulled out a flashlight to show us where we'd be going. Then we dosed ourselves liberally with bug spray and Yulirus and I clambered into the boat.

Yulirus looked nervous, and I wondered if he was remembering the small craft that had brought him to Florida, and how he'd had to claw through the mangroves to reach land.

Ike unhooked the hitch and jumped into the boat. He moved up to the controls as we started to slide slowly down the ramp. He got the engine going and we moved the rest of the way into the water, and then through a marked channel out to the Atlantic.

There was little breeze and the air was close and humid, with a tang of salt. We motored slowly through the open water in a light chop for about half an hour, past mile after mile of mangrove swamps. The boat's navigation lights were the only illumination, so we saw millions of stars above us, including the hazy outline of the Milky Way.

"We so small," Yulirus said beside me, as he pointed up to the stars. "Is so much world."

I agreed, but just because we were an infinitely tiny speck in the universe didn't mean we were trouble-free. I watched Ike expertly navigate us past a headland and then turn into a narrow channel.

"This is Saddlebunch Harbor," he said. "That's Pelican Key to our port side. We're going to head up this way and around the back."

I leaned out the side of the boat to watch, though I couldn't see how shallow or deep the water was. "The captain of the incoming boat has to know these waters well," Ike said. "The channel between Saddlehill Key and Pelican Key is very shallow. We'll have to navigate carefully—can't go out with the engine roaring."

I thought about that for a minute. "You're saying the captain of this boat is an experienced smuggler?"

"Wouldn't surprise me. We don't patrol this area much because there's nothing here but mangroves. You can't easily drop people off or hide away to make a transaction, so the Coast Guard and the DEA concentrate on other areas that are easier for drug traffickers."

That reminded me how porous Florida's borders are. I'd gone to Canada once during spring break, and we'd had to wait in a long line of cars to have our IDs checked. I'd read stories of how condo dwellers on the miles of populated beach from Miami north had been out for early morning walks and stumbled over rafters landing, many of whom had simply disappeared into the city streets.

We settled into place, and the very gentle rocking of the boat in the tide was soothing. The mosquito repellent did its job, and I went into a trance-like state for a few hours, thinking about my mother and my brother and my future with Lester.

Then Ike elbowed me. "Hear that?" he said in a low voice.

I listened carefully and heard the very faint thrum of an engine. "Someone's coming," Ike said. "Without lights."

He pulled out a unit that resembled a handheld video camera. "I was lucky I could check this baby out for tonight," he said. "This is a thermal imaging monocular, which lets us spot warm bodies out in the ocean ahead of us."

He lifted it to his eye and then slowly moved his head and the device inch by inch across the horizon. "Still too far away to see," he said. "But we should get ready."

He pulled the anchor and we crept forward out of the sheltering channel, right up to the edge of the mangroves. We were still camouflaged, but we had a much better view of the ocean. The boat's sound grew louder, though it was still far away and the sound was difficult to distinguish from the lap of the waves.

My heart was thrumming faster and I gripped the edge of the gunwale. I looked over at Yulirus, who was shivering.

The approaching boat finally turned on a single navigational light at the prow, and Ike held the monocular up against his eye again. Then he handed it to me. "Take a look. I have it on the black hot setting, so human beings show up in black against the white color of the boat."

I hefted it up to my eye and didn't see anything. Then I shifted as I'd seen Ike do, and suddenly something appeared to disturb the darkness. As I concentrated I could make out the prow of a boat, with one person at the helm, and another behind. The boat moved up and down as it crested the small waves.

"Doesn't look all that seaworthy," I said, as I handed the monocular to Yulirus.

"You'd be surprised," Ike said. "Often smugglers use boats that look run down, but have big engines under the hood. Cuban mechanics are way smarter than American ones because they've had to make do with old cars and boats and makeshift parts for decades."

Suddenly Yulirus gasped. "*Madre de dios!*" he said.

"What's the matter?"

"Elpidio is with man driving boat."

Chapter 27

False Friends

"Are you sure?"

He handed the monocular back to me. "I have known him for many years. I am sure."

Well, that screwed things up.

"Do you think he wants to stay in the States?" I asked. "If he stays here, that cuts his ability to find more art to steal in Cuba."

"What if he try to kill me again?"

"Why would he do that?"

"So he go direct to buyer."

Cut out the middleman, I thought. My mind raced through possibilities as the smuggler's boat bore down on us.

One, Elpidio was trying to double cross Yulirus. He had no idea that the Bureau was involved; maybe he thought he could kill his old friend and take the painting to the buyer himself.

But why involve Yulirus at all, then? It would be easy enough to sneak in the way Yulirus had, though with more advance planning to get him from this remote backwater to Miami.

Perhaps Yulirus was his plan—get off the boat with the painting, then kill Yulirus and steal his car? Well, my car, but again, Elpidio hadn't counted on me being there.

I had assumed that the captain of the boat would hand off the painting and then return to Cuba. Roger haunted me then, reminding me that I might have made an ass of myself and Yulirus.

Yulirus and I hadn't discussed my role because we had not contemplated having to explain me to someone who was merely an intermediary. If anything, Yulirus could have said I was his driver.

We'd have to go with that. The boat had no official markings, and neither did my Mini Cooper.

Crap. My back seat was minimal, at best. We had planned to put the painting back there. Maybe I should have borrowed Lester's SUV while he was away.

I turned to Ike and spoke in a low voice "You carrying handcuffs? Weapon?"

"My service pistol is in a thumb holster under my shirt. Cuffs and other equipment in my car back at Sammy's Creek. You think there's going to be trouble?"

I explained who Elpidio was. "I don't know what his plan is, but it can't be good."

I pulled out my phone and was relieved to see that I had a couple of service bars. I texted Miriam as quickly as I could to tell her Elpidio was on the boat, and ask what to do.

As the Cuban boat approached, my phone dinged with an incoming message. Standing behind Yulirus, I was relieved to see it was from Miriam, directing me to wait at Sammy's Creek for her to arrive.

Then I stepped over to Ike. "Can we take it slow back to the dock? My boss is at a motel on the other side of A1A in Sugarloaf Shores and she's coming to meet us."

"Can do."

The Cuban boat pulled up alongside ours, and Ike held the stern close as Elpidio jumped on board. He was short and stocky, with bushy eyebrows and black hair that had gone wild in the ocean wind.

Then the captain handed the painting over to him. There was a dodgy minute when both boats rocked away from each other, and I thought Elpidio might lose his balance and let a half-million-dollar Spanish Old Master drop into the Atlantic, but Yulirus grabbed Elpidio's belt and dragged him back into our boat, and the captain let go of his end of the painting. Elpidio stumbled backward, a death grip on the frame.

The Cuban captain skillfully turned his boat to port and then headed back out to the open sea. Elpidio regained his balance and set down the painting alongside the fighting chair in the well at the stern of Ike's boat. It was wrapped in heavy brown kraft paper, and plastic wrap over that. He'd certainly taken more care with it than I had with the pile of boxes back in my apartment, waiting to be trucked to Doral.

I stayed in the background as Elpidio embraced Yulirus, my hand hovering near the service pistol holstered under my fishing shirt. They spoke to each other in rapid Spanish, and then Elpidio turned to me. "*Quien es este?*" he asked.

Yulirus introduced me as the friend who got him the boat.

"*Yo soy* Angus," I said, trying to make it clear with my bad accent that I didn't speak Spanish—which was close to the truth—and reached out to shake his hand.

He hesitated. Meanwhile, Ike had turned the boat north to head back to Sammy's Creek. Finally Elpidio took my hand.

"*Gracias.*" Then he turned back to Yulirus, who told Elpidio we were going to the dock where my car was.

The ride back to Sammy's Creek was agonizingly slow. Ike told the three of us he was going without lights to avoid detection by a regular police patrol. That meant he had to go slowly to avoid mangrove roots. Elpidio seemed to understand, and he nodded.

As we approached the boat ramp and Ike maneuvered the launch into position, I scanned the area. I saw my car, and Ike's truck, but didn't see Miriam's car. How long could I delay? It was going to be awkward to get the painting into the back of the Mini Cooper and there wouldn't be room back there for either Yulirus or Elpidio. One of them would have to stay at Sammy's Creek.

Maybe I could generate an argument between the three of us that would delay us enough for Miriam to arrive. I was conscious of my service pistol at my waist. When would I have to draw it? What if Elpidio was armed, too?

Ike expertly backed the boat up the ramp, and I jumped out to handle the trailer hitch. While I did, Elpidio and Yulirus were talking, but I couldn't understand them.

When the boat was secure, Ike cut the engine. Yulirus hopped out and opened his arms to receive the painting from Elpidio.

It was big, and he stumbled backward a few feet. Elpidio jumped out after him, landing awkwardly on his right ankle.

That's when Miriam appeared from the shadows behind the map display. She held up her gun in her right hand and a powerful flashlight in the other. "Elpidio López, you are under arrest," she said, and repeated it in smooth Spanish.

Elpidio looked from Yulirus to Miriam and said, "*Hijo de puta!*" I wasn't sure if he aimed those words at his old friend or my boss, or just threw them out into the air. Then before any of the rest of us could move, he ran to the edge of the paved area and dove into the shallow water.

I repeated his epithet in English and handed my phone and my gun to Ike. Then I took off after Elpidio, unbuttoning my shirt as I ran. I was down to my slacks and boat shoes by the time I reached the water's edge.

The water was shallow there, only two or three feet if I recalled from the navigational chart. Elpidio was lucky he hadn't broken his neck when he dove in. He was swimming toward Cuba in an awkward sidestroke, favoring his left arm.

"You'll never make it," I said. "Don't make me come in after you."

Yulirus joined me and spoke to Elpidio in rapid Spanish, most of which I couldn't understand. I think he was trying to tell Elpidio that our real interest was in the buyer of the painting, not in him.

Elpidio wore out quickly, and he was treading water as he spoke to Yulirus. Finally he began paddling back toward us.

The riprap was slanted so I had to direct him around to the boat ramp, which he could climb up. He was soaking wet and bedraggled as I approached him with Miriam's handcuffs. I was pissed because I was sure that as junior agent, I would have to drive him to the police station, wherever that was, and he'd soak my passenger seat.

Before I could get the cuffs on him, Yulirus darted in front of me and punched Elpidio hard in the stomach. He staggered backward, and I just avoided a gout of sea water gushing from his mouth.

"*Eso es por intentar matarme en la Habana*," Yulirus said.

Yeah, if someone had tried to kill me I'd be angry, too.

As I slapped the cuffs on Elpidio, Miriam began reciting his Miranda rights in Spanish. In the distance, I saw the rotating lights of a cop car approaching.

I ought to have been thinking of what to do next, but all I felt was relief that no one had been shot, and that my car wasn't going to get wrecked.

Chapter 28

Plan A

As the bright headlights of a snazzy black SUV illuminated the island, it felt like I was part of an artist's tableau. Elpidio faced the street, his hands bound behind him by the cuffs. I stood to one side, Miriam to the other. Yulirus stood under the chickee hut by the map, holding the Murillo, with Ike Jiskani beside him.

When the SUV pulled to a stop, I saw the words Monroe County Sheriff emblazoned on the side, beside a silver star. Two young uniformed cops got out, and Ike stepped up to talk to them.

"Hey, Ike," the heavier of the two said. "What have you got for us?"

"I witnessed the gentleman in the handcuffs jump from an unmarked boat into mine. Intel provided by the Bureau and its informant indicates the man is a Cuban national named Elpidio López, who came here to deliver a stolen painting to a buyer."

The cop nodded toward Yulirus. "That the buyer?"

Ike shook his head. "The intermediary. I'd appreciate it if you could take Mr. López into custody and process him to Krome while we let the Bureau continue its operation."

"We can do that," the slimmer cop said. He took Elpidio by the shoulder and led him to the SUV. As he stepped up, Elpidio cast one sad look back at Yulirus, who ducked his head.

I found my shoes and buttoned up my shirt as Miriam turned to Ike. "Special Agent Miriam Washington," she said. "Thanks for your help this evening."

"Beats spending a shift waiting for poachers," he said. "My pleasure. You have a vehicle here?"

"Black sedan parked up on A4a. You mind bringing it down for me?"

"My pleasure." He took the keys from her and beeped the fob, and her headlights flashed up on the street above us.

She waited until he was gone to say, "Well, here we are. Good work under pressure, both of you."

Yulirus nodded.

"I'm glad I didn't have to go into the water after him," I said.

"Though I have no doubt you would have," Miriam said. "Fortunately Mr. López was smart enough to realize he wasn't up to a ninety-mile swim."

"And that's if we'd been in Key West," I said.

Ike drove Miriam's car down the ramp and popped the trunk, and then he and I carefully lifted the painting inside, our hands slipping a couple of times on the wet plastic wrap.

"You know where the motel is?" Miriam asked me.

"Saw it on the way in."

"I'm in room 101. See you both there in a few minutes."

She thanked Ike, shook his hand, and executed a neat U-turn to head back up the ramp.

I thanked Ike, too. "We pick up refugees through here periodically," he said. "Cubans, Haitians, even some Chinese and Africans. Every time I see them head off with the cops I feel bad knowing what's ahead of them at Krome. Tonight, not so much."

"Yeah, I know what you mean. You've got to feel sorry for people who are so desperate to get to America they do everything they can. Too bad doing anything about it is above my pay grade."

"Yours and mine both," he said, and he turned back to his brother-in-law's boat.

Yulirus and I got into my car. The cabin, which sometimes felt too small with Lester and me jammed into it, was comfortingly close that night.

"Are you all right?" I asked Yulirus.

"My hand hurt." He shook out his right hand. "Friend of my mother, he try to teach me boxing in Cuba, but I am not strong enough."

"Elpidio will remember that punch."

"What happen to him now?"

"I don't know. That's up to Miriam, and to the police."

We drove the rest of the way through the darkness, my headlamps the only illumination, until we reached U.S. 1. It was silly that we had to wait so long for a green light when there was no other traffic, but I was an agent of the U.S. government and expected to follow the law.

A crescent moon hung low over the palm trees, and a few neon lights splattered color on the pavement. A convertible full of young women, yelling and singing along to a Garth Brooks song, zoomed through while we waited for the light to change. Long after they had passed, we heard echoes of "Friends in Low Places" in the otherwise quiet night.

I pulled into a parking space at the motel, which looked like it had been dropped in from a Jetsons' cartoon, and we walked to Miriam's room.

When she let us in, she had already unwrapped the painting, ditching the plastic wrap in a tiny trash can and carefully folding the kraft paper. She had moved all the lamps in the room around to focus on the painting, which she had propped up on a round table next to the kitchenette counter.

Seeing it there, the focus of attention, was a "come to Jesus moment" like the ones I had experienced in churches in Italy, all the religious fervor of generations focused into a single object of reverence.

Behind me, I heard Yulirus whisper an awestruck *"Dios mio."*

Miriam began peering at the painting with a monocular in one hand and a high-powered flashlight in the other. She handed the light to me and I held it as she carried out her examination. From the way I'd seen her look before, I knew she was looking at the signature, the brushwork, the way the paint sat on the canvas.

I wondered if she had felt the same chill of recognition and faith that Yulirus and I had. But perhaps that had happened while she was alone in the room with the painting, and she had absorbed that emotion and was using it to focus her investigation.

Eventually she stood back and I shut off the flashlight. "There's more work to do-- X-rays, paint analysis and so on before we can be certain this is a Murillo. But I'm confident that it's worth moving forward to confirm."

We were all quiet for a moment, absorbing the knowledge that we were likely in the presence of a 15th century Spanish Old Master painting, one that had survived centuries of adoration, travel, neglect, and now a rough sea voyage to be with us.

"What happen now?" Yulirus asked Miriam.

"Now we move to the next phase of this operation. You or Elpidio call Alvaro Vela Blanco, and get him to agree on the phone that he knows he's accepting a stolen painting. We arrange another handoff, and this time we arrest Diaz."

"You make it sound so simple," I said.

"And if everything works smoothly, it will be."

"If something goes wrong?"

"We find a plan B. And then a C, if necessary. You know what they do if they run out of names for hurricanes, don't you?" she asked.

"They go to the Greek alphabet," I said.

"Let's hope we never get to plan Omega."

We left the painting in Miriam's custody and went to the room she had booked for us. Twin beds, last renovated in the 1950s, but I didn't care. I used the bathroom, skinned down to my briefs, and slipped into one of the two beds. As Miriam had suggested, I stuck my car keys under my pillow. I was asleep before Yulirus got out of the bathroom.

I woke around seven, while Yulirus was still asleep. I put on a pair of running shorts and a tank top, and grabbed my keys. I slipped outside for a quick run. I had a lot to process, and physical activity was the best way to give my brain a chance to do the work for me. I hoped that Yulirus was smart enough to stay in the room until I returned.

Otherwise it wouldn't be hard to catch him—there was only one road out of the Keys. And if he was stupid enough to run, with so much waiting for him back in Weston, then he would get what he deserved.

The sun was rising over the Atlantic in a pale-yellow shimmer, streaking the restless water and glistening through the leaves of the palm trees. The motel was situated on a small island, and very quickly I was running along the side of a low bridge connecting one islet to another in the roadway's relentless trek toward Key West.

I had views to both sides. To my right was Florida Bay, flat and calm. Far out I saw a couple of small fishing boats already trying their luck for bonefish, tarpon and snapper. To my left was the Atlantic Ocean, growing more and more golden with the rays of the sun. A steady stream of traffic passed me, RVs and convertibles and pickups towing fishing boats. I hoped the Garth Brooks fans from the night before had made it to their destination safely.

I slowed my pace, waiting for a break in traffic when I could cross the highway and return to the motel on the other side, and eventually caught one, sprinting across the two lanes of pavement and turning back. The steady pace helped me organize and compartmentalize my thoughts. I had to get Yulirus back to Weston, then meet Lester and his rental truck in Wilton Manors. We'd move, return the truck, settle in. I needed to be present that day, to show Lester I was committed to him above my job. Problems with the painting and Yulirus's future would be there on Monday morning.

Yulirus was still asleep when I returned, but by the time I finished my shower he was awake. I drove out to a local coffee shop I'd seen on my run and returned with coffee and pastries. Miriam had already texted me that she was on her way back to Miami, and would see me on Monday morning.

Yulirus and I were on the road by eight-thirty. Neither of us spoke much on the long trip. I concentrated on the scenery, memorizing places I wanted to visit with Lester sometime. A1A was busy, lots of people heading to the beach for a relaxing Sunday, and at one resort the parking lot was on the bay side, so there was constant traffic across the street and I had to move slowly.

"I think about Elpidio," Yulirus said, when we had passed through the sprawl of Key Largo and we were on a long, narrow stretch of land that connected us back to the mainland. "How I feel when I am with police. Lonely and frightened. Is all because of him, or I am still at my work in Habana."

I took a deep breath. "Yulirus. He tried to kill you. If you had picked him up without me and Miriam and Ike, he might have stolen the boat and dumped you in the ocean."

"We are in painting class together at university," Yulirus said. "Elpidio, he is much more talented than me. He often come to help, hold my hand over brush, show me how to shade. Then when I apply for master's program, he help me study. Already he know so much about art. He recognize pieces by way the artist paint, by chiaroscuro, subjects."

He frowned. "He so talented. Hundred years ago, he have a wealthy patron, paint beautiful canvases. But no room for someone like him in Castro's Cuba."

"Did he go to graduate school with you?"

He shook his head. "No, he want only to make art, not evaluate it or categorize it. But life for artist very difficult in Cuba, so he find this other way to get money."

"By stealing paintings."

"*Si, claro que si*. But what else?"

I didn't know. I was lucky that what I liked to do, accounting and analysis, was also what I was good at, and I'd been able to find jobs that paid me to use and improve my skills. Danny had a natural charm and a gift for languages, a love of art and travel and other cultures. I had thought he'd be a professor, but that didn't seem to be in the cards.

Now he wanted to be an agent, like I was. I could see him as one of the Bureau's legal attachés, stationed in a foreign country, absorbing the culture and helping agents track down criminals. The Office of International Operations or OIO supervised the Legats.

The problem with that approach was that a Legat needed to have several years of experience as an agent, and then more time in a supervisory role above that. So it wasn't likely that Danny could jump right into a legat role with the Bureau.

He spoke Italian—but that wasn't a prime language for the Bureau. Spanish, Mandarin Chinese, and Arabic were much more in demand.

That left the CIA. He had many of the characteristics they looked for in agents—fluency in a foreign language, sensitivity to other cultures. He was energetic, in good physical health, and coped well with stress. But he was eager to get through college and start working.

Would he be willing to go through another eighteen months in school for the Clandestine Service Trainee (CST) Program? Could he stand up to the pressure of more education, under more stress?

We rode the rest of the way in silence. I dropped Yulirus in Weston, where Jesse was relieved to see him.

Then I called Lester. "I'm on my way home now."

"Everything's loaded from my place. You need help with your stuff?"

"I'm mostly packed, but my car's pretty small."

"We'll head over there now. We still have some room in the back."

I drove immediately to Wilton Manors, where both Camilla's car and Jonas's were in the driveway.

I parked on the street and walked inside. A French country kitchen had exploded in our living room. Tablecloths overflowed from boxes. Dinnerware was piled on every surface. Curtains were draped over the sofa and chairs.

"Great, Angus. You can help us," Camilla said.

"Didn't Jonas tell you? I'm moving out this afternoon."

She turned to him. "Really?"

He looked sheepish. "Guess I forgot."

"Jonas. If we're going to be business partners you have to tell me everything, whether or not you think it's relevant. Write things down if you can't remember them, for Christ's sake."

He started to argue with her, and I held up my hand. "Sorry, guys, but Lester is on his way over here with a truck. Can one of you clear a space for him in the driveway?"

Camilla glared at Jonas, who said, "I'll go."

He walked out, and I said, "Sorry. He's kind of a flake, as you probably already know."

"I don't know if this business is a good idea anymore," she said. "I sent all the revisions you made to our business plan to my father. He thought they were excellent, but that they revealed," and she used finger quotes for "underlying flaws in the plan."

"Ouch."

"Well, better to know that now than later. The biggest problem is that Jonas can't get his father to match the investment my father's going to make. That gives us an unequal partnership, which complicates a lot of stuff. And lately, the more we work together the more I see him making dumb mistakes. Like not telling me you're moving out so soon. In our plans, we counted on you sticking out the rest of the lease so Jonas wouldn't be out of pocket."

"I know I only gave him a week's notice. I can pay my half of February."

She waved her hand. "You can work that out with him. But seriously, would you go into business with him?"

I gulped. I had realized that I liked Jonas, but he still had a lot of growing up to do, when it came to both business and dating.

"I admire him for taking those classes where he met you," I said. "He recognized that he hated his job and needed credentials to get a better one."

"He's not exactly a scholar. Neither am I, and I still got better grades than he did."

I looked out the living room window and saw Jonas approaching, after parking his car on the street. "Look, I'll help you guys however I can," I said. "Pro bono, at least for the first few months. Keep an eye on your revenue and expenses, and help you head off any problems that come up."

"That would be great!" She rushed over and put her arms around me, and kissed my cheek.

"What did I miss?" Jonas asked as he walked in.

"Angus is going to help us," Camilla said. "Like a sort of silent partner."

I wanted to interrupt, but I saw a big truck start backing into the driveway. I'd work things out more clearly with Jonas and Camilla later. Consider our agreement a plan A, that could evolve, just as the arrangements with Alvaro Vela Blanco would.

Chapter 29

On the Move

I met Lester's friend Tony, another beefy bodybuilder, though apparently straight, from the way he continued to talk about women as we loaded my stuff into the truck. I'd noticed that in straight guys sometimes. Around gay men, they seemed nervous and determined to attest their hetero bona fides.

It was surprising in the end how little I had. Tony was an expert at sliding my athletic gear into unexpected spaces, and my boxes of books and clothes lined up like a series of soldiers at the back end of the truck. "Good work, dudes," Tony said, and held up his fist for both of us to bump.

I followed the truck in my Mini Cooper down to Doral. It felt weird to be leaving the house in Wilton Manors, though I was sure I'd come back to help Jonas. This had been my first place in Florida, and I had experienced a lot there. Even though I'd be with Lester, I'd miss it.

Lester and Tony did most of the unloading of Lester's furniture, though I carried boxes, clothes and gear. Then Lester had to get the truck back and drop Tony off. I was alone in this new apartment, not knowing where anything went. It felt like my first day in the dorm at

Penn State, when I got there before my roommate and didn't know which bed to pick.

I realized that I hadn't spoken to my mother or my brother enough that week, especially since my mother was jump-starting her whole life. I sat on a chair I recognized from Lester's kitchen and dialed Danny's number.

"Hey, bro, I'm on my way back to Happy Valley right now," he said. Because so many people came to State College from distant corners of Pennsylvania and never wanted to leave, the town had acquired that third name. University Park was the college campus, State College the town, and Happy Valley the hippy-dippy name that encompassed it all.

"How's Mom holding up?"

"Well, she started to work, which I think is a good thing, although she's already complaining about the computers and the other women and how far her office is from the employee parking lot."

"That sounds like Mom. Always look for the gloomy side of life."

"Remember when you read me *Winnie the Pooh* when I was a kid and we both agreed she was Eeyore?" Danny said.

"Oh, yeah. Candy Miller had a birthday party where the kids had to pin on his tail, and after the party you convinced her to give you the poster and the tails. And we put it up on your wall and every time Mom was miserable to one of us, we stuck a tail and a pin on the donkey's ass."

Danny laughed, and it was great to hear such joy coming from him. "She wasn't so bad," he said eventually. "I mean, now that we look back on it. She was just trying to keep her head above water."

"I know, and I admire her for it. But she could be a pain in the ass, even after she married Roger and didn't have to worry about money."

"I know." He paused for a moment. "You think any more about Dad?"

I let out a deep breath. "Honestly, I haven't had the time,

between this case and moving. I'm sure it'll catch up to me eventually, and whatever happens I'll work through it."

Then I told him about retrieving the painting the night before, and Miriam's belief that it might be an original Murillo.

"Man, I'd love to see that," he said. "And what's up with Lester?"

"I'm sitting in our new apartment. He went to return the rental truck."

"So you're in a liminal space," he said. "Between two parts of your experience. A threshold." He snickered. "Did Lester carry you through the door of the apartment?"

"I think that's supposed to happen after you get married," I said. "Which is definitely not in the immediate future."

"I don't know, he sounds like a guy to hold onto."

I heard someone in the hallway. "That's him. Gotta go. Travel safe."

Turns out it was a neighbor. I'd have to get accustomed to the closeness and noise of apartment living again. But that motivated me to get up off my ass and start hanging up my suits and shirts in the closet, and lining my shoes up next to them.

I had no furniture of my own, so I'd have to share Lester's bureau, and I decided to wait for him to unpack the rest of my clothes. Instead I moved into the kitchen, where there was a dishwasher, to my delight. I unwrapped all Lester's dinnerware – he only had place settings for four—and ran all that stuff, and the glasses and silverware, in a load.

I moved the table by the window and placed the chairs around it, and fiddled with everything else. I found a dumpster at the edge of the parking lot and I had already trashed most of the boxes and packing materials by the time Lester got back.

"You didn't have to do all this by yourself," he said, when he looked at the apartment. I had made the bed, laid the pillows on the sofa, and so on. "But it looks great."

He plopped heavily on the sofa. "I could do with a beer after all that driving and loading," he said. "You didn't happen to find the cooler, did you?"

"I did, and I put everything in the fridge. I'll get you that beer."

I brought one for him, and one for myself, and I sat beside him on the sofa, then moved closer to cuddle up. "I stink," Lester said. "Need a shower."

"Don't mind." I rested my head on his shoulder, though shifted so I was smelling the air around him, not him. "Our first place together."

He clinked his bottle against mine. "Not our forever home, but it'll do for now."

It pleased me to know that Lester had an idea of a forever home for us in the back of his mind. I had no idea where we'd end up, and I didn't mind, as long as we were together.

Miriam called late in the afternoon. "You get Yulirus back to Weston?"

"Yup. What's going to happen to Elpidio?"

"He'll go through the same system that Yulirus went through. Though we may have to make a deal with him, too, if we want to catch Vela Blanco."

"Yulirus talked a lot about him as we drove. He doesn't sound like a bad guy, just trapped by circumstance and making the best out of what he had."

"We'll see. In the meantime I stopped in Coral Gables on my way home, and met a friend of mine who teaches at the University of Miami."

"On a Sunday?"

"For the chance to authenticate an Old Master? He didn't mind at all. I left the painting with him, and you and I will go back down to his studio tomorrow to see what he's come up with."

"First impression?"

"He agreed with me on all the key points. And when we took the painting out of its frame, there was a very, old faded note that seems to include the name de Haro. That's the family who last owned the picture, correct?"

"Yes," I said. "So it's got to be real, then?"

"It could be by a follower or a student of Murillo," Miriam said. "Just because it has the de Haro name on it doesn't mean it's authentic." She paused. "Though it does add to the provenance."

By the time I hung up with Miriam I was excited, and Lester suggested we go out for a run, then a shower before dinner. I agreed, and we went slowly, circling around the lake. We found the clubhouse and gym, and a coffee shop on one corner that served both residents and neighbors.

It was a fun evening. We went out for sushi, then came home and christened the new apartment, and both of us fell happily asleep. My last waking thoughts were of Yulirus, who had a happy path ahead of him, and Elpidio, who was stuck at Krome. I was developing a pattern —use Jesse, then help him. The same with Yulirus.

Was it my responsibility to help Elpidio, too? Or just use him to get to Vela Blanco?

Chapter 30

Authentication

Monday morning it was weird to drive to the office from Doral. I had internalized the trip from Wilton Manors so that I didn't have to think, but leaving the apartment I had to make conscious decisions—left turn, right turn? Which way was the highway?

It was a relief to get onto the Turnpike and head north; at least I knew the way from there. When I got in, I spent a couple of hours documenting everything that had happened that weekend, and then it was time to accompany Miriam to Coral Gables to meet Professor Kyle Roberts, the art historian. He was a skinny guy, only a few years older than I was, in jeans and a Hawaiian shirt.

In our business suits and sensible shoes, Miriam and I didn't look like we belonged in the messy studio, surrounded by paint splatters and canvases. The art on easels looked like student work, a combination of oils and watercolors and pencil sketches.

"Interesting development since I saw you last," he said to Miriam after the introductions. "I was so careful removing the backing from the painting yesterday that I didn't realize there was another painting sandwiched in there."

"Another Old Master?" I asked.

He shook his head. We were in a long room with a line of windows on one side. At the near end, a group of chairs and easels were clustered around a low pedestal, like a round coffee table. At the far end was an office and a laboratory, as well as lots of art supplies like paint and brushes. The room had the sweet and somewhat chemical smell of paint.

"No, a contemporary painting," he said, as he led us down toward the lab. "Very carefully packaged in tissue paper, and then slid between the painting and the backing."

I looked at Miriam. Our last case had involved gold coins hidden in the frame of a painting. She raised her eyebrows. "Can you tell anything about it?"

Roberts shrugged. "The painter has some talent, certainly." He pointed us to a small oil painting, perhaps three feet wide and two feet high, on an easel by the windows. We walked over to it.

It was in what I recognized as an impressionist style. Small, thin, visible brush strokes with an emphasis on portraying light. The subject was an old mill somewhere in the countryside, and the water in the mill race vibrated with light. It wasn't what I'd call photo-realistic—the walls of the mill looked old and weathered, in an impression, if you will, of decay contrasted with the vibrancy of the foliage around it, including a majestic palm tree off to one side.

Roberts pointed at the bottom left of the canvas. "It's signed last year, with a single name. Looks like Elpidio."

"Elpidio López," I said. "The man who arranged to have the Murillo smuggled from Cuba."

"Interesting," Roberts said. "I ran some more tests this morning on the main painting. The hallmarks are all there—the right paper, the right paint, the right kind of strokes to be Murillo. Still possible, of course, to be of his school, but given what we know of its provenance, that a painting of this subject matter was sold to the de Haro family a year before Murillo's death, I'd say this is an original."

"Worth?" I asked. Ever the accountant.

He quoted the same numbers I'd heard before. Perhaps a half-million dollars at an Old Master auction, maybe more if there was interest from specific collectors or museums.

"What are you going to do with it?" he asked Miriam.

"For now, use it for bait. In the end, it will have to go back to Cuba. It belongs to a small museum out in the countryside, but I would imagine it will end up in the *Palacio del Centro Asturiano*, the museum of Spanish art in Havana."

"So you'd like to wrap it up again? Include the Elpidio painting?"

"Let's wrap that separately," she said. I watched as the two of them carefully reassembled the Murillo, using only the materials that had come with it. Elpidio's painting was in its tissue, with heavier kraft paper over it to protect it.

We walked back to Miriam's car. The UM campus was lovely, with a sparkling lake at the center, undergrads in shorts and T-shirts kicking a soccer ball, others heading to class or lounging in the shade reading. I was lucky to go to college in the United States, to study what I wanted and build my own career. Yulirus had been lucky, too, until Elpidio tried to run him over.

Elpidio, however, hadn't had the chance that I had. He was a painter of some talent, at least according to Kyle Roberts, and he had been forced to steal the work of other artists in order to survive.

I carried the larger, heavier painting and she had the smaller one. "What do we do now?" I asked.

"Yulirus has to get in contact with Alvaro Vela Blanco and set up the handoff. I want to be in the background on that conversation, however, so I can be sure that Diaz acknowledges he's receiving stolen goods."

I nodded. "I'm sure the conversation will be in Spanish, so I can't help you there."

"I am intrigued by this other painting, though. What's it doing there? Does Diaz know it's coming? Is he supposed to buy it, or help López make connections with American dealers?"

"I can go down to Krome tomorrow, assuming I can get an interview with him."

"Good." We got to Miriam's car, and carefully loaded both paintings in the back. At the Miramar headquarters we stowed both paintings in one of our secure vaults.

Then I called Yulirus and explained that Miriam wanted to hear the conversation between him and Vela Blanco. "Can you text him and make an appointment for the call? Maybe this evening?"

"How I know what to say?" he asked.

"Miriam will tell you, in Spanish, and we'll both be there while you're talking. Remember, we need him to acknowledge that he knows the painting has been stolen."

"I nervous, Angus," he said, giving my name the Spanish pronunciation, an-Goose. "Why no have Elpidio make call?"

That was a good question. "He's in Federal custody. We can't make arrangements for him to get out and be part of the painting transfer. Plus we don't trust him."

"You no get him same deal as me?"

I tried to phrase my response avoiding any colloquial expressions like 'out on a limb for you' or 'in deep water.'

"What Miriam did for you is very unusual, Yulirus. For the FBI to get involved in the case of an illegal immigrant. We were lucky that Jesse took you in, and that the judge was sympathetic. We can't go back to him a second time for a second immigrant."

"But Elpidio..."

"No buts, Yulirus. You agreed to carry all this out when we agreed to step up for you through the immigration process. I don't want to but we could go back to the judge and tell him you stopped cooperating."

Suddenly Jesse was on the line. "You're an asshole, Special Agent Green. Can't you tell how frightened you're making Yuli?"

"I may be an asshole," I said calmly, though I wanted to tell Jesse Venable what I thought of him. "But I have a job to do. I've treated

Yulirus very well so far and I want to keep that going. As long as he does his part."

"Fine. I'll see that he sends the text and we'll let you know when the call is scheduled."

Then he hung up.

I was sure I could have handled that better. Miriam would have been smoother, more iron fist in velvet glove. I had to listen to her more.

While I waited to hear back from Yulirus and Jesse, I called Krome to make an appointment to see Elpidio López. Miriam wanted to know why he had included his own painting with the Murillo, though I didn't know her motive. Maybe she was hoping for more details that would help us indict Vela Blanco.

You'd think with a name like Elpidio he'd be easy to locate, but the woman on the other end of the line wanted his inmate number. "How can I get that?" I asked.

"You'll need some specific information that only the inmate can provide. Birthdate, birthplace, and mother's maiden name should be enough. The Monroe County deputies are trained to ask those questions before they bring people to us."

I wanted to ask if I should find out about his favorite pet, his childhood best friend, or the first school he had attended, but I held my tongue.

I called the Sheriff's Office and identified myself. I had to leave my office phone number with them so that someone could get back to me on a verified line.

Bureaucracy. And I couldn't complain about it because I'd ensconced myself in the middle of such knots and tangles when I signed up with the Bureau.

It only took a half hour to get a call back from a deputy at the Marathon substation, the one closest to where Elpidio had been picked up. The woman who called had a charming Bahamian accent, and she provided me all the information I needed, though she did stumble on Mamanantuabo, the tiny town north of Camaguey where Elpidio had been born.

We didn't have any kind of inter-agency special phone number to call, so every time I called Krome I had to go through a whole authentication process to prove who I was and what agency I represented. This time the agent insisted on calling the main FBI number and being transferred back to me to agree to schedule an appointment.

Once she was satisfied I was who I said I was, I had to explain what my business was with Elpidio López.

I was stumped. I was going there to ask him about the painting he put in with the Murillo, but that kind of fishing expedition wasn't going to skate easily with ICE. So I went back to another version of the truth. "He smuggled a valuable artwork into the United States on Saturday night. Before we can authorize sending him back we need further information about his contacts in the U.S."

She thought that was reasonable, and made an appointment for me on Thursday afternoon.

I kept working for the next couple of hours, wondering when I would hear from Yulirus, but there were always forms to fill out and emails to answer.

A few minutes before six, Jesse called. "The guy's going to call Yuli tonight at 8. You and Miriam will be here?"

"I have to check with her. Hold on." I put his call on hold, called Miriam's cell, and she agreed. She had some more work to do so she said she'd meet me in Weston.

I went back to Jesse. Trying to smooth him over, I said, "You want me to bring something for dinner? I can pick up takeout."

"Yuli's cooking. *Pollo a la plancha.* Chicken marinated in orange and lime juices, with rice and beans. I suppose there'll be enough for you."

"Thanks, Jesse. I'll be there in forty-five minutes."

"Bring a bottle of wine, as long as you're coming."

I called Lester. "I have to work late tonight," I said.

"Really, G-Man? I thought we could settle into the apartment together. If you know what I mean."

I knew, and so did my penis, which stiffened uncomfortably in my slacks. "We signed a year lease, Lester. That's 364 other evenings we can spend together. And I'll be home eventually."

"Five hundred twenty-five thousand six hundred minutes," he said, and because he wasn't singing, it took me a moment to recognize the lyric from *Rent*. "Plan to spend some of those minutes with me, all right?"

"Will do."

It was funny, when I agreed to move in with Lester I was more worried about his travel, that I'd be alone in the apartment in Doral when he went to trade shows and conferences. I hadn't counted on my missing dinners with him because of work.

But he knew I loved him, and that my job was important to me, as his was to him. We'd work around these small problems in the future. Or at least I hoped we would.

I stopped at a wine store near the office on my way north. "I deliberately got a bottle that needs chilling," I said, when I handed it to Jesse as he answered the door. "I don't think anybody should drink before this phone call."

"Yuli's Cuban. He could drink a whole bottle of rum and not feel a thing."

"Even so." I sniffed the air as I walked in behind him. "That smells great."

"He's a good little cook. Only makes healthy food, though." Despite Jesse's grumble, he smiled. He had traded his triple-X T-shirts for one that showed off the additional weight he had lost, so he looked a lot less like a contestant on one of those six-hundred-pound-life shows.

For the first time since I'd met him he wasn't wearing enormous sweatpants, either, having slimmed down enough to wear some off-the-rack khakis. He even moved more smoothly with the walker, as if he hardly needed it.

Yulirus was in the kitchen, plating the food, when we walked in. Jesse and I sat and Yulirus served us, then sat to eat as well. Though the setting and the food were homey, there was an underlying tension in the room that I didn't know how to relax. I wished Miriam was with us.

The chicken was fragrant and tender, the rice the perfect consistency to mix with the soupy black beans. "This is delicious," I said. "Where did you learn to cook like this?"

"My abuela," he said. "Every day after school, I help cook dinner." He smiled bashfully. "I no cook as good as her, though."

"Are they still alive? Your grandparents and your mother?"

He shook his head. "All gone. No one for me to go back to."

That made me think of Elpidio, and what his whole story was. "Elpidio put one of his own paintings in with the Murillo," I said. "You have any idea why he did that?"

"He say something about how maybe this man will help him sell his own paintings," Yulirus said. "But nothing more."

We ate slowly, and I tried to get Yulirus to relax by asking him about his childhood in Havana, how he developed his love of art, and so on, but it was difficult. Each memory triggered renewed nerves about the call, and I was glad when the gate announced that Miriam was there.

At last we could make the call and see what kind of actor Yulirus could be, knowing how much was at stake.

Chapter 31

Strength

I was happy to let Miriam take over. She set up equipment so that she could hear the whole phone conversation, while I helped Yulirus clear the table, to take his mind off what she was doing.

Then slowly and carefully she walked Yulirus through what she wanted him to say, mentioning key words that he wrote down on a white lined pad. By the time eight o'clock approached, he was much calmer, and I admired the delicacy she'd used with him.

He was great—until the phone rang, and he started to shiver.

"You can't do this to him," Jesse protested. "Look at him."

Yulirus took a deep breath. "I must do this, *Papi*." Then he answered the phone.

The whole conversation was in Spanish, so I could only follow a few words. Instead I watched Miriam. She was intent, listening and translating in her head, nodding to Yulirus, pointing at words on the page.

Finally Yulirus said, "*Claro*," and ended the call. Then looked at Miriam. "I do all right?"

"Very well." Miriam turned to me and Jesse. "Yulirus did an

excellent job of explaining how Elpidio got hold of the painting," she said. "Vela Blanco tried to stop him, and even said that he knew the painting was stolen."

"That's great!" I said.

"That's a fundamental building block to our case, now that he's admitted he's buying a stolen painting."

"So Yuli is done then," Jesse said. "You've got your confession from this guy."

Miriam shook her head. "Not until we have a physical handoff of the painting."

"Why can't you get this other guy to do it? The one who stole it."

"Because Elpidio López is in custody at Krome," I said. "And we've already played that card once, to get Yulirus out. It's not going to work again."

I looked at Miriam. "I heard the word *miércoles* in that conversation. Does that mean the handoff is going to be on Wednesday?"

"It does. Nine PM, in the parking lot for the Diaz Industries building on Brickell Avenue in downtown Miami." She looked at Yulirus. "Make yourself available then. We'll be in touch with the details."

Then she turned to me. "Come on, Angus. We've still got a lot of work to do."

As we walked out, she said, "How would you feel about staying with Yulirus and Jesse until the handoff?"

"Whatever you need." Lester wasn't going to be happy that I was out of the apartment for the next two nights. But he'd lived alone before moving in with me, so he'd get over it.

"Good. Go home, get your clothes, then come back here. I don't trust Jesse Venable at all. Now that Yulirus has his paperwork I wouldn't be surprised if Jesse tried to get him to skip out on his responsibilities."

"Yulirus is scared," I said.

"I understand that. But he was a gay man in Castro's Cuba. That must give him some strength, right? You understand that."

It was a lot different from being gay in Scranton, or coming out in the supportive atmosphere of Penn State, but yeah, I got it. Yulirus was strong, and he'd make it through the next two days with me by his side.

When I got back to the apartment, Lester was lounging on the sofa watching a football game on TV.

Wearing only his jockstrap.

"Well, that's a nice sight to come home to," I said, dumping my messenger bag on a kitchen chair.

He looked at me, smiled, and shut off the TV.

That was all the invitation I needed. I started shedding my clothes and he pulled down his jockstrap, and we went at it like rabbits. Very horny rabbits, even though we'd just had sex the day before.

We didn't even leave the living room. When we were finished, we were both on the floor cuddled together. "That was just what I needed," I said, kissing the back of his ear. "But I have to take a shower and head out again."

He turned to look at me. "What?"

"I have to babysit Yulirus for the next two days." I explained about the handoff on Wednesday night. "But I'll be home after that. And then nothing more on my plate."

"Until you get a new case," he grumbled. He pulled himself up so he was leaning against the sofa. "I need to go up to Gainesville and meet with the people who work the UF circuit. I can drive up there tomorrow morning, spend the night, and be back Wednesday."

"You'd do that? That's so sweet."

I was thanking him for doing his job, the way I was doing mine, but it was kind of him to work around my schedule.

"Do something for me, though. Take a picture of that dildo you said is on the dresser."

I blushed bright red, and Lester laughed. "Good. You know just what I want to see. Text it to me tomorrow night."

"And what are you going to do with that picture?"

He grinned. "That's between me and my K-Y."

Then he swatted my butt. "Better get in that shower and get moving. Don't want to give Yulirus time to run away."

I showered and packed, and when I finished Lester was back on the sofa watching his game, though he'd put on a T-shirt and shorts. I kissed him goodbye and hefted my duffle bag.

This time I didn't bother to creep up on Jesse and Yulirus. I parked in the driveway and Jesse answered the door. "Not surprised to see you," he grumbled. "Come on in. We're working on that bottle of wine you brought."

I put my duffle in the guest room, where the big dildo still sat on the dresser, and even though no one was there to see me I felt myself blushing.

The three of us quickly demolished the bottle of wine, and Yulirus opened a second as we all told stories. It was fascinating to hear Jesse talk so openly about growing up queer in a small town in Indiana. "I didn't know what it meant," he said. "I hated taking showers after gym class because looking at other boys gave me a boner, and they'd tease me and call me names."

He shrugged. "None of us knew what a faggot was then. It was just a name you called someone, but it was bad. Then one day in English class we read an excerpt of some book, and the narrator was staying in some seedy hotel where he said the desk clerk was a fruit."

He frowned. "I'd never heard that term, but it blazed into my brain. I thought I was destined to end up like that, working some crappy job, that I'd never be able to have a real life."

"Oh, *Papi*," Yulirus said, and squeezed his hand.

"I looked on TV and the only men I saw I could tell were gay were the real over-the-top ones, like Paul Lynde and Liberace. I saw the way they used their flamboyance as a shield over them. So I started cultivating that. I was always ready with a self-deprecating wisecrack, and the other kids laughed. Laughing with me, not at me." He smiled. "I liked that."

"How did you get out of Indiana?" I asked.

"I studied my ass off, for one thing. Got the only academic scholarship awarded to a boy from my county to study at Ball State in Muncie. One day I stumbled into the art museum on campus, and I was hooked. By the time I graduated with a degree in business, I had memorized every item in that building."

He poured us all another glass of wine. "Then I moved to Chicago. Worked a bunch of different office jobs, spent my weekends in museums and my nights in bars. I was a lot better looking back then, and I got lots of offers."

There was a certain way he turned his head when he looked at Yulirus, when I could see the echo of the man he'd been.

"Then they started dropping," Jesse continued. "Men I met in bars. Men I had roller-skated with along the lakeshore. Men I slept with."

He shivered. "It freaked me out. Winter of 1982 I lost my job because I mentioned I had a friend who had died, and I said to hell with this snow, I'm going to Florida. I drove down here and started collecting my unemployment insurance, and I got a part time job at an antique store in Sears Town. Betsy's Bits-n-Bobs, something like that."

He leaned back in his chair. "That's where I met my first thief. Didn't know what he was, back then. He'd come into the store with a silver service, a Rolex watch, a diamond ring. He always had a story. His mother died. He picked up the watch at a yard sale. That kind of thing. Then he stopped coming in, and I thought the police must have busted him."

I was fascinated. When I'd arrested Jesse originally, I never thought about how he had begun his life of crime.

"Then I ran into him at a bar. Bought him a couple of drinks and he told me he'd found a pawn shop that didn't ask questions, that gave him more cash than Betsy could. The next day I walked past the place, just out of curiosity, and saw a help wanted sign in the window. I walked in, dazzled the guy with everything I knew about art, and what I'd learned at Betsy's about antiques, and he hired me."

He shrugged. "You know the rest, if you've read my record." He struggled to stand up, and Yulirus jumped to help him walk down the hall to his bedroom.

I thought about my brother then, his love of art and Italy and all the beautiful things in the world that cost money. I was determined to see that he didn't drift into a life of crime like Jesse, even if it meant worrying that he was in danger with an organization like the CIA.

I went to sleep soon after that. When I woke at sunrise, the house was quiet, and I grabbed a key and went for a long, looping run through the manicured streets of Jesse's development. By the time I returned, Yulirus was in the kitchen.

"I'm going to take a quick swim and cool down," I said. "Towels?"

"In cabinet by pool," Yulirus said. "Jesse, he will still sleep another hour."

I could have gone into my room and found a bathing suit, but the pool was sheltered from the neighbors by a screen of palms and low shrubs, and Jesse was still asleep. So I shucked my running clothes and dove naked into the deep end of the pool. I swam a dozen laps, then wrapped myself in a towel and climbed out of the pool.

It felt naughty and transgressive, not something that a proper FBI agent would do. But I was horny and missing Lester, and Jesse's house, with all its naked male art, didn't help.

I relaxed for a few minutes, then showered and dressed. When I came back to the kitchen Jesse was eating an egg-white omelet stuffed with mushrooms and green vegetables, and Yulirus offered to make me one, too.

Yulirus had to take Jesse for physical therapy that morning, so I had the house to myself. I settled at the dining room table, made sure the VPN was running on my laptop, and got to work, answering emails and reading bulletins.

An hour in, Miriam called and we talked about the next night. She was liaising with the Miami police department about security around the parking lot, and she gave me a series of small assignments of people to contact.

Jesse and Yulirus returned around noon, and Jesse went right to bed for a nap. I worked on FBI business for the rest of the afternoon, until I began to sniff delicious smells coming out of the kitchen. I walked in to find Yulirus in a tank top and tight shorts, stirring a mélange of meat and colorful vegetables. "That smells great," I said.

"My picadillo," he said. "Is a Cuban dish, only I make with ground chicken to be healthier for Jesse."

I leaned against the counter. "What do you want to do when you finish writing up Jesse's collection?"

"I like help him," he said simply. "He say that maybe I can stay here after I finish."

"And give up your career? To take care of a sick old man?"

I knew it sounded heartless as soon as I said it, but I couldn't take it back.

"Jesse say maybe I am consultant," he said, pronouncing the word carefully. "I learn a lot about other kinds of art by researching his collection. He say he know other rich people, and maybe I help them document their collections, maybe even advise with buying and selling."

I nodded. "That sounds good. You are a lot younger than Jesse. You have to make sure you can get by on your own."

He gave me a teaspoonful of picadillo to taste, and my mouth was in heaven. "Then again, maybe you can cook, too." I was reminded of what Miriam had said, that growing up gay in Castro's Cuba had made Yulirus strong. As long as we didn't put him in mortal danger during our arrest of Alvaro Vela Blanco, he'd be all right.

Chapter 32

Handoff

I spent Tuesday evening at Jesse's house. He was still tired from his physical therapy and he was angry at me because I wouldn't let Yulirus out of his obligation to go with Miriam and me the next night. That put Yulirus on edge, too, and a couple of times he dropped serving spoons and banged into appliances. Even though the picadillo was delicious I was eager to leave the two of them and go back to my room.

The big dildo sat on the bureau, taunting me, and I wondered if Lester was in Orlando. I texted him a photo of it, and almost immediately he texted back. "U r evil wcb later."

While I waited for him to call back, I logged in to my mother's accounts. She had gotten her first paycheck on Friday and deposited it in the bank. Then I called her to check in.

"I'm doing fine," she said. "Danny was here this weekend, but I sent him home early on Sunday. Honestly, you boys don't need to keep watching me. I'll be fine. As long as I don't think too much about Roger."

"That's good, Mom. How's the job?"

I listened patiently as she explained the ins and outs of medical billing, and the personal stories of the other clerks. "I'm going out for a drink after work on Friday with Delia and one of the other gals," she said. "I told Danny not to bother coming in. He needs to focus on his schoolwork and on his job. I don't want that bar to let him go before he finishes his degree."

I had worked at La Scuola for years before Danny started at Penn State and I knew the guys there would look out for him. But she was right, he needed to focus on his schoolwork. After I hung up I looked at the class he had mentioned, Risk Analysis. There was a lot of finance involved, and I worried he didn't have the background in it. Macroeconomic Risk and International Finance seemed like it was a section that even I'd have trouble with, because so many of my classes, both in my undergraduate degree and my master's, had been focused on the United States economy and tax laws. I made a resolution to do some reading on the subject myself, once this case was finished, and then call Danny on the pretense of a chat and see if I could help him.

Lester called later that night, and we had some fun on the phone involving the dildo, though I was conscious that it was a work of art and I didn't want to damage it. Or myself for that matter.

The next morning I ran and swam again, and I was happy to have done so because when Jesse was awake, the energy in the house was angrier and more volatile. Jesse snapped at me twice over breakfast.

When I excused myself to go into the guest room and get some work done, he said, "Yeah, go push around your papers and manipulate your numbers while other people put their ass on the line."

I had had it with his attitude. "I got shot in the parking lot of the Miami Beach Convention Center last year, and I shot back in return. I stabbed a man on a roof in Venice to get the painting you sent me there to retrieve. And don't forget that I jumped on that boat to go after a very nasty person while you stood comfortably on the dock."

"Angus chase Elpidio when he run away," Yulirus put in. "He is good man, Jesse. You be nice to him."

"I'll be nice to him when he's finished with us," Jesse growled.

BRACKISH WATER

I spent the afternoon double and triple checking to make sure that everyone and everything was in place for the meeting that night with Alvaro Vela Blanco. At one point I stood in the guest room staring at a painting on the wall and realized it was the same size as the Murillo. That gave me an idea.

Miriam joined us in Weston that afternoon, and she brought the Murillo with her.

"Angus is going to be with you tonight," Miriam said. "I have a hand truck in my car. He'll be dressed as a laborer you hired to help you carry the painting. He'll stand in the background and he'll be right there for you if anything happens."

"You have a gun?" Jesse demanded.

I was wearing a pair of my oldest jeans, which were faded and had a hole in the knee, a white T-shirt with nothing on it, and a cheap windbreaker I had bought when I was in college. I opened the jacket to show Jesse my gun in its thumb holster.

Then I pulled up the right leg of my jeans, to where I had a knife with a wicked blade strapped to my leg. I'd only ever used it to cut open packing tape, but I was comfortable handling it.

"So what happens exactly?" Jesse asked.

Miriam smiled tightly and sighed. "Mr. Vela Blanco will come out of the office building. There is a lamp post by the front door where he will examine the painting. If he verifies it is the Murillo he is expecting, he will activate the transfer to Elpidio's Cayman Islands account on his phone. There will be an eight-digit verification code, which he will write down for Yulirus. He will also give Yulirus his cut of the deal, $5,000, in cash."

Jesse wanted to come with us, but Miriam politely and then strongly declined. I was still arguing with him as I carried the Murillo out to my Mini Cooper and stowed it carefully in the back.

"You come back to me, all right?" Jesse said to Yulirus. He balanced himself against the walker and opened his arms.

Yulirus stepped into them, and kissed Jesse on the cheek. "Of course, *Papi*. We call you soon."

Despite his bravado, Yulirus's body shook as he lowered himself into my car. He took a few minutes to calm down, and I did the same. There was no real danger awaiting us. Alvaro Vela Blanco was a respected member of the business and exile community in Miami. He was the son of a multi-millionaire, and even if he wasn't as rich as his father, people like that didn't get their hands dirty.

I didn't expect him to be armed, though I wouldn't be surprised if his driver was. For all its positive publicity, of sun and sandy beaches and tropical drinks, there was a dark side to the city and a man of Diaz's wealth and position needed to feel safe. I consciously worked at shifting him in my mind from a bad guy under investigation by the FBI to a successful businessman who might cut the occasional corner.

"There are police there?" Yulirus asked as we got onto the highway.

"Under cover. You won't even notice them until they step in to arrest Diaz."

"But me? Will they arrest me?"

"Nope. And I'll drive you back to Jesse's as soon as you're done."

Yulirus slumped against the passenger window. He kept tapping his foot, which I took to be a good sign. If he was nervous, he'd be careful.

Traffic moved sluggishly on the highway that led us into downtown Miami, the occasional sports car accelerating fast and darting between lanes, and I kept expecting to hear the crash of metal on metal. I was glad that we'd left early enough that I didn't have to worry about being late, among all the other things I was concerned about.

A couple of big tour buses were transporting the athletes from an out-of-town college to the football stadium, which had already undergone two name changes since I'd been in town. A vanguard of motorcycle cops guided the buses, moving smoothly in and out of traffic. Air conditioner repairmen, who were worth their weight in gold in the hot Miami climate, jockeyed with SUVs shrink-wrapped with advertising banners. There were dozens of state-issued license plates, supporting everything from the Olympics to wildflower conservation. Even the Miccosukee and Seminole Indians had their own plates.

Once we were on the long, curving exit ramp that would drop us down into the city, I began worrying again. I knew how many cops would be there, where they would be stationed, and how Miriam hoped the handoff would go. But in any operation, I had learned, there were offbeat factors that could screw things up.

Suppose the parking lot wasn't empty, as Vela Blanco had promised. Or that there was an accident on Brickell Avenue with lots of police and rescue vehicles. There were any number of reasons why Vela Blanco could call things off, or things could go wrong.

I was clutching the steering wheel, and I tried to relax. I had to set a good example for Yulirus. "Your wire comfortable?" I asked.

He shrugged. "Is okay."

As we waited at the light at the end of the ramp there were few cars around us. I turned right and crossed the bridge over the Miami River, which separated the Brickell district from downtown. Unlike the narrow streets of the inner city, with two- and three-story buildings leaning in, the pavement broken and treeless, Brickell was shiny new. I drove slowly down the tree-lined street, past fancy hotels and high-rise headquarters of foreign banks.

The Diaz Appliance headquarters weren't on Brickell Avenue itself, but instead on a curving street one block east where all the buildings faced Biscayne Bay. The block we aimed for was deserted, though the windows of the office towers were lit and a Chinese restaurant was open a block away, red-toned light streaming from its windows.

I pulled up in front of the building and looked around. There were no other cars in the small visitor lot, though the building had a garage where I presumed Vela Blanco kept his car. I couldn't see anyone around us, and I hoped that the undercover cops were in place.

With shaky fingers, Yulirus retrieved his cell phone and called the number he had for Vela Romero. "*Estoy aqui,*" he said. He listened for a moment, then added, "*Bueno.*"

He put the phone in his lap. "He is here soon. What do we do?"

"Let's get the painting on the hand truck. I'll stand behind you in the shadows, but I'll be close enough to intervene if anything goes wrong."

"What go wrong?" Yulirus asked, his chin quivering.

"Hope for the best, plan for the worst," I said as I got out of the car. "Like I said, I'll be right behind you."

By the time I had unloaded the painting and stacked it on the hand truck, I heard an awful groaning noise, and Yulirus looked at me with fear. "*Que es eso?*"

"It's the garage," I said, pointing to the metal grate, which had begun to rise. A gray Bentley sedan slid out elegantly, as soon as the gate was up.

The car pulled up beside us, and a driver in a black suit got out, then moved around to the back, where the trunk lid rose silently. Then the rear window lowered.

"Go," I whispered to Yulirus.

Vela Blanco had changed things up. Instead of coming out of the building, he'd emerged in his car from the garage. But he'd still want to inspect what he was buying, wouldn't he? I wouldn't transfer forty-five grand to an unknown bank account without verification.

Once he verbally agreed with Yulirus that this was the painting that Elpidio had stolen from the museum in Cuba, we would move in and arrest him.

But he wasn't getting out of the car. Yulirus walked over and spoke to him, but because I didn't have a receiver I couldn't tell what they were saying. Finally Yulirus motioned to me and I walked toward him, towing the hand truck. "Put painting in trunk, please," he said.

That wasn't supposed to happen. We weren't going to give Vela Blanco physical custody of the painting at any time. I looked around. The parking lot still appeared to be deserted, which meant Miriam hadn't gotten the confession she wanted. And I hadn't seen Vela Blanco hand any cash to Yulirus either.

"Where's the cash?" I demanded. "You promised me five hundred to come with you."

The driver, who I'd ignored while focused on Yulirus and Diaz, stepped out of the shadows with a handgun pointed at me. "There won't be no money for either of you tonight," he said, with a heavy Spanish accent.

Well, crap. We knew that Vela Blanco was a crook, but only suspected him of white-collar crime like money laundering. I wasn't connected to Miriam, so I couldn't rely on her for advice. I shrugged and began pushing the cart toward Yulirus. "I'll collect from you later," I said as I passed him.

I turned my body as I reached down toward the bottom of the painting, resting on the hand cart. But instead of grabbing it, I bunched up my pant leg and moved it up so that I could unstrap the knife.

"No funny business," the driver said.

"Just getting a good grip on the painting," I said. "It's heavy. You don't want me to drop it, do you?"

Using all the strength I'd developed from boxing with Lester, I jammed the knife into the right rear tire of the Bentley, then twisted it. To cover the noise, I started coughing loudly.

Then I hefted the painting up and settled it into the trunk. I pulled down on the trunk, and the driver said, "Easy. It goes itself."

I used the cover of the lowering hood to reach down and remove my knife from the tire. I hoped I'd made enough of a cut to keep them from getting too far.

When I stood up, I saw the snout of a gun pointing out of the back window and aiming at Yulirus. The driver was raising his gun arm, too.

"Get down!" I grabbed Yulirus and ducked behind the Bentley, and we stumbled for the cover of the building.

"Police officers! Stay where are you are!"

I couldn't tell where the voice was coming from, but the driver decided it was best to get out of there. He jumped in the car and took off.

Yulirus and I leaned against the building. "What did he say to you?"

"He show me gun. He say if I don't give him painting he kill both of us."

"You did well," I said.

"But he has painting and you don't arrest him." He began crying. "You send me back to Cuba now. And Elpidio, too. And he is angry with me because of what I do, and he kill me."

I put my hand on his arm. "No, Yulirus. You're staying here."

I didn't know where the police cars had come from, but I saw two cruisers with lights flashing head down Brickell Bay Drive behind the Bentley. I hoped they stopped him soon, because if he made it to the highway there was no way the cops were engaging in a high-speed chase that might endanger civilians.

Miriam emerged out of the darkness. "What happened?"

I kept my hand on Yulirus's shoulder as he explained.

Then I said, "They won't get far, though." Miriam looked at me, and I pulled the knife out of my pocket. "There's a wicked cut in the right rear tire."

"Good thinking, Angus."

She told me to take Yulirus back to Weston, and that I could go home after that. "We'll reconvene in the morning to see how we proceed."

"Don't you want to wait to know if the police catch him? Won't we have to go to a station and make statements?"

"I need to talk to the SAC," she said. "Not only have we screwed up this operation, but we've also probably tipped our hand to Vela Blanco that we're on to him. I'm sure that if they pull him over, he'll lawyer up. And I wouldn't be surprised if he has a faked bill of sale already prepared for the Murillo to show anyone who tries to arrest him."

"Only it's not the Murillo," I said.

She looked at me curiously. "It's not?"

"Last night I was thinking through different scenarios," I said. "I was worried that Vela Romero might pull something funny. So I found one of the paintings in Jesse's collection that's the same size as the Murillo. I wrapped it up the same way in brown paper. That's the one in the trunk of the Bentley."

"Where's the Murillo then?"

"In my car. And Alvaro Vela Blanco is now the proud possessor of a large oil painting of two big, hairy men engaging in anal intercourse."

Chapter 33

Starting Over

Miriam began to laugh. "What were you going to do if he asked to see the painting?"

"If everything was kosher I'd admit that I made a mistake and dragged out the wrong painting. Oops. My bad. And then he would have seen the right painting and given Yulirus the money, and you'd have arrested him."

"This should be a lesson to me," Miriam said. "You are so cute and eager, Angus, with your red hair and your gym-toned body. I forget how sharp you are and sometimes I underestimate you." She shook her head. "I won't do that again."

I put the real Murillo on the hand truck and pushed it over to where her car was parked, along a side street. "I'll make sure that the SAC knows about your initiative," she said.

"It could have gone wrong in a bunch of other ways."

"Which I'm sure you had already planned for."

I shrugged. "I had a few ideas."

She laughed. "I'm sure you did."

I walked back to where Yulirus waited for me by the Mini Cooper. "Jesse like that painting," he said.

"We'll get it back for him."

We were quiet on the drive back to Weston. As we approached the guard gate, Yulirus said, "What happen now?"

"I can't be sure, but I believe that with Vela Blanco under arrest, we can subpoena—make a legal request for – his documents. If we're right, we'll find evidence of other, bigger crimes. He may never even go to trial for this."

"Will he find me and hurt me?"

"He will be too busy dealing with his lawyers. But we'll keep in touch with you."

We went into Jesse's house together, and Yulirus hugged him and told him what had happened while I gathered up my stuff. "You owe me a painting, Special Agent," Jesse said when I returned.

"I'll get it back for you."

"Or you and that hunky boyfriend of yours will end up posing for one."

My dick stiffened a bit at that idea, but I pushed it aside. "You convince the Special Agent in Charge that's what you're owed and we'll talk."

It was nearly midnight by the time I got back to Doral, and Lester was still in Orlando, so I settled for a quick text to let him know I was all right, and then went to sleep.

The next morning, I woke up early and confused. Where was I? My house in Wilton Manors? Jesse's place in Weston? No, I was in my new apartment in Doral, the early morning sunlight making the tan carpeting glow. I looked over at the other side of the bed.

Empty. Lester was still in Orlando, but he'd be home that night.

Home. The apartment we were going to share. Someday, perhaps, we'd look back at this place and say, "Remember it?" And we'd talk about the memories we made there.

With no Lester there were no memories to be made. I pulled on a T-shirt and shorts and went for a run. I met a white stork picking at insects in a shallow pond, who was unflapped by my passing. A few other joggers with whom I exchanged perfunctory nods. Then I rounded a corner and the sun came out from behind some clouds, shining directly on the balcony of our unit.

Something about the way the light hit reminded me of the Murillo, and the figure of Saint Joseph standing beside his young son. I would have been about the age of the boy in the picture when Cameron Green died, but his memory had a vividness that connected me to Joseph, who had agreed to raise Jesus as his own son. My father—for I still insisted on calling him that—had done that for me.

I was no Jesus, nor was Annette Green a comparison to the Virgin Mary. But the three of us had made our lives together, welcoming Danny to join us.

A pain sliced through my gut, causing me to double over. One morning my father had been there at breakfast with us, tousling our hair and making sure we ate our oatmeal. Danny and I left for school like any other day. It was only when we came home and found our mother weeping in the living room with Aunt Jenny that we knew things had changed irrevocably.

They let us see him the next day, after he'd been worked on at the funeral home. He wore the same kind of suit as he did when he went to work, and the only thing that was different was that his eyes were closed. I was tall enough to see over the edge of the casket, but I had to hoist Danny up.

He had begun crying, and I wrapped my arms around him and carried him back to a pew, where the two of us sat, holding hands, as mourners came to pay their respects to our mother. A couple of times people came over to us—a cousin of Cameron's, a couple of his co-workers. They all said the same things—that he had loved us both so much.

I straightened up and wiped the tears from my face, and ran the rest of the way back to the apartment. I could let my mother's revelation turn my life inside out, or I could move forward, knowing that a kind man with an inquisitive mind had taken on the task of raising me before I even emerged from my mother's womb.

According to Scripture, Jesus knew from a young age that he was the son of God. When he was twelve years old, the family traveled to Jerusalem, where Jesus disappeared. Mary and Joseph found him in the temple courts, among the teachers, and he said, according to the book of Luke, "Didn't you know I had to be in my Father's house?"

My father's house was the one Cameron had made for us, and always would be. He was my father, and no revelation could ever change that.

After a shower, I dressed and drove to headquarters in Miramar. It was a much shorter drive than the one from Wilton Manors and I didn't have as much time to think on my way and plan my day. All I knew was that I was eager to learn what had happened to Alvaro Vela Blanco. Had he gone back to his million-dollar home in Cocoplum, unwrapped his newest acquisition? What kind of Cuban swear words might he have used when he realized he'd been outsmarted?

I dropped my messenger bag in my office and went looking for Miriam. She was in her office with another agent, an older guy from the money laundering unit. "The Bentley's tire collapsed on the access ramp to I-95," Miriam said, when she looked up and saw me in her doorway. "Caused a shutdown and a traffic jam while Vela Blanco and his driver were arrested and the car was towed away."

I nodded.

"This is the end of our involvement," Miriam continued. "I want you to hand off everything you have on this case to Agent Cutler. Then you're back on Vito's team. Agent Cutler will handle getting Mr. Venable's painting back to him."

"What about a green card for Yulirus?"

"Out of our hands. I'll have the SAC write something for the file that commends Mr. Diaz for his help. Then his immigration attorney can use that when he comes up for renewal in a year."

I nodded. Well, I'd done my best for Yulirus, and come through on everything I had promised. "What about my appointment with Elpidio López at Krome today?"

Agent Cutler knew what was going on. "Document everything

about your meeting and pass it on to me," he said. "We may need to intervene with ICE to keep him in custody until we settle this case against Vela Blanco."

I walked slowly back to my office, through the narrow hallways, past other agents and their assistants doing their jobs. I felt at loose ends, though I still had to complete a report on Elpidio López.

I passed a painting on a wall, which resembled the lot where our headquarters stood before all the chrome and glass had come in. It was a wild landscape of sawgrass and the occasional palm, a testament to what had been there before us.

I realized with a start that I cared about what happened to Elpidio López as much as Yulirus Diaz and Jesse Venable. It was his word against Yulirus's whether he'd actually tried to run Yulirus down or merely steered to close to him.

Maybe I was turning soft very early in my career at the Bureau, but I hadn't sensed any menace in López, just a guy trying to get by. As we all were, as Joseph had done when confronted with Mary's pregnancy, as Cameron Green had done with me.

For Elpidio López things were only going to go backwards. He'd be sent back to Cuba, perhaps prosecuted for his crimes. Even if he was set free, what else was there for him but to go back to what had made him a living before? Was he a good painter, as Kyle Roberts had speculated? If so, was there a visa program he could get into?

I hurried back to my office and researched special visas for artists. What I read disappointed me. There were three types of artist visas: the P1, the P2, and the P3, and Elpidio López didn't qualify for either of the first two. He wasn't internationally recognized, he hadn't been invited to a conference or a presentation, and he wasn't sponsored by any group back in Cuba.

The P3 might offer more flexibility. He was over eighteen, qualified in his field, and able to communicate effectively about it. However, he was in the U.S. illegally, so at the very least he'd have to go back to Cuba and apply for the visa, if he wanted to stay in the States and paint. It wasn't much, but it was a small ray of hope.

As I was driving to Krome, I tuned my radio to the all-news station. The background of world events was soothing as I thought about everything I had been involved with, from getting Yulirus out of Krome to Roger's death and my mother's new life. There was a whole lot of starting over going on, including my move in with Lester.

It was lucky that I'd been to Krome a few times in the last couple of weeks because I was pretty much on auto-pilot as I drove there and parked. I went through the standard routine before I met with Elpidio López in another nondescript interview room. "We arrested Alvaro Vela Blanco last night," I said. "The FBI may ask the Immigration service to keep you here until he goes to trial."

He looked even more unhappy than he had when I walked in. "Here? In this prison?"

I shrugged. "You broke the law."

"He was going to help me," he said in an anguished voice. "Señor Diaz. To show my painting to his rich friends and to gallery owners. I was going to stay here and paint."

He started to sob. "Now I have nothing."

I hated to see the man's life in ruins. Yes, he'd made some bad decisions. But did that make him a bad person? Did he deserve to have his life destroyed, his art suppressed?

"We showed your painting to a professor of art at the University of Miami," I said.

Elpidio looked up.

"He thinks you have talent."

"I do," he said defiantly. "I have many paintings, back in Cuba. I could show you, but my phone was ruined when I jumped in the water."

I noticed that his English was much smoother than Yulirus's, perhaps because he had done business with Americans other than Alvaro Vela Blanco.

An idea started percolating in my head. "All the same style? Sort of like Impressionism?"

"With a Cuban eye," he said.

I hesitated. My next question was surely inappropriate, but it might be the key to his survival.

I leaned forward and said, in a low voice, "Do you ever paint men? Naked men?"

He looked down at the table, and I had my answer even before he said quietly, "Yes."

"Are there other clients you have stolen artwork for?"

"Why?"

"Because it's going to take a while to bring Alvaro Vela Blanco to trial. If you can help us with other cases, there is more reason to keep you here."

"There are two others in Miami," he said. "The rest, they all went to Europe or the Middle East."

"Two others can help. I'll need details."

I pulled my pocket notebook out and gave him my pen. As he wrote I thought about what I could do. I was so caught up in ideas that I didn't notice when he had finished, until he pushed the book back to me.

He had listed two names, and the paintings he had stolen for each, and the museums they came from. Then on another page he had sketched a quick portrait of me.

I was flattered, of course, but even more surprised by his talent. The face that peered back at me from the page was my own, lost in thought. It was something I thought Lester would like very much.

"This is beautiful, Elpidio."

"I can do much better with the right materials."

I pocketed the pen and the notebook and stood up. "I'll see what I can do about getting you someplace better to stay while you wait for the trial."

It took longer than I expected to organize. I had to get Yulirus to say that he held no grudge against Elpidio, and for Jesse to agree to fund a studio where Elpidio could paint. Jesse's attorney said that there would be no conflict in his sponsoring Yulirus for one type of visa and Elpidio for another.

My accounting skills came in handy then, as I put together a year-long business plan for Elpidio. He would pay Jesse back in paintings—an old tradition of impoverished artists. And Jesse would introduce him to private collectors and gallerists.

I discovered how I could get Elpidio's work packed and shipped from Cuba to Miami, so he would have a stock of work to sell immediately. And I researched the names Elpidio had given me, and the paintings he had stolen.

Then I presented the whole deal to Miriam one afternoon.

She read through what I gave her, and then looked up at me. "Really, Angus?"

"He's clearly talented," I said. "Professor Roberts at UM thinks so. And it's a shame to keep him locked up at Krome because we need him for our case. This way he can be productive—a reward for him helping us."

"And you think he'll stay? Why not just disappear?"

"Miriam. You know art and artists. We give this guy a studio where he can paint, and a place to sell his work. We aren't going to end up charging him, in exchange for his testimony. So why would he run?"

"Because he might be sent back to Cuba?"

"Not if he can qualify for the P3 visa. With help from us.

The Special Agent in Charge was a bit more skeptical. "You have some capital with me, Angus," he said. "Based on your smart thinking when we arrested Mr. Vela Blanco. You sure this is the way you want to spend it with me?"

"I can stand on my own, sir," I said. "I'm happy if I can use whatever is at my disposal to help someone else."

"You have a penchant for helping criminals," he said. "Jesse Venable. Yulirus Diaz. Elpidio López. You sure you wouldn't be better off as a social worker?"

"With all due respect, sir, something that I learned at the Academy in Quantico has stuck with me. Many people commit crimes because they feel they have no other options. The best way to rehabilitate them is providing them with a way forward that doesn't lead them back to crime."

I took a deep breath. "Mr. Venable is probably the most law-avoiding of the three men you mentioned. But his age and his health have caught up with him, and because I've been helping him with his financial records, I know he has the means to continue his lifestyle without resorting to crime."

The SAC narrowed his eyes. "Helping him how?"

I shrugged. "I'm an accountant. When he came back from prison his finances were a mess. Unpaid bills, unrecorded income. I cleaned it all up for him."

"Because you wanted to show him a way forward."

"Because I have some talents. And I want to use them to help people."

"The Bureau has found your talents helpful so far as well." He looked over at his screen, and clicked the button to authorize our part of López's release. "Keep up the good work."

That wasn't the end, of course. It took more maneuvering through ICE to get Elpidio released into Jesse's custody, to move him into the spare room in Weston, and get him set up in a small studio in a strip shopping center a bike ride away.

But eventually it all happened. I framed the sketch Elpidio had done of me at Krome and gave it to Lester, and then one day he and I went to Elpidio's studio and posed for an oil portrait. It wasn't the kind of thing Jesse Venable would put on his wall, but it was something I could show my mother, and that Lester and I could hang in the living room of the apartment in Doral, where we had begun to live together quite well.

Lester's parents announced that they were taking a cruise out of Miami from Christmas to New Year's and asked if the four of us could get together. I said I'd be delighted to meet them, and then said, "What if I invited my mother and Danny down for Christmas, too? We could all have Christmas Eve dinner together. Then your parents would go off on their cruise. You'll probably be busy that week with all the parties, and I can hang out with my mother and my brother."

"That sounds like a plan," Lester said.

"I can even take a day and drive them down to the Keys. Show them where Yulirus and Elpidio came in. Maybe some of my other great locations."

"I doubt your mother would like brackish water and mosquitoes."

I shrugged. "You never know what you'll accept until you start to wrap your head around it."

Acknowledgments

There is a real Kyle Roberts with a degree in art history, but I have merely borrowed his name for my purposes. There is, to my knowledge, no real painting named *My Father, My Apple*. Readers who like their visuals can check out the Murillo work called *The Good Shepherd* and imagine Joseph on the left side of the canvas and an apple in Jesus's hand. I did significant research to choose a Murillo as my subject, because I wanted the painting to reflect the father-son theme at this at the heart of this book.

The quote that Danny finds does not come from the Bible; instead it is from a book called *The Life and Glories of St. Joseph*, by Edward Healy Thompson, M.A. who cited it from a legend collected by the fifteenth-century scholar Isidoro de Isolano.

The quote Angus remembers is from the poem "Florida" by Elizabeth Bishop.

There was a real store in the Sears Town shopping center in Fort Lauderdale called Betsy's Odds-n-Tiques, though my use of it in this novel is purely fictional. Betsy took many items on consignment from me and my mother when we started slimming down our collections, and it was great fun to go there and browse through all her dusty shelves—and then collect cash at the end!

I am grateful to the FBI for the opportunity to attend its Citizens Academy and learn about policies and procedures—and to get to play with some of the weapons that agents use. However, my use of FBI policies and procedures is in no way intended to represent the attitude of the Bureau.

My fellow members of Mystery Writers of America have always been helpful, answering questions about police procedures and how to write better crime fiction. Part of this book was written while on a sabbatical sponsored by Broward College, where I was until 2022 a professor of English on the South Campus.

Randall Klein, then working as an editor in New York, recognized something about Angus in my first submission, and then shepherded *The Next One Will Kill You* through its first edition with Diversion Books. Since then he has been a great sounding board and freelance editor.

Kelly Nichols has come through with another terrific cover. And I greatly appreciate my beta readers, who have helped me find errors and fix awkward phrasing. Bless your hearts Andy Jackson, Judith Levitsky and Tim Brehme.

This is the fourth book in the Angus Green series of FBI thrillers. More information on the first three can be found at my website, www.mahubooks.com.

If you've enjoyed reading about Angus, I hope you'll check out some of my other work. Randall has said that I have a particular skill at writing male relationships—in families, relationships and workplaces, and I believe that carries through in everything I write.

My Mahu series is about an openly gay Honolulu homicide detective, Kimo Kanapa'aka, who discovers more about himself in each installment, while also showcasing the shadier parts of a sunny paradise. These books are currently available at many e-retailers and in print. Some are in audio, with others to follow.

The Have Body, Will Guard series focuses on a pair of men who are partners in both life and the close protection industry. They travel the world making it safer for LGBTQ+ people, one case at a time. The first of those is *Three Wrong Turns in the Desert*—my very favorite of the books I've written. This series is gradually moving into audio and is also available widely.

It would be impossible for me to write a book about fathers and sons without dedicating it to my own father, David Plakcy. I share some of his stubbornness, which led to a lot of drama when I was growing up. But as time wore on I realized that he loved me a great deal, and that he was trying to mold me into someone who could, like Angus, Kimo, Aidan and Liam, survive a difficult world.

I was fortunate to be able to spend the last years of his life with him, in a high-rise condo my parents had bought for their retirement. He spent his time snoozing on the balcony, overlooking a big lake, and he loved to be able to look down at the clear water and spot large fish. The love of water in all its forms has been a constant connection between us, and the fact that I live near the ocean is a testament to how deeply he ingrained that love in me.

Part of this dedication also goes to my husband Marc and our golden retrievers, Brody and Griffin, who provide me with love and support.

To Marc: Somewhere in the crowd there's you.

Author's Notes

Thanks for reading! I'd love to stay in touch with you. Subscribe to one or more of my newsletters, Gay Mystery and Romance or Golden Retriever Mysteries, via my website, www.mahubooks.com and I promise I won't spam you!

Follow me at Goodreads to see what I'm reading, at BookBub for bargains, and my author page at Facebook where I post news and giveaways.

If you liked this book, please consider posting a brief review at your vendor, at Goodreads and in reader groups. Even a short review help other readers discover books they might like. And there are often specific vendor promotions I can sign up for, only if I have a certain number of reviews posted at the vendor. Thanks!

This is the fourth book in the Angus Green series. Have you read them all? They are available widely in e-book and print.

1: *The Next One Will Kill You.* While investigating a jewelry heist with its roots in Fort Lauderdale's gay neighborhoods, Angus must learn how to use his education, his intelligence and his good looks without losing track of who he is and what he stands for. The street quickly teaches him that the only way to face a challenge is to

Author's Notes

assume that he'll survive this one--that it'll be the next one that will kill him.

2: *Nobody Rides for Free.* Angus's second case takes him from Fort Lauderdale's seamy underbelly to boisterous beachfront bars where big-fish Russian emigres launder illegal cash. He'll befriend a beautiful Russian-American undercover agent and rekindle a romance with a man who makes him feel protected. In the end, he'll learn the truth of a saying he learned as a boy -- there is a price to pay for every decision we make. Nobody rides for free.

3: *Survival is a Dying Art.* Angus, who knows nothing about art and speaks no Italian, may be in over his head as he is assigned to befriend, and ultimately betray, a Fort Lauderdale con. But with the help of his Italian-speaking brother and his art-loving boyfriend, he may be able not only to retrieve a lost painting, but solve a smuggling case and potentially save thousands of lives.

Contents

1.	Barbershop Boys	1
2.	End of Nowhere	11
3.	False Friends	21
4.	Island Visit	27
5.	A Lot to Unpack	35
6.	Setting in Motion	43
7.	Convincing	53
8.	With Both Feet	65
9.	Transitions	73
10.	New Beginnings	83
11.	The Man	95
12.	Roger That	99
13.	Baggage	105
14.	Canned Potatoes	111
15.	Global Security	119
16.	Once a User	127
17.	17: My Father, My Apple	135
18.	A Good Son	147
19.	Trust	153
20.	Worms	159
21.	Alvaro Vela Blanco	167
22.	Shadows	175
23.	Good Mood	181
24.	One Year	189
25.	Additional Focus	195
26.	Hawk Channel	203
27.	False Friends	213
28.	Plan A	219
29.	On the Move	229
30.	Authentication	235
31.	Strength	243
32.	Handoff	251
33.	Starting Over	261

Acknowledgments 271
Author's Notes 275

www.ingramcontent.com/pod-product-compliance
Lightning Source LLC
LaVergne TN
LVHW011947060526
838201LV00061B/4236